SEX, HEAT AND HUNGER: PART 1

THE DARK AND DAMAGED HEARTS SERIES, BOOK #3

WHITLEY COX

Copyright © 2017 by Whitley Cox

All rights reserved.

No part of this book may be reproduced in any form or by any electronic or mechanical means, including information storage and retrieval systems, without written permission from the author, except for the use of brief quotations in a book review

ISBN: 978-1-7750910-5-9

DISCLAIMER

Please do not try any new sexual practices (BDSM or otherwise) without the guidance of an experienced practitioner. The author will not be held responsible for any loss, harm, injury or death resulting from use of the information contained in this book.

Make sure your e-reader files are stored and locked properly so no one under the age of eighteen can access them.

And on that note, I'd like to thank you for purchasing this book, and I hope you enjoy it. I certainly enjoyed writing it.

Thank you.
Whitley Cox

For the husband:
My love, my life, MY EVERYTHING.

Thank you for loving me, even when I'm going bat-shit cray-cray.

Hello!
I just wanted to thank you for buying my book, and I hope you enjoy it. I certainly enjoyed writing it.

This is book three of The Dark and Damaged Hearts Series; there are ten books altogether in the series.
Each story or "couple" has two books, part one and part two.

This is Sex, Heat and Hunger: **Part 1**, Book 3 of The Dark and Damaged Hearts Series.

Sex, Heat and Hunger: **Part 2** will be available **April 29, 2017!!**

As a way to just mix things up and try something new, I do the prologue from the hero's point of view, just to give you a taste of the way he thinks, but from Chapter One until the end, you're in the heroine's head

Thank you again from the bottom of my heart, and enjoy!
xoxo
Whitley Cox

PROLOGUE
JAMES

Damn it; it's empty. I hesitated for a second; the bottle poised high in the air before I thought better of it and set the dead soldier down on the liquor cabinet instead, crouching down to rummage around inside again in search of another. *There's probably a long-forgotten bottle of Baileys or Cognac in here somewhere, but today is a day for scotch, twenty-five-year-old scotch. He's been gone twenty-five fucking years and this day still hasn't gotten any fucking easier.*

It should have been me.

We'd be running this town together if he were here. He was my best friend, and I couldn't even save him.

I can't go home. No one's home anyway, because I have no one.

Finn's gone too. Been dead for almost a year but I still smell his wet fur in my den where he sprawled in front of the fireplace. The office is empty. It should have been OUR office. I sent them all home early, couldn't stand their fake smiles and worried stares, not that I care. Not that it matters, not that any of it matters. I've been drunk since lunch. But I need more. I need to be numb. Only then can I fall asleep and not think about him.

I could walk to a liquor store and head home, but then I'd be home, alone, drinking, and that's what I did all fucking day.

There's a pub up the street. I could go and drink there for a while, ignore people, but at least I wouldn't be alone. Or I could call that chick, the one I call when I need to get off. What's her name again? Nah, she's not even hot, nice enough, but she needs to put on a few pounds and stop dying her hair that godawful lemon color. Guess I'll walk to the pub. But it's so bloody cold outside. I could cab. Fuck it. It's only six blocks. I'll walk. Maybe it'll tire me out so I can go home and pass out.

Son-of-a-bitch, the place is packed. What day is it? Friday? Yeah, I guess so. And there's a hockey game on—damn it. Is there a seat anywhere? I should just leave. This was a bad idea. Shit, I don't want to be alone right now. I just want to drink alone in a room full of people until I pass out that's what I want.

I hate this month. I hate this day. I hate my life. I just want it to be over... There's a seat.

"Scotch neat, please. No, not that stuff. I want that dusty bottle up there." I pointed to the scotch on the top shelf, the expensive shit with only two ounces missing from it. The bartender poured me two fingers, and I grunted a thanks.

Why is someone talking on their phone in here? Get up and go.

"Oh God, what happened?" *Any conversation that starts out that way has to be interesting...* "Oh no, that's okay," she continued. "It was a bit of a last minute plan to meet up, anyway. Our schedules were just open at the same time. I know Alyssa is really busy right now, we just haven't hung out in a while and were going to grab a drink. I'll call her tomorrow. I hope she feels better soon. Food poisoning sucks. If there is anything I can do, come over and hold her hair or something, let me know... That's okay. Take care, Steve, and good luck... Bye."

Don't look straight at her! I'm not into chitchat right now, but her kindness and that sweet and sexy voice is intriguing. All I could tell from my peripheral was that she's blonde and young, perhaps too young. *Oh God, please don't have me old enough to be her dad. What's she drinking? I hope it's not some stupid, ridiculously difficult and sugary martini that just screams high-maintenance and pretentious.*

Thank God. It's clear with a lemon. No nonsense. Vodka maybe? Is she going to leave now that her date isn't showing up? Do I care? But where did her friend eat so I can avoid that place? Shit, Shaw if you start talking to her then she may never shut up.

"Where did your friend eat?" The words come out before I can stop them.

Well, fuck me, she's gorgeous! Those eyes, hazel with flecks of gold, humor, and intelligence running just beneath the surface. And that mouth, oh my God that mouth! I felt my cock twitch as she parted those beautiful lips just so. *I would love to fuck that greedy little heart-shaped mouth. And the hair, honey blonde down her back, rippling like a mermaid's. Why do I have such a thing for mermaids? Who the fuck cares?* I want to grab it and pull her toward me. I need to have my hands in it as she's on her knees, looking up at me with those big doe eyes. *Why is she staring at me? Does she not speak English? What the fuck? Of course, she speaks English, you idiot, you just heard her on the phone. Say something, woman!*

"Uh, her boyfriend didn't say, apparently she had some fish that was off." But I'm too busy gawking at that penetrable mouth. *What did I ask her again?*

She's staring, looking right at me, right *through* me. *Does she already know that I'm a miserable fuck-up? She knows, doesn't she? Everything that I am, or more accurately, everything that I'm not. And yet she still hasn't run away. Cut the crap, Shaw, who do you think you are? Am I that drunk? Is the room spinning? Does she feel it too? The electricity crackling in the air between us, the earth shaking, time standing still?*

She's still staring, what did I ask her? Now you're an even bigger fool, say something, you ass. "You'll have to find out and make sure you avoid that place." *Smooth Shaw, real smooth.*

"Yeah, that's a good idea."

She feels it too, I can tell, she's not looking away from me. The pull, the crackling, the shaking, time standing, she feels it all too.

"I'm James. What's your name?" *Please don't be something stupid like Rainbow or Epiphany or Storm. I don't think I could handle it.*

"Emma."

1

EMMA

"Hey, Emma, wait up."

"What's up?" I reached for my purse and coat, tying my scarf around my neck. I'm not looking forward to the walk to my car as the night is frigid, the wind's whipping fiercely off the water. I loved working in the inner harbor, but damn it got cold.

"I... I was wondering if you'd like to get a drink tonight? Or maybe dinner?"

I liked Wendell, well enough, but only as a friend and co-worker, nothing more. He just wasn't my type. He looked as if he would blow over if the breeze were anything above a small-craft warning. Half of my body cast a bigger shadow than he did and his wardrobe didn't help him look any bigger either—skinny brown corduroys with an oversized mustard yellow cardigan and black turtleneck. And he was always talking about craft beer. But I can't recall one time he's ever said he likes any that he's tried. Just like every other hipster out there, he's glomming onto a trend he secretly loathes, simply because it's hip. And those white ear-buds! For heaven's sake, way to ostracize the real world there, bud. They're always in his ears. Unless he's teaching, of course, then they're hanging out of his pocket. But the moment he's out of the classroom they're back up. The man refuses to take them out of his ears, even when we speak, so I never know if he has indeed heard me.

"Uh, um, thanks for the offer, Wendell. But actually, I have plans with a girlfriend tonight, sorry. I need to go home first to change and have a few things to do before I meet her, but I'll see you Monday."

"Oh, uh. All right, no worries. I just thought I'd ask. Can I walk you to your car?" Chocolate eyes blinked dolefully through his thick hipster glasses.

"Yeah, sure. Is your car parked in the same lot?" I pulled my gloves on and grabbed my phone, shoving it into my pocket.

"I don't *own* a car," he boasted. "I bike or walk. I prefer to do my part and keep my carbon footprint as small as possible. You should consider biking to work."

His attitude abruptly shifted, from apprehensive and unsure, to conceited and smug. I gritted my teeth and felt the hair on the back of my neck stand up.

"I'll give it some thought," I said, as I punched the button on the elevator in frustration.

"You should," he said almost snidely, joining me and standing uncomfortably close, despite how much space we had. "I read a book that says within in the next thirty years we're all going to have to wear gas masks when we go outside because the air is going to be so polluted."

"Was that perhaps a fictional book? I think thirty years is a little too soon. But I wouldn't doubt it, eventually. Besides, I live too far away to bike or walk, and I do take the bus when I can."

"And I only shower three times a week," he added, nodding with self-satisfaction. "Cuts down on the amount of freshwater I consume. And I have a rain barrel on my balcony so I can do dishes."

"Good for you." I scrunched up my face, trying hard not to sniff to check if I could smell him, but making a shit job of it. Did he stink? I couldn't tell. "I live in a condo on the third floor. I don't think my downstairs neighbor would appreciate it if my rain barrel overflowed onto his deck seven months of the year. And I'm at the gym every day. I need to shower, no way around that one. But I recycle and compost, use energy-saving light bulbs, do what little things I can to help our precious earth, you know, reusable grocery bags and all that."

His eyebrows disappeared beneath his heavily gelled side-swept hair. Why did I feel like I was being persecuted for showering every day and not catching rain on my balcony? Was Wendell really that pretentious?

"You should *really* consider switching to an electric car then, or one that runs on bio-fuel," he droned on, as he followed me out into the darkness. "I've seen what you drive, and it's not very green or earth-conscious."

"Thanks, Wendell." I sighed as I began fishing and fumbling in my coat pockets with gloved hands for my keys. "Another thing I'll give some thought to, though, I really can't afford a new car right now. Let alone a Prius or a Leaf. It's all about priorities."

"Well, your priority should be saving the earth."

"Yes, well..." I huffed, "... my priority is keeping myself fed, clothed and with a roof over my head, but, to each his own. Here we are, this is my car. Thanks for walking me. You have a good weekend."

At this point, all I wanted was to get away from this obnoxious hippy hipster-douche. We'd never chatted this much before, alone, and I found his judgmental, holier-than-thou routine more and more off-putting. I hoped Wendell would take the hint and walk away but instead, he came up behind me, boxing me against my car. I shifted to face him, desperately reaching for the door handle behind me.

"I like you, Emma," he whispered.

Really? You like me even though you think my carbon footprint is too big?

He took half a step forward and closed the gap even further. His face mere inches from mine, his breath smelled funny, like burnt toast and onions.

What the hell had he eaten earlier?

"I... I uh... thanks, Wendell, you're nice too." My eyes darted around the dark empty lot, searching for another human being, another person, anyone to help defuse this increasingly uncomfortable situation.

"I'd like to take you out." His lips were inching closer. I turned my head to the side, desperate not to let him kiss me or smell his foul breath any longer than was necessary.

"That's uh... flattering." I put my hands on his shoulder and pushed him away from me gently. He was so boney, did this man avoid food like he avoided showers? He didn't budge. Jesus, for a waif he was surprisingly strong. "But I... uh, I *have* a boyfriend."

"Really?" he asked as he backed away half a step. I leaped at the opportunity to open my door. "Since when?" He looked at me skeptically, his eyes black holes framed in startling white plastic, shining fiercely in the orange glow of the streetlamp.

"It's uh, really new. Just a few weeks but it's serious. I'm sorry." I winced, sighing inwardly and visibly relaxing as he backed away another two steps.

"Really? You're not just saying that to avoid going out with me?"

I shook my head and bit my lip, trying hard to come across as earnest. I'm a terrible liar.

"All right then well... have a good night." He shrugged like he thought I was the one losing out, then jammed his hands into his pockets and walked away without looking back.

I breathed another sigh of relief and jumped into my car, locking it as soon as I got in, giving a small "thank you" to my invisible, non-existent boyfriend, and wishing that he wasn't so non-existent or invisible. It'd been nearly a year, and I finally felt like I might be ready to try dating again, but Wendell? No way in hell!

I arrived at the pub around eight fifty, early, as always, in hopes of snagging a nice quiet corner booth. Unfortunately, though, the place was packed, hockey game—shit! I climbed up on an empty stool at the bar and ordered a drink, vodka with club soda and a lemon wedge. Very few calories, no sugar, and no scurvy—bonus! I didn't really feel like making small talk with random strangers, so I brought out my phone and started checking emails while I waited.

I got caught up reading hilarious forwards from my dad, so by the time I looked at the clock, it was nine twenty. What was up with Alyssa? I texted her.

E: **Where are you? I'm at the bar, left side.**

Five minutes passed and no answer.

E: **Everything okay?**

Five more minutes passed, now it was nine thirty and still no sign or contact. I called, hoping that she was just her usual tardy self and that she'd say she was on her way in a cab.

"Hello?"

"Steve? It's Emma, where's Alyssa? She was supposed to meet me at the pub half an hour ago. Why are you answering her phone?"

"Emma? Oh hey! Yeah, umm I don't think she's is going to be able to make it tonight, she's puking her guts out right now."

"Oh God, what happened?"

"Her office went out for a goodbye sushi lunch today, and she must have eaten some fish that was off because she's been throwing up since she got home at five thirty. She had to cancel her spin class and hasn't left the bathroom for hours. I didn't know you guys were meeting up tonight. Otherwise, I'd have let you know earlier. I'm really sorry."

Alyssa taught spin twice a week at the gym I belonged to, which is where she and Steve had met. He was a newbie member who had fallen *off* his stationary bike mid-class, but fallen *in* love with Alyssa, instantly, and got her phone number that night despite his clumsiness.

"Oh no, that's okay. It was a bit of a last minute plan to meet up, anyway. Our schedules were just open at the same time. I know Alyssa is busy right now, we just haven't hung out in a while and were going to grab a drink. I'll call her tomorrow. I hope she feels better soon. Food poisoning sucks. If there is anything I can do, come over and hold her hair or something, let me know."

"Okay, thanks. And sorry to make you sit in a bar all by yourself."

"That's okay. Take care, Steve, and good luck."

"Thanks, bye."

"Bye."

"Where did your friend eat?"

In the midst of my phone conversation with Steve, the bar stool to my right had been vacated and re-occupied without my noticing. The thick as molasses voice came from a guy in a three-piece dark gray suit, black leather dress shoes, and an understated but none-the-less impressive Rolex which peeked from beneath the cuff and also revealed a light dusting of dark hair at the wrist.

His hands were huge, like *super* huge! You can tell a lot about a person from their hands, and these were capable hands. Looked to be the hands of a man who worked hard and didn't just push a pencil all day; with trimmed nails, plenty of calluses, and the occasional scar to show he dove right in when it came to dirty work. A man's man in gentleman's clothes.

But more noticeable than his big hands, which I suddenly ached to have on me, was the most intoxicating scent of the man. An alluring mix of spice, woods, and confidence, like he'd just chopped down enough trees to make a log house and then swiped Old Spice under his arms—it was hot. I looked up from my phone, straight into piercing cobalt blue eyes and flicked down to a cocky but adorable smirk on an even more adorable mouth—scratch that—a sexy, delicious and unbelievably kissable mouth. My core tightened as I envisioned that mouth traveling down my body and ending between my legs.

Holy shit! Where did that thought come from? More to the point where did you come from Mr. Sexy Mouth?

My jaw hung open for what felt like hours but was probably closer to two or three seconds as I took in tall, dark and dangerously handsome sitting next to me, sipping on a glass of some belly-warming amber liquid. He was attractive. Boy was he attractive. An older face, maybe mid-thirties, there was certainly nothing *baby* about him, hard and with edgy angles and bold lines. Perhaps that's where the dangerous came into play? His eyes locked on mine and I felt as if the whole world had been put on pause; the air sparked and sizzled between us. Did *he* feel it too?

"Uh, her boyfriend didn't say, apparently she had some fish that was off," I said, shaking my head trying to regain my composure.

"You'll have to find out and make sure you avoid that place." His voice was gravelly and so deep I shivered inside as I continued to stare at his mouth.

"Yeah." I swallowed. "That's a good idea."

"I'm James. What's your name?" He extended his big right hand across his body and held it out for me to shake. I took it and immediately felt an electrifying surge of lust run through me. It ran from the tips of my fingers that were wrapped around his warm, powerful hand, right down to my toes, lingering in places that hadn't been touched by a man in far, *far* too long.

Please don't be old enough to be my dad.

"Emma," I squeaked.

"Nice to meet you, *Emma*. That's quite a firm handshake."

"I was thinking the same about you. So many men I shake hands with give me feeble shit because I'm a woman. They must believe that they'll crush my hand. But I can handle it."

He chuckled a thick and warm rumble that spread through him and came out in a broad and diabolical grin. "I bet you can. May I buy you another drink, *Emma*, seeing as your friend is otherwise indisposed. Or are you going to head home, now that you're dateless?"

I bit my lip. "Well, I was going to head home... but sure, why not?"

"His name is James Shaw, he's thirty-eight, into running, fishing and woodworking, and he's the owner of J.P.S. Developing Inc. here in Victoria," I blathered into the phone Saturday afternoon.

"Really? You found all that out? And you met him at the pub? Or did you Google him?" Alyssa asked. She was feeling better, not a hundred percent or well enough to go to the gym, but at least she'd stopped puking when I'd called her the next day to catch up and fill her in on my encounter with Mr. Firm-Handshake-Sexy-Mouth.

"No. I found it out the old-fashioned, non-creepy-stalker way, by talking to him. I'm not going to *Google* him. Not yet anyway. And why are you so shocked that I met someone? It's not like I was out clubbing and started making out with a random guy on the dance floor and then took him home. I'm not twenty-one. And I didn't even *do* that when I was twenty-one, you know that. *And* I didn't go home with James either. I behaved myself, thank you very much."

She laughed over the phone. "I don't know. You just don't strike me as the type to meet someone at a pub or bar that's all. Let alone a gorgeous business tycoon. Nobody meets anyone at a pub anymore, not since our parents were on the dating scene. It's all online dating, some terrible hook-up app or through mutual friends. But more importantly..." Her tone changed, ready for the dirty details. "... you made-out with him?"

I nibbled on my bottom lip and bobbed my tea bag in my mug before lifting it out and tossing it into the compost. "Well, call me old-fashioned if you like, but I did meet James at a pub. And yeah, we made-out, kind of. We kissed in the cab. But who knows if it will amount to anything."

The evening had gone quite well in my opinion. We'd grabbed a booth as soon as one became vacant, ordered nachos and talked for nearly two hours. We'd covered all the first date kind of topics, and even though it wasn't a date, it ended like one—in a shared a cab as the taxi had to skirt his neighborhood on the way to my condo building.

When the cab pulled up to his house, my eyes went wide. Oh my God, what a house it was; a two-story masterpiece made of dark wood and stone, with big windows, a three-car garage, and a wrap-around porch. And although big, it wasn't ostentatious or gaudy. Rather shyly, he admitted to designing and building it himself and even in the dark of night I could tell this man had taste. The air had continued to pulse and flicker around between us all night. By the time we got into the cab, it was fully charged and so was I, even though he hadn't made a move all night, he hadn't even touched me. It'd been years since I'd dated and wasn't sure what to expect, was he going to kiss me? Invite me in? Another handshake? Oh fuck, a hug? What?

He fished around in his wallet and handed the cabbie a fist full of bills, murmuring, "And that's for the lady too, keep the change."

I protested, but he wouldn't hear of it, and then he leaned in, grazing my cheek with the backs of his fingers. I closed my eyes and licked my lips readying myself for the goodbye kiss. The chill of the evening quickly banished by the heat he generated low in my belly, his look long and probing. Only he didn't kiss me, he moved to the side of my head, his breath warm and stirring, the smell of scotch and his masculine scent driving my senses wild.

"I'd love nothing more than to invite you in and ravish your body until breakfast, but you said you have a gym class in the morning, and if you stayed over you wouldn't get there on time, I'd make sure of it. And..." He nipped my earlobe, making my whole body convulse. "...you, Emma, why you're more than a one-night stand."

Grabbing the back of my head roughly, he kissed me, hard and deep, his mouth swallowing my surprised gasp. Thrusting his tongue into my mouth and spreading my lips, delivering slow savoring licks that made my pussy tighten and long for him to do the same thing lower down on my body. I melted into him, went lax as he pulled me close, allowing him to lead the kiss, matching his plunges and thrusts with my own, sucking on his soft tongue. I whimpered when he bit my lip. It'd been way, way too long since anyone had done that. Eventually, he pulled away with a wolfish smirk. I was panting as I licked my swollen lips. I can only guess what my face looked like, shock? Lust? Wanting? Wanting more, that's for sure.

"Goodnight, Emma," he said, opening the door.

I gulped. "'N-night... James."

"Wow! That sounds hot," Alyssa exclaimed. "Like something out of a romance novel, a real bodice ripper. But the big question is—does he own a pair of Crocs?"

I chuckled. "No! And thank goodness for that! I did manage to slip in that question at some point. It would have been such a pity if he'd said yes."

"What was his deal-breaker?"

"Smoking, like so many people. I guess smoking is one of mine too. But I'd probably put Crocs above smoking."

"Well, duh!" She snorted. "He'll call, for sure."

"Yeah? Well, we'll see—oh, oh, hold on I'm getting another call...

shit, shit, shit it's him! What should I do? Let it go to voicemail or answer it?"

"Fucking answer it! And then call me back immediately! Bye. Good luck!"

I let it ring a couple of more times before I pressed "accept." Not so much as to play hard-to-get or make him sweat, but to simply compose myself. I hadn't felt this giddy or ridiculous about a man since high school.

"Hello?"

"*Emma*." He growled. Oh my God that voice. "How was the gym?" The way this man said my name made my knees weak and my panties wet. I could feel the warmth and pull of his rock hard body through the phone.

I swallowed. "Hey," I replied, trying to sound as relaxed as could, even though inside I was a jiggly blob of goo. "Tough as hell, so in other words, amazing."

"A glutton for punishment are you?"

"No, just a firm believer in no pain no gain."

He chuckled softly. "Meet me for lunch today."

My eyes flashed to the clock on my microwave. "It's already one o'clock."

"Okay, meet me for *linner*."

"Did you just say *linner*?"

"Yeah, let's get linner or lupper or whatever you'd like to call it. I don't want to wait until actual dinnertime to see you. I'll come and get you. Twenty minutes."

I looked down at my yoga pants. Shit, I'd have to change. "Um... okay."

"See you soon."

It didn't occur to me until after we'd hung up that he had no idea where I lived. He hadn't asked for my address, and I hadn't told him last night. How was he going to find me? Did *he* Google *me*?

2

"I'll have an Earl Grey tea with milk and honey, a glass of water and the Thai Chicken Salad please."

"You're ordering tea?"

"Yeah, what's wrong with that? I'm a major tea enthusiast, a bit of a granny, really. I even belong to a Tea-of-the-Month club, but Earl Grey is my favorite." I grinned, trying my best to come across as cute and free-and-easy. Meanwhile, inside I was so incredibly nervous I was sweating under my boobs, and I could feel damp patches under my arms.

"Fair enough."

I didn't think it was possible, but he looked even more handsome in jeans and a tight black t-shirt than he did in his suit last night. His dark wavy hair was tousled in a run-your-hands-through-it-after-a-shower kind of way, and his blue eyes had a sparkle of mischief that I hadn't detected in the pub lighting.

"So, I haven't been able to stop thinking about you or that kiss," he said, his lips turning up into a wicked smirk. "I needed to see you." He was so matter-of-fact that it caught me off guard. There was lust in his eyes, but also an edge, he was keeping his walls up. Was he worried I didn't feel the same?

"Um, wow, you don't beat around the bush do you?"

He lifted one shoulder cavalierly. "I'm a busy man. I don't have time for games. When I see something I want, I go for it. And I want you."

"Ummmm." I wasn't sure how to respond to such a comment. I looked down at my paper napkin. I'd shredded to confetti.

"Look," he started, "I didn't invite you to come in last night because my observations told me that you're not that kind of girl. You're not a prude, but you're also not easy. You like to be treated like a lady, enjoy sex but you just don't have it with random people. Am I correct so far?"

I slowly nodded.

"And I'm guessing you don't do one night stands."

I nodded again, shrugging sheepishly.

"Well, that's pretty much *all* I do," he continued. "But if it's not you, I'm not interested in making you change. But I'm a very busy man, and I don't have a lot of time for relationships and dating. I'm being very upfront about what kind of person I am and what kind of partner I would be. I love sex, I'm *very* good at it, and I would prefer to have it with someone I enjoy spending time with and respect. And I would very much like for you to be that person. I want to take care of you, spoil you, but above all else fuck your brains out. I just won't be a typical hands-on always home, always around boyfriend. Don't expect sweet text messages and phone calls every night that's just not me. I'm too busy. And I'm definitely not the boyfriend, marrying, settle down and have a family type of guy."

"Ummm." I fidgeted in my seat, unbuttoning and removing my black cardigan with as little seduction as I could muster; eager to cool off as I was quickly becoming hot and bothered from the come-hither stare this forward man was giving me. I could feel the flush of arousal creeping up my chest and neck, certain that my cheeks were a rosy pink, showing James just how nervous and turned on he was making me.

Suddenly I was rethinking the red sweater I had on underneath as I'm sure my pit-stains were noticeable. The man was making me sweat.

"So, what are you asking me, then?" Wow, that was easier than I thought, my voice only cracked a tiny bit, maybe he hadn't even noticed? "Are you asking me to be your girlfriend on what's technically our first date? Or a fuck-buddy but more than a fuck-buddy? I'm not saying no, I just want to know what it is I am agreeing to."

Yay, me, that was well articulated, and without any hesitation or dropping of silverware, I rock!

"I want you. Simple as that. I want to fuck you. I *need* to fuck you. I don't remember the last time I *needed* to fuck someone as strongly as I feel the *need* to *fuck* you."

I stared at him, my eyebrows shooting up to my hairline, while my eyes just blinked and blinked and blinked.

"But you need to know I live only in the now and won't make any promises about the future. What I *can* promise, though, is that when we are together, I will take care of you. I want to take you out as my date to special events, have you share my bed as often as you want to, and spend time together when it's convenient. I don't play head games and don't like labels such a *boyfriend* and *girlfriend*, but for lack of a better term, that's what we would be. However, I never share. We would be exclusive, so it's a take it or leave it kind of thing. I'm not a good guy, and I'm not boyfriend material. We have no future. It's all about making each other feel good in the now, for as long as the arrangement works for the both of us."

"Jesus, this got serious quickly," I muttered. "And you certainly have a gift for rhetoric. Have you considered running for office?" That earned me a half-smirk. "But take care of me? I'm twenty-six and very independent. I don't need anyone to 'take care of me.'" I put my head down and stared at my knotted hands. "God... I can't believe I'm having this conversation on a first date. This is so messed up." The waitress must have sensed the tension at the table— hopefully, she didn't pick up on it being *sexual* tension—and quietly placed our plates in front of us. James shook his head when she offered him pepper, so she took off.

He took a deep breath and cut into his steak, put the fork full of meat to his lips and hesitated, looking me in the eye, his expression blank and unreadable. And then he placed the steak between his teeth and pulled the meat off without having it touch his lips. I don't know why he did it, but somehow he knew how it would affect me. It was as hot as hell. I wanted to jump his bones, throw him down on the table, rip his shirt open and have the buttons go flying, as I rode him hard and fast.

"I understand very well that you are an independent woman, Emma, I saw that immediately, and I couldn't admire you more. That doesn't mean I still couldn't bring you tea when you're cold, rub your feet after a run or draw you a bath after a hard day at work. I'm proposing a trial run, but I don't want to do the initial *dating* thing. I want to start this with you, now, today. We'll go on dates as we go, but I want to be with you, now. I don't have time to do the traditional 'date and get to know you, then become a couple' thing I'm just too busy. I have a charity gala I am supposed to attend next Saturday, so you'll come with me. If you're not happy at any point, just tell me and we'll end the arrangement, plain and simple. But I don't have time to date casually. I need to know that we are together. Today."

"Rub my feet? Bring me tea? Those sound like things a *good* guy would do?" Once again I surprised myself with my steady voice, especially because inside I was shaking like a leaf.

He chewed his meat and gave me another salacious grin but shook his head. "I couldn't be further from a good guy. I just know how to make a woman purr."

God this man was something. Brazen, bold, smart, sexy as hell and he was asking me to be his "girlfriend."

What's the worst that could happen? I die from too many orgasms? Not the worst way to go that's for sure.

Confidently, I looked him in the eye and with a small, and I hope sassy and promising smile, I shrugged and said, "Okay." Then I put my head back down and dug into my *linner*. I peeked up from the corner of my eye and could see that he was smiling, his shoulders relaxed, and he no longer looked like he was bracing himself for a letdown.

"And how does everything taste?"

It'd been almost four full minutes since either of us had said anything; we just sat in silence and ate our meal all the while exchanging hooded glances and smirks. Barely acknowledging the waitress with little more than murmurs of thanks, we continued to look at each other through bites and swallows of our food. I found myself mesmerized by the way his throat undulated as he swallowed; watching as his Adam's apple slid sinuously up and down was somehow incredibly erotic. I was longing to kiss it, run my tongue over it. Slowly I felt a foot touch mine under the table, gently rubbing against my boot.

Was he playing footsies with me? Yeah, I guess he was.

As much as my body was screaming to take James to bed and have him make good on all that he'd promised, my mind was prevailing in the battle as it usually did. I wasn't ready. I needed a night alone in my bed to process our arrangement. I hadn't been a relationship for quite a while, and that relationship had been toxic.

I needed some time to sort out what I had just agreed to. Yes, he was smart, kind, handsome, successful, and confident, the list went on and on, but was he funny? I'd seen glimmers of humor in him, and he had a sense of humor, but he hadn't made me laugh, and that was very, very important to me. For too long I'd been in a relationship that only made me cry, and I just couldn't do it again.

"Emma? Where'd you go?"

I snapped back to reality.

"Do you need the night to sleep on everything I've asked you? It's all right if you do. But would you like to come over for a drink, no sexual strings attached. I'm not going to try to lure you into my house and seduce you with wine, music, and ambiance." His nose wrinkled as he gave me a rare but meaningful smile. "Well, okay maybe I am. But I believe you're strong enough to resist my charms if you need more time to think."

Aha, humor! Yes!

I swallowed, thanking the waitress as she took away my plate. "Sure, I'll come over for a glass of wine. But, only ONE glass. I need to keep my wits about me and my pants on. And you're right. I would like some time to think. I'm still getting over a harsh breakup."

"Fair enough. But we'll see about those pants." He winked, flashing me another beautiful smile. "I'll get our coats."

The next thing I knew I was sitting on the soft brick colored leather couch in James' living room with the fire blazing, Jack Johnson playing in the background, and the most fantastic merlot swirling around in my glass. I'm not sure if it was the wine or just the warmth of the fire and cashmere blanket I was curled up in, but I felt comfortable in his home. It didn't feel like a bachelor pad at all.

With an open concept living room, kitchen and dining room, the layout was spacious, functional yet cozy. And even though he was a successful man who could probably afford a much grander house than this, he chose not to live a lavish lifestyle; everything inside had a purpose. Although, when I asked him why he had four spare bedrooms and a two-bedroom garage apartment, he just shrugged and said that they were attractive selling features.

He had superb taste in decorating; shiny hardwood floors, with dark earth tones of browns, coffees, and greens accenting the camel-hued walls throughout. Offset to great effect with landscape paintings and artifacts he'd collected while traveling which he'd placed in just the right places. His house was anything but flamboyant or pretentious; it felt like a home.

I asked about the photograph of a Chocolate Lab sitting on the mantle, and he grew quiet, explaining that he'd had to put Finn down almost a year ago because the dog had had a stroke. I still hadn't brought myself to open up my laptop and Google James, and maybe after tonight, I wouldn't need to.

The conversation continued to flow free and easy throughout the evening. Though each time I asked a question, he would answer it with as little information as possible. He definitely didn't like talking about himself or his feelings. Everything he said was fact based, spoken with very little emotional attachment, and when I asked questions about his family, he'd unobtrusively change the topic. He didn't come across as robotic per se, just aloof. I chalked it up to first-date jitters and hoped that in time he'd bring down the walls and let me in. After all, it was only our first date, our first day as a couple, our fifth hour spent together, how much could I expect from him?

We cuddled on the couch and kissed. There was some heavy petting, a hand up my shirt and some very skilled dry humping, but nothing beyond first base.

Or was grinding considered second base? I have no idea.

At times though, it seemed like he wasn't just holding back for me but possibly for himself as well. Perhaps he needed time too? I know he'd said he wanted to be together now, right this minute, but even when I went to put my hands down his pants, he'd stopped me.

For a man who said he didn't "do" relationships, and that he was the furthest thing from a "nice guy," he was awfully nice and respectful. I could feel his erection through his pants when we were a mess of tangled limbs making out like ninth graders, and I knew that unless I left soon, my willpower would be jumped and beaten to a pulp by my libido.

As he drove me home, we made plans for the following weekend. Saturday was the all important charity gala celebrating the restoration of the cancer clinic. It was being held at a local golf club, and James was on the guest list because his company had been a major benefactor, donating money, time and manpower to the cause. And that wasn't all. After I'd practically nagged it out of him, he reluctantly revealed that he was going to be recognized for his philanthropy and involvement with the organization. Saturday was a big deal.

The kiss when he dropped me off was more like the kisses we'd been sharing on the couch, slow and languid with tongues massaging in and out while our lips caressed and teeth gently nipped.

"Can I come up?" he asked, his breath warm and inviting on my neck. Clearly, he'd decided to give in to the demand of his libido, his hesitation from earlier had obviously been pummeled and beaten until it was no more. His need for me drove me wild. And oh how I wanted to give in too. Oh how I wanted to taste James. Feel James. Be with James in every way. But no, I needed time.

I pushed away from him and plastered myself against the door of the car, giving us more than an arms-length distance. He cocked an eyebrow and looked at me quizzically.

"You're a redolent aphrodisiac, James. I can't smell you, be right next to you and form a coherent thought. You hypnotize me. I want to say yes, and when you kiss me like that I *need* to say yes, but I know that I have to say no. I need some time. Please be patient with me."

His smile nearly made me come on the spot, devilishly triumphant and sexy. The man was getting his own high knowing the effect he had on me.

"What does *redolent* mean?"

"Good smelling. You smell amazing. What is that? Is that just your natural smell? Because if so that's just not fair."

He smiled again and reached for me. I hesitated for a millisecond but all resistance, however momentary, was futile, and I fell back against his hard body, dissolving into him, letting his mouth devour mine and making me kick myself hard for saying he couldn't come up and spend the night.

3

Sunday, Monday, and Tuesday flew by, as I was so busy with work and trying to finish painting my entire apartment, a foolish endeavor I'd begun a few weeks ago. For those three days and nights, I spent most of my downtime in old, ratty clothes singing away to the radio while I tried to return my home to order.

Monday took me back to the gym for a quick workout, and I managed to catch up with Alyssa a bit before and after she gave the spin class. She seemed to be in perfect health after the sushi incident, and her big news was that she and Steve were going on their first holiday together. Her law firm was sending her to Miami in April, for a conference, and Steve had managed to get the time off as well—her excitement and nerves seemed to be running neck-and-neck.

Tuesday I snuck in my usual lunchtime run around the park, showered in the staff office bathroom, then taught my regular late conversation classes to my ESL students all afternoon until nine o'clock.

James didn't call. He had warned me that he was a busy man, so I didn't think anything of it, or at least I tried not to. But my insecurities niggled in the back of my mind daily. I was bummed that I had to wait until Saturday to see him again; it felt like forever. He had said that he'd take care of me when he was around, but had insisted that he wasn't one of the "good guys" and that I shouldn't expect him to give me the time and devotion of a "normal" boyfriend. I still didn't really understand what that meant, but I figured I'd find out soon enough.

I was just getting out of my car and walking into the gym after work on Wednesday when my phone buzzed an incoming text message from James.

James: **What are you up to?**

Emma: **Just walking into the gym. You?**

J: **Trying to figure out what to do for dinner, what are you having?**

E: **Haven't thought that far ahead, probably some sort of chicken and salad combo when I get home. My go-to meal.**

J: **When will you be home?**

E: **7:45-8:00-ish, depends if I stop for groceries or not.**

Should I text, "call me later?". I really wanted to hear his voice, but was that too needy? Screw it.

E: **Call me later?**

J: **You bet. Have a good work out. xo**

E: **Thanks. xx**

I walked into the gym with an added spring in my step and a stupid grin on my face. During my whole kickboxing class, I couldn't peel that dumb smile off, which made it tough to keep kicking my own face in the mirror when my "opponent" was beaming back at me like an idiot.

I was just jumping out of the shower at home with a towel around my head and nothing around my body when there was a knock at the door.

Towel still on my head, I threw on my silk mid-thigh, black kimono dressing gown—one of my only souvenirs, albeit an expensive one from my time teaching English in Asia—and opened the door.

And in he walked, putting a fabric collapsible cooler and bottle of wine on my kitchen counter, kissing me on the cheek as he passed by. "I brought dinner."

Damn, I'd almost forgotten how freaking gorgeous he was; my tall, dark and handsome man with a strong, firm handshake and the sexiest most kissable mouth I'd ever tasted.

"Hi," I panted, already breathless from wanting him.

"Hi. Where are the plates?"

"How do you know I don't already have dinner ready, or that I haven't already eaten?" I sassed, putting my hands on my hips and following him.

"Do you? Have you?" He didn't stop moving about my kitchen opening drawers and cupboards, finding what he needed.

"No," I demurred.

"Well, then go finish getting out of the shower, and I'll put dinner together," he said with such authority and control that I couldn't help but listen.

Shrugging my shoulders, I walked back to the bathroom and began drying my hair. We'd spent all of a few hours getting to know each other, and suddenly we were a couple, already? Good God, he was bringing me dinner and rummaging around in my kitchen making an awful racket. I didn't know how to feel; things had moved quickly. Was I ready for this? Did I have a choice?

I wasn't sure where this evening was going to end, but I wanted to be prepared for anything. I moisturized my freshly shaved legs, put on the cutest pair of tank top and shorty short lacy black pajamas that I could find, and then threw my silk dressing gown back on. I quickly pick combed my curls and scrunched in some gel before grabbing my deodorant and giving my pits one quick swipe as I left the bathroom.

By the time I got back to the kitchen, James had poured us both a glass of a lovely and—according to the label—very rare Argentinean malbec. I didn't even want to think about the price, but expected it to partner well with the beautiful salads he had prepared; greens, blackberries, nuts, cheese, vegetables and grilled chicken. I began to salivate. There were two place settings at my counter bar and a pillar candle glowing and giving off a very wintery and cozy scent. Cinnamon and apples maybe?

"Wow. You work fast. Did you make this salad? It looks fantastic. Are those pine nuts?" I grabbed a few nuts from one of the salads and popped them into my mouth; I was famished after my kickboxing class. Ramona, the instructor, is tough. She knows how to push you to the point of almost puking, and it's addictive, in masochistic kind of way.

"Have a seat and dig in. I'm just going to do the dishes in the sink and then I'll join you," he said, plopping the tongs and big salad bowl into the sink.

"Oh, don't wash up." I patted the seat next to me. "I'll do that. It's the least I can do after you took care of dinner, come sit down, the dishes can wait."

He finished drying his hands and came over to sit next to me, planting another kiss on my cheek and scooting his chair closer to mine, so our legs touched. His proximity and clothed leg touching my bare leg sent shivers up and down my body. I crossed my legs and squeezed, this was going to be a difficult night to get through if I intended to wait until Saturday to sleep with him. My nipples tightened against my tank top and pushed against the silk of my robe. Did he notice?

I took a bite of my salad and closed my eyes as the harmonious blending of flavors burst across my tongue. A vinaigrette like I'd never tasted before; spicy, grainy mustard, a hint of smoky and sweet woodsy maple notes, finishing with a citrus bite that had me all but licking the bowl by the time I'd finished. I looked up and saw him staring at me with a curious half smirk. The flash of his grin made my heart stop for just a moment. Did I have food on my face, lettuce between my teeth? Was I inhaling it like I came from a family of twelve wrestlers? Was I eating too much? What?

"Do you like it?" he asked, with genuine curiosity and perhaps even a bit of hope in his voice.

"It's unbelievable. Delicious doesn't do it justice. It's... orgasmic." I used my finger to wipe my bowl clean, licking off the dressing.

"Orgasmic? Well if that's how you orgasm we're going to have some issues. I'll never know when you've climaxed. You just sat there and ate the salad with your eyes closed and a tiny smile on your face. Is that how you come?"

I wasn't prepared for such a personal comment to come out of the blue and spat out my wine... everywhere.

"T-that's not what I meant," I stammered, wiping my lips and the counter top with my napkin. "I just meant that the salad was pure pleasure. It was wonderful, thank you." I could feel my face getting hot; it was probably as red as the Malbec.

"So, I will know when you come?"

"Yes," I whispered, staring into my wine glass; this was a very weird start to our impromptu date. I dared to peek at him out of the corner of my eye; he was finishing his salad with a shit-eating grin on his face. Oh, this man.

"Am I making you uncomfortable, Emma? You look scandalized."

I grabbed his empty salad bowl as well as my own and walked them to the sink. I filled the sink, pumped the soap and watched the water foam and froth as I weighed his question and my response.

"No, not uncomfortable," I finally said. "You just shocked me with your frankness. I'm extremely comfortable talking about sex, in any capacity with virtually anyone, well... minus my mother and my grandmother. But even with my mum, I can have an adult conversation about sex. We just don't get into personal details. I'm not going to text my mum and be like, 'Hey you should really try out this new position, it's great.'"

He barked a loud and hearty laugh that made my lady parts tingle as he took a sip of his wine and then came over to the sink to start drying. "Can you now? So, I can ask you *any* question about sex, your experiences, preferences whatever, and you will answer honestly and not go all red in the face or spit wine all over yourself?"

It was true; I didn't have a problem talking about sex now. In the past, I would have, for sure, because every time I'd tried to talk about it with Tom, he would chastise me, make me feel wrong and dirty, and not in a good way. But being with Max and Alex had changed me, helped me become much more comfortable with the topic. In fact some days it was *all* we'd talked about.

I gave him a playful elbow in the ribs. "Yes. Can I ask you the same questions and expect honest responses? It's not a one-way street."

"Of course." One shoulder casually lifted half an inch. "I'm an open book. How many men have you been with?"

Really? We were jumping, right into our fuck-numbers? Wow!

"Three. You?"

"Zero... men."

I rolled my eyes and hit him gently with the tongs that were in my hand.

"A hundred and twenty-six."

A hundred and twenty-six? Holy shit! That's almost five times as many women as years that I've been on this earth. I started doing the math in my head. Okay, the man was thirty-eight, so let's say he started having sex around sixteen, and from then until now he slept with roughly five women a year, that's only a hundred and ten women. Throw in some serious relationships, followed by a binge of one-night stands after a breakup. I took a deep breath, suddenly a hundred and twenty-six didn't sound *that* outrageous.

"Em? Where'd you go?"

I shook my head and swallowed. "Uh nowhere, sorry. Just uh... just doing some math."

His mouth twitched as though he were trying to keep from smiling. He knew he'd shocked me.

"Sorry, what did you ask me?" I asked, trying to keep up with his line of questioning.

"Have you ever been with any women?"

"No."

"So, I guess the question about threesomes is out? If you've never been with a woman and you've only been with three men."

I raised my eyebrows and then became exceedingly focused on scrubbing the bowl that was in the sink.

"So you have?"

"Yes," I admitted.

"Two men?"

"Yes."

"When?"

"About nine months ago when I was in Europe traveling."

"You just met two guys and had sex with them?"

I couldn't tell if there was a hint of disproval in his voice or not. I hadn't told anyone about what had happened in Europe. I'd told Alyssa that I'd met a couple of guys and slept with them. But I hadn't gone into any greater detail, and she hadn't asked, so I never told her. She just seemed happy that I was getting over Tom and moving on.

"Well, no, not exactly. Are you going to get all judgy on me? Because I don't have to tell you if you don't want to know. And regardless of the fact that I've had sex with two men at the same time, my number is still significantly smaller than yours. And I bet it wouldn't be too much of an assumption to say that you've probably had a threesome once or twice yourself." I hoped that he didn't detect the frustration and fear in my voice. This revelation could send him packing and out the door, depending on what kind of guy he was.

He grabbed the bowl from my hand and put it on the counter. Then he took both my hands and led me over to my comfy micro suede sofa

"I'm not going to get *all judgy* on you. I just want to know you—everything about you, the good the bad, the clean the dirty. If it helps, yes, I have had threesomes but never with men. I've had two, with two different sets of women. And I'm not ashamed of them. We were all consenting adults. I don't have many regrets... don't have time for them."

"Okay," I said slowly.

Do it like a Band-Aid, woman, just get it all out and let him decide for himself.

"It's just that it wasn't just sex with Max and Alex. We were *together*. All three of us. Well not all *three* of us. They are heterosexual best friends, but they behave more like brothers. They grew up together, their families were neighbors since the boys were five and their birthdays are twelve days apart. In a word, they are inseparable. We met on a flight from Paris to Ibiza."

Not sure how much to tell James, I did some self-censoring; I'd desperately needed to sow some wild oats and have a little fun and had chosen Ibiza because of its reputation for being a crazy party island. I'd been looking, hoping for, no, *craving* an innocuous fling with a sexy

European, but instead I'd found two drop-dead gorgeous hunks of Australian manliness.

I continued, "I was stuck sitting in the middle seat, and they were on either side of me. Why they didn't just pay for the middle seat is beyond me, they're enormous, in a muscly kind of way, and I was incredibly uncomfortable jammed between them. Sorry random tangent... anyway, they're software developers from Australia, and their company is rather successful, so they were on a bit of a working holiday. Fortunately, they have the luxury of working wherever as long as the Internet connection is decent.

"We shared a cab from the airport because as it turned out, we were all booked at the same resort. The boys wanted to upgrade to the presidential suite and asked if I wanted to join them as we would each have our own room as well as a kitchen, living room, office, dining room and private balcony. We were friends for a while before anything sexual happened. They made me feel safe, and best of all I didn't have to travel alone anymore. I didn't much care for it."

My mind drifted back to the night they'd asked me to join them...

"So uh, listen, Lovey," Max said, taking a sip of his water, "do you remember our drunk dinner conversation last night? The one about Al and me sharing a woman?"

"Yeah."

We were sitting at what had quickly become one of our favorite restaurants in Ibiza. One that Manny, our favorite bartender at the swim-up bar had recommended. The place was just down the road from our resort and tucked down a small alley with no sign on the door or overhead. The food was authentic, cheap and filling. And after you got past the fact that you had to walk through a Spanish family's backyard to get to the rooftop terrace bistro, it was the best food and wine we'd found yet.

"Well, we were wondering if maybe... 'cause we've always wanted to try... to uh, share a woman. Would you be interested in a—" But Alex cut him off.

"What Max is trying to say is, would you be interested in having a threesome with us? We've always wanted to try it. We think you're hot as hell and it might loosen you up a bit."

"Uh..." I grabbed my water glass and chugged fiercely, letting their offer sink in. Though I'm not sure, it ever would. The entire notion was insane.

"You don't need to give us your answer right away," he added. "Think about it. But we think it could be fun. We find you incredibly gorgeous, smart, sexy, funny, easy to be around, and although I can't speak for Max, I would like nothing more than to lick your clit until you scream."

Max nodded in agreement. I gasped, and wicked grin took over Alex's mouth. A mouth I'd done nothing but dream about for the past week.

He went on, "The only reason we haven't tried anything with you until now is that we both want you and we don't want to fuck up the dynamic we have going on by making you choose. Plus, you're kind of damaged... no offense. If you don't want to then just say no and we'll pretend we never had this conversation."

"We also respect you," Max added. "You're more than just a piece of ass. You're our friend."

"Right." Alex nodded. "What he said. But let's not pretend like we haven't caught you checking out the both of us."

I hid my eyes sheepishly, looking up at them beneath my lashes. It was true; I was checking them out, constantly. Both had become the male leads of my fantasies. And I was spending an awful lot of time locked in my room with my mini travel-vibrator lately and was getting worried it might break down on me with overuse. I'd had to replace the batteries twice already.

"I've, uh, I've never had a guy do that to me before." I looked down into my lap and twisted my linen napkin around my index finger until it started to turn purple, unwilling to look them in the eyes.

What if I'm too vanilla for them? Too inexperienced?

"Do what?" Max asked softly, he reached for my hand, lifted it from my lap and stilled my twitching palm. He was grounding and calm, and immediately I felt better.

"Put their mouth on me there before. Tom refused to go down on me. He thought it was dirty."

"Did you go down on him?" Alex asked.

I nodded. "All the time, it was his preferred way to get off."

"Selfish asshole." He snorted. "I love eating pussy. And I bet you have a very pretty little one."

Abashed, I blushed, hiding my eyes from his penetrating, mind reading gaze. I could feel the heat creeping up my neck; embarrassment with a healthy dose of arousal if I'm honest. Jesus, Alex really didn't hold back. He just said whatever was on his mind. It was hot, but also a little frightening.

Truth be told, I'd always wanted to have two guys make love to me, one inside me, while one ate me out. I'd watched it in a porno once, it had looked so hot, just seemed so primitive and carnal, and although it was porn, it didn't look like the actress was acting, she definitely appeared to be enjoying herself.

"Listen, Em," Max said, "you don't have to answer right now. Just think about it. No pressure. But, I believe we can help you. It seems like this Tom guy really did a number on you. You're a beautiful, sexy, sensual woman and you have a right to pleasure." He shrugged. "We could show you."

I lifted my head and scanned their handsome faces; their eyes honest and eager. I'd already spent enough time with them to know that they would be patient and gentle with me, not pushing me any further than I was ready, guiding me and teaching me along the way. And I needed it, needed it so badly. Wasn't that why I'd come to Ibiza? To get laid! And now I had two devastatingly handsome men asking to make love to me, not one, but two! Could I handle two? My body was already humming with the thought of their lips on my skin. And they were right; I was damaged. Tom *had* done a number on me. The man had ruined me.

So, going with the theme of this entire trip, self-discovery and rehabilitation of both my mind *and* body, I looked them in the eyes, squared my shoulders, pushed out my chest, took a deep breath and said, "Okay..."

I looked back up at James, his expression still hadn't changed, but he gave me a small nod, encouraging me to continue.

I pressed on, "We went out for dinner the following night and had a few drinks, but none of us were plastered, just enough liquid courage to reduce our inhibitions and increase our spontaneity.

"And the whole experience was incredible. I felt sexy and desirable. They were gentle and patient because they knew that it had been awhile and that my sexual experience was limited. They understood that I needed to take things slow, but at the same time, they made my body come alive. They fucked me hard. They screwed my brains out until I couldn't keep my eyes open and I was pushing them off me because my body couldn't take anymore. They made it all about me. And one night ended up not being enough, we all kind of fell in love with the lifestyle. They had a woman whom they could fuck when they wanted and was eager to please and learn, and I had two gorgeous men who adored me and provided me with orgasms on demand.

"We got along incredibly well and flew to mainland Spain a week later, backpacked all through the hill towns, took a train to Italy, spent a month there and finally ended in Greece for our last month together. We saw the sights as friends and companions, goofing off at all the major historical attractions and then providing one another with pleasure and comfort at night. And there was never any pressure to have sex. If I wasn't into it, they never pushed or bullied me. It was always safe and consensual. And often I only slept with one of them. They worked out a system, and we had sex when we needed and wanted to. But it wasn't always three people fucking like monkeys on ecstasy, it was somehow all really easy.

"We parted ways after Greece, I came home, and they headed back to Australia. We still send email updates, follow each other on social media, but we agreed that what happened in Europe stays in Europe. They are two of my best friends, and I owe them a lot. They brought me back from a very dark place, and I am incredibly grateful to them for that. They awakened my sexuality. They made me *like* sex." I exhaled and searched for my wine but then frowned when I realized it was all the way over on the kitchen counter.

"How..." finally breaking the long and awkward silence that had seemed to fill the room, James scrunched his eyebrows, "how do you fuck guy A and have guy B go down on you without guy B getting repeatedly smacked in the chin with guy A's ball sack?"

I opened my mouth and closed it a few times like a fish, more surprised that that was where his mind had gone, that his first response to my admission of being part of a three-month relationship with two gorgeous Australians was how not why.

Did this mean he was okay with what I had done and was trying to lighten the mood?

"I mean gay or bi-sexual guys probably wouldn't care to have a ball sack in their face or whatever, but it would certainly make my johnson droop if some wrinkly taint landed on my head."

I couldn't withhold the laugh; he'd managed to paint quite the visual.

"Um, well, guy A lays on his back and the girl lies on top of him on her back sliding him into her that way. Both guy A and the girl need to spread their legs, and it's best if this is done on the edge of a bed. Then guy B positions himself in between their legs and eats the girl out that way."

He tilted his head to the side and pursed his lips as if trying to picture the position with three naked bodies writhing in pleasure. It was an adorable look on him and made me want to kiss those lips, but I was still really nervous about his reaction.

"Were you guys doing any drugs?"

"No." I shook my head. "I don't do drugs, and they don't either. Alex's uncle died of an overdose when the boys were ten—they were the ones who found him in their fort in Alex's backyard so, understandably, they're heavily against narcotics. That's not to say they don't drink like sailors, but no, we never did any drugs."

"Good," he said, nodding absentmindedly. "I don't tolerate drug use."

"Neither do I."

He made a mock pout and nodded once more. "Huh. Well, that all sounds hot. It takes a lot to shock a man like me, but you've managed to do that. Good for you. At least you got it out of your system because I can't say we'll be having any three-ways. I don't share. But more importantly, what did Tom do to you? Can you tell me about that if you're willing?"

And just like that, his momentary flash of possessiveness was over. He got up for a moment, retrieved our wine glasses and the bottle then topped us both up.

I continued to talk. I told James how Tom and I had been together since high school and all through university. I mentioned going to China to teach English, then coming back after Tom begged me to, and how subsequently he dumped me a month later because the girl he'd been cheating on me with was pregnant.

I explained how Tom was sexually oppressed; that he preferred only two positions, missionary, and spooning, as he believed it was emasculating to be beneath a woman, even during sex. Alex and Max had done more than just help me forget Tom and realize there were much better people and lovers out there, but they helped me realize that *I* was a better lover. That sex wasn't dirty, and neither was I and that a woman on top is hot as hell, not emasculating.

James and I snuggled on the couch for a while, kissing and talking. He was such an interesting person; he'd traveled the world, worked all different kinds of jobs from dishwasher to tree-planter. It blew my mind that he'd seen and done it all.

Our bottle of wine was long gone though I'm pretty sure I'd consumed the majority of it. I knew that James held off drinking more because he wasn't sure if he was going to be driving home or not—that made two of us. I wasn't sure where the night was going either.

Should I ask him to stay over? Could we sleep in the same bed and not have sex?

I think I needed more time...

Suddenly he jumped up from our nest of limbs and blankets on the couch. "I can't do this anymore."

"C-can't do what?" What had I done? Was he really okay about my past with Alex and Max? Or had he realized he couldn't accept me after having a bit of time to think? Maybe he thought I was a pathetic loser for letting Tom bully me for so many years?

"I can't sit here and not know what your pussy tastes like. I know we have this unspoken agreement that we are going to wait to sleep together until after the gala on Saturday night, but I can't wait until then to taste you. And I need to know what you sound like when you come."

He fell to his knees and pulled my legs around, so they rested on his shoulders. Pushing my shorty-shorts and thong to the side, he blew cold air gently on my most sensitive area. I was already wet from all our kissing; my legs parted shamelessly, and I sucked in a breath as he gently drew a finger around my opening. His hands were confident and skilled and the man took what he wanted. And I was more than willing to give. He continued to swirl his finger around my wet and swollen slit, deliberately not pushing it inside like I wanted him to, like I needed him to. And then his mouth was on me; his tongue swirled around my clit in rhythmic circles then he thrust his finger into me, pushing in and out at just the right speed, my hips started to move, matching his rhythm.

"Jesus you're tight," he mumbled. I pushed my pelvis into his face trying to get more pressure in the right places. "And greedy, how long did you say it's been since you've had sex?" He slipped another finger inside me, and I nearly fell off the couch. My hands slid into his thick hair as I rode his face.

"I... it's been a while, oh ah... uh, nine months." My eyes were closed, and I chewed on my bottom lip, grinding myself against his face.

My body was a maelstrom, my nerves unsure of what was happening, but relishing the discovery. I began to lose focus on the rhythm, my hips weak and jerking randomly as I tried to delay my destination, the journey just felt so damn good. He coaxed my body to the brink, just enough to make me writhe, but not enough to make me come. Over and over, like playing a fish on a line, he'd reel me into the edge and then let me slide back down, playing with me, toying with me.

Cleverly, he remained focused on my clit, speeding up his efforts until a single stroke would set me off, only then did he move lower and thrust his tongue inside me, soft shallow dips and plunges, gentle and provocative laps of warm velvet against my sensitive flesh. Ready to combust, I whined and moaned, begging and pleading with him to let me come. Tightening my grasp on his hair and pushing myself into his face just as I let go.

"Oh fuck. Oh God. Oh God, oh, oh, ah, ah... oh God. Don't stop."

My release continued to build and spread and swell as his efforts never ceased. Finally, I had to push him off me I was so tender. Every lap of his tongue sent shivers up my spine and made my legs twitch until I felt I was going to get a Charlie Horse. I wasn't ready for multiples, not just yet. I melted into the couch heavy limbed as he gently removed my legs from his shoulders and placed them on the cushions so I could lay down flat.

"I like the way you come," he said sitting back down on the couch and draping my legs over his lap, licking his fingers. His face appeared flushed, and a beading of perspiration glistened on his forehead like a badge of honor. "Little whimpers, cursing and then praying to a higher power. As if he had *anything* to do with your orgasm." He chuckled softly and then started massaging my feet. "So, am I correct to assume that we are going to wait to sleep together until Saturday after the gala. The whole 'third-date rule?' Though, I'd consider this our third date. Can I spend the night?"

"I... um, just give me a second to collect myself," I said out of breath as I flopped an arm over my eyes and tilted my head back against the couch, peeking out to look at him.

His wicked grin made me want to jump up, straddle him, and ride his blatant erection until neither of us could form a complete sentence.

"What you did right there is making it *extremely* difficult for me to want to wait until Saturday. But maybe we should. I've never really dated, so I don't know this whole 'third-date rule.' But, hold on a minute," I sat up and looked at him, "are you considering the night we met to be our first date?"

He shrugged and continued to smile. "A guy can try."

I giggled, desperate to have that smiling mouth give me more and more delicious orgasms.

"I just… I just don't want to rush things. I'm enjoying getting to know you. But that doesn't mean I can't help *you* out and relieve some of the stress." I repositioned myself on the couch pulling my feet away from his grasp and grabbing at the zipper on his jeans.

"Oh no," he protested. "I'm not interested in repayment." He took my hands and brought them to his lips, kissing each fingertip, and the inside of my wrists. "I got what I wanted. I got to taste you and hear you come. That's enough for me tonight. And if you want to wait until Saturday then that's okay. I'm enjoying getting to know you, too."

I snuggled up next to him, pulling the blankets up and over our legs. "Would you like to spend the night? We could just sleep? Or at least try to just sleep."

"I would love to spend the night," he purred. "And I can *just* sleep if you can *just* sleep." He smiled those perfect pearly whites again, and I couldn't stop myself, I tackled him and peppered kisses all over his face; finishing with one on his lips that lingered and grew more intense as the minutes ticked by.

4

"You look lovely," James said accepting the coffee I offered him in my kitchen the next morning. Kissing my temple, he walked past me and dropped two slices of bread into the toaster with the familiarity and nonchalance as if this wasn't the first morning we'd ever done this.

"You don't look too bad yourself there, stud. I could stare at you in a suit all day." He smiled and opened my fridge, grabbing the peanut butter. He'd slung his jacket over the bar stool and was just sporting the vest and pants; his back muscles flexed as he screwed off the lid of the jar. Watching with lust-filled fascination, I licked my lips, gulped, and took a sip of my tea. Suddenly I was parched.

"Thank you for letting me spend the night. Even if we didn't do anything, I enjoyed sleeping next to you." He came up behind me as I peeled a hard-boiled egg, planting feather light kisses along my shoulders, the heat from his lips causing all kinds of dirty thoughts to embed themselves in my mind. These were going to be a *long* two days!

"Thank *you* for staying, and for the uh, the preview of what I'm to expect on Saturday," I said looking over my shoulder.

He winked. I sipped my tea and sprinkled some salt and pepper on my egg, leaning against the counter, drinking in his gorgeousness. The toaster popped up his bread, and he began to smear peanut butter on his toast liberally. I watched with a wry smirk as he continued to slather it onto the slices until it was nearly an inch thick.

He turned to face me mid-bite asking, "What?" while continuing to chew with a sassy grin.

"Nothing..."

"You think I put too much peanut butter on my toast? Go on, say it. Everybody else does."

I smiled. "If someone tells you that you put too much peanut butter on your toast stop talking to them. You don't need that kind of negativity in your life. Trowel on the whole jar for all I care. Do what makes you happy."

I walked over and scooped a large dollop of PB out of the jar with my finger and sucked it off provocatively, causing his eyebrows to shoot up his forehead. He let out a husky laugh and put his toast on the counter before grabbing me in a boob-crushing hug against his chest. His body shook with laughter as he bent his head low to kiss me, our peanut butter laden lips and tongues gliding over one another in a nutty tango. I rested my arms on his shoulders and toyed with the soft hair at the nape of his neck, twisting it around my fingers and pulling until I received the sought after growl of approval against my mouth.

"Where'd you come up with that?" he asked still laughing and holding me tight.

"I saw it on a meme." I grinned, licking a smidgen of peanut butter off the corner of his mouth, he growled again and reclaimed my mouth. And then the make-out session started all over again.

Thursday and Friday trickled by like sands through a never-ending hourglass. James had called twice on Thursday after we'd parted ways reluctantly that morning and headed to work, and again Friday afternoon while I was at lunch. But, I was starting to over-think our upcoming date to the gala would I be enough glitter on his arm like the candy I was meant to be? Would I be enough for him? And more importantly, would I be enough for him in bed at the end of the night?

Alyssa and I caught a movie on Friday night after spin class, to make up for our missed drinks the week before, and hopefully, we had burned enough calories to earn the extra-large buttery popcorn we ordered. I filled her in on the past week and how James had surprised me with dinner on Wednesday and that we'd spent the night together, but nothing happened. Well not nothing, I did have a mind blowing orgasm.

"I'm nervous about Saturday," I said as we watched the trivia questions come up on the screen at the theater. Without missing a beat, we both said "Reese Witherspoon" to the blurred picture on the screen.

"Nervous about what?" she asked, quietly pulling her gym water bottle out of her purse and taking a sip. "The gala? You'll be fine, wear the royal blue dress that you bought for my sister's wedding, it's so hot, and you'll knock his and every other dude's socks off."

I shook my head. "No, not the gala, *after* the gala. The sex. I feel like I'm putting all this pressure on Saturday night. Maybe we should have just screwed on Wednesday when he slept over. What if I have too much wine or champagne and act like an idiot in bed? Or I over-think it like I'm prone to doing and can't get off? 'Cause that's happened too, you know. Your mind wanders, and then you can't get back to your almost orgasm. I just start making lists of things I need to do the next day. Or groceries."

She nodded and agreed, saying that she would often start thinking about work in her head when she was having sex and sometimes couldn't get off because she was so worried that she'd messed something up on an important document.

"Or what if I'm lame in bed and not adventurous enough? He's been with *a lot* of women. He's experienced. Way, way more than me. And if his cock skills are anything like his tongue skills, he's going to be incredible."

The screen went black, and the room began to dim. The reminder to turn off your cell phones came on, and the theater became aglow with the back lights as dozens of phones were turned off.

"Then have sex with him before Saturday night," she whispered, shoving a giant handful of greasy popcorn into her mouth.

"When? Tonight? After the movie? I can't show up there at midnight and jump his bones. Especially not sober. That's a drunken booty call kind of thing."

"Well, how about tomorrow after your workout? Call him and find out if he's home. Then go over there in your regular clothes all showered and clean from the gym with your endorphins high, and just say you want to have sex now. So there isn't any expectation or pressure looming over the evening. That you want to sleep together in the middle of the day when you're just normal people in normal clothes doing something normal people do."

I wrinkled up my nose in thought. It wasn't such a terrible idea. "You don't think he'd be weirded out by that?"

"*Pfft, n*o, he's a guy. And you're going over there to have *sex* with him. He'll love it. And then you can have a relaxing evening at the gala and go home and screw again without any pressure or stress. Been there done that."

"*Shush!*" Came a voice from the back.

Oh relax, it's the bloody previews.

But we stopped talking anyway. I had a lot of thinking to do. Alyssa's suggestion made a lot of sense. And I was, for some very strange and inconvenient reason, most aroused around one o'clock in the afternoon.

5

Saturday morning's class at the gym was hard, harder than usual. Perhaps it was because I'd put in extra effort or that I'd gone early and run five miles on the treadmill beforehand, but I was limp and tired by the time I got home.

Could I go over to James' house with the intention of just fucking him to get it over with?

That's a terrible way to put it, but that's precisely what I intended to do. I wanted this man more than anything, but I was also nervous about sleeping with him. I quickly dressed after a meticulous shower and put my hair in a messy bun after I'd dried it.

I got dressed, making sure to pick an outfit that didn't scream "trying too hard." One quick dab of blush on my cheeks and some glossy lip balm, I was out the door. And then I sat in my car and rang James. When we'd talked on the phone over the past week, he had been the one calling. This was the first time I'd called him, and I was nervous, still unsure of what to say.

"Emma, hi."

"Hey, what are you up to?"

"Just got out of the shower, I managed to run about twelve miles today."

"Wow, good for you. You staying home for a while or heading out?" I asked.

"Home for a bit. I've got some emails to catch up on, then I'm going to run out and pick my tux up from the dry cleaners. Why?"

"Oh, no reason. Just interested in how your day is going to pan out before I see you. I like to think about what you're doing while I'm doing what I'm doing." I rolled my eyes at myself.

Did that sound as stupid out loud as it did in my head? Yes, yes it did.

"Oh, I like that too. What are your plans for the day?"

"Just getting dressed and then going to go grocery shopping and run some errands. Nothing too exciting. But I should let you go. I'll see you tonight."

"Okay, well... thanks for calling. This is the first time you've called me. I like it. Enjoy your afternoon. I can't wait for *tonight*." His emphasis on the last word spoke volumes about his intentions, laden with promise and seduction. It sent a ripple of lust right up my spine and down again. I was aroused and perhaps a little frightened, but frightened in a good way, like when you go to a horror movie or ride a roller coaster. You like being scared for just a moment, it makes you feel alive and gets your adrenaline pumping—and that's certainly what James did for me. My engine was revved up, and I was ready to go.

My mind wandered to what the man had planned for this evening, so much so that there was silence on the other end of the phone, and I realized he was waiting for me to reply.

Oh shit, what did he say?

I quickly rummaged through my horny brain, and my seemingly empty short-term memory, only to come up with dick-all, so I took a shot in the dark. "Uh... yeah, me too. Bye."

There was a whiskey-thick chuckle on the other end, followed by a slow and deliberate. "*Bye.*"

Did he buy it?

It was hard to tell, he's such a perceptive man. Maybe he knew I was lying. I've never been very good at lying. Well, at least he was home. I was committed to it now.

I parked my car in his driveway roughly ten minutes later, confident that he wasn't aware of my intentions and that the long grumbling gravel path from the road to the house hadn't given me away. I walked up and knocked on the door as butterflies did back flips in my belly and my body trembled and my core tightened. I craved James at this point, was starved for his touch and his lips on my body again, he was already becoming as necessary as air. I saw his shadow in the mottled glass on either side of the big French doors.

Did he know it was me just by my silhouette?

"Emma? This is a surprise. Is everything okay?" He moved out of the way and motioned for me to enter the house. I could feel the heat of his big, hard body and the masculine scent of his skin, fresh from the shower was intoxicating. He had me spellbound the moment I stepped across his threshold. I would do anything for this man. I took a gulp, steadied my breathing and looked up into his eyes. How was it he made me nervous but wanton at the same time?

"I, um... I don't want to wait. I can't wait until tonight. I need to, uh... w-we need to fuck... *now*."

"Okay." He shrugged, and instantly he was on me with the nape of my neck in his hand and his lips crushing mine.

God, he was hard, damn hard. That was fast! He savored my mouth, tasting and jabbing with his velvet tongue, grinding the iron-hard length of his rod against my belly. I'm not entirely sure how we managed to get to his bed as quickly as we did, especially since his room was upstairs. But in no time at all, I was flat on my back with his excitement pressing into my hip. My coat and scarf were removed on the way from the door to the bed, and James was pulling at the hem of my shirt to bring it over my head.

I had ransacked my stash of wild and daring undergarments; it'd been hard to choose between the leopard print balconette and the classic red and black plunge push-up. I went with the push-up, figuring I'd save the jungle print for another night.

My shirt was off, and he groaned in appreciation at the sight of the red and black classic brazier; a long and nimble finger dipped beneath the hem of the bra to pull on a pert nipple for just a second. His other hand came up, and soon he was caressing both of my breasts, kneading them with soft rhythmic squeezes. One hand drifted up into my hair, and he pulled free my messy bun, fisting my hair and tugging my head closer, devouring my mouth with his, swallowing my pants and gasps as he ground and rolled his hips skilfully against mine, teasing me, taunting me.

He stopped for just a moment to unzip my boots and throw them to the ground, and I took the pause to catch my breath and lean back on my elbows and watch this handsome man undress me. I was no longer nervous; no, the butterflies in my belly were no longer apprehensive, they were excited. Hot and bothered and so turned on.

Relieving me of my socks and delivering a devilish bite to each big toe, he then stood up, ready to dominate my body again. But I pushed myself to a sitting position, my legs dangling over the bed, kicking playfully and I reached for the hem of his shirt. Kissing a trail from his bellybutton toward his chest I lifted it over his head, licking and tugging at each of his nipples, continuing on to his neck and cheek and along the curve of his strong, masculine jaw, tasting him. I bit his lip and pulled lightly, delighting in the carnal groan that emanated from the back of his throat.

"Oh, Emma." In a surprisingly sweet gesture, he reached up and softly ran the back of his hand against my cheek and down my neck, eyes staring into mine, stripping me bare and leaving me raw and open. He gulped. "I... I need you so badly. I don't know if I can go slow."

I continued to hold his gaze, and a sassy smile caught my lips as I shrugged. "Then don't."

He pushed me back to the bed and quickly unzipped his pants stepping out of them. I decided to do the same and shimmied out of my jeans. When I looked up, he was staring at me, like a lion stares a gazelle right before it pounces. Eyes ablaze with heat and hunger, he was starving too. Every hard, luscious inch of him exuded sin, sex, and seduction. I was finally seeing him almost entirely naked—he'd slept in boxers and a t-shirt at my house—and then man was a work of art, a magnum opus. Designed by the heavens, bronze skinned, chiseled and toned. But not like a gym monkey who picks things up and puts them down for the sake of seeing his traps flex. No, James' muscles were gained by honest, hard labor, from working with his hands like a man's man. A soft dusting of hair ran from his bellybutton down beneath his boxers, and a small patch sprinkled his chest between very defined pecs; just enough to be manly, not so much for me to mistake him for a bear. He truly was a masterpiece.

"Take 'em off," I purred as I playfully snapped the waistband of his black boxer briefs.

Without a word and without taking his eyes from mine he obliged. His erection sprung free and rested against his belly. Dear lord, he was big! I hesitantly leaned forward to touch him. It was like a freaking snake, and a small part of me expected the thing to haul off and bite me. I took him in my hands, his skin was so soft, yet he was so hard, he was beautiful. He wasn't circumcised which was all right with me, none of the guys I'd been with had been, so I really didn't know any different. I ran my hands up and down his length cupping his soft hairless balls and tugged them ever so gently.

He inhaled and gave a moan when I put my lips to the tip and kissed it, bringing my tongue out and gently caressing the silky purple head, flicking and probing the small hole at the top, and continuing to run my hand up and down his shaft. I licked the veins that coursed the length of him, watching with lust and intrigue as every muscle in his body became rigid, poised to fuck as hard as his eyes promised. He had tangled his hands in my hair and gently pushed my head forward, so I took in more of him. I was a little hesitant to deep throat him right away. It'd been a while since I'd had a cock in my mouth. I'd need to work up to it and relax my throat otherwise I'd gag, and it'd all be over. I'd been pretty good at suppressing my gag reflex before, with Alex and Max, but I just needed a moment; James was big.

"Ah, fuck..." he moaned. "Yes... suck it hard. I love your greedy little mouth."

Another guttural groan and he began to move my head faster and harder, begging for me to take him deeper into my mouth. I relaxed my jaw and pushed forward until his cock knocked my tonsils. I didn't gag. The salty taste of pre-cum dripped onto my tongue and down my throat as his breath hitched, and his rhythm grew more erratic.

Was he going to come? Could he go again so quickly if he did? I needed to fuck. I came here to fuck!

Almost as soon as I finished, that thought he pulled out of my mouth. His shaft slapped against his belly as he pushed me back to the bed, pulling the cups of my bra down and taking a nipple into his mouth as he gently tugged and pinched the other one. He lightly bit down, and I gasped, bucking my hips into him, desperate for some kind of friction. He switched breasts and delivered the same sweet torture to the other one, flicking his tongue against the sensitive bud and sucking gently and then harder.

I was lost in the magic of his warm and devoted mouth. His tongue continued to travel lower, grazing down my torso, tracing a path of sexy little circles around my bellybutton. He kept both hands on my tits, continuing to torment them with twists and pinches. Slowly he moved his hands down my sides tickling me as he went, planting kisses on my inner thighs and behind my knees; deftly pulling my thong off, he tossed it to the floor to join the rest of our clothes.

"Do you wax or shave?" he asked, his voice like thick molasses.

"Shave," I panted. "I used to wax but hated the waiting period between waxes where I was hairy again. I'm not very patient. And I hate hair."

He chuckled low and deep in his throat. "I like that you'll be bare every day. Nothing between your pussy and whatever I decide to do with it." Then he plunged his tongue between my folds, and inside me so fast I nearly kneed him in the skull.

Using his fingers to spread me open, he licked through my folds before sucking on my clit. I was already going crazy, bucking my hips into his face and burying my hands in his hair as the fluttering dips of his tongue into my trembling core kept me riding the edge. But I didn't want to come this way; I wanted him inside me, I needed to feel him inside me, but oh God it felt so good.

"Oh God, don't stop! No stop! No, don't stop! Oh, stop... I don't want to come this way. I'm so close... I-I need you inside me." My voice was no more than a strangled whisper as I fought to stave off my release.

"Impatient *and* indecisive." He chuckled, lifting his head up with that mischievous smile, his lips glistening with my wetness. He leaned over to the bedside table and opened up a drawer. I put my head back down on the bed waiting as I heard the telltale sound of a foil wrapper.

Before my mind could wander any further, he was over me again and teasing my entrance, kissing me hard on the mouth. I could taste my arousal on his lips and tongue, and it only spurred me on. I clawed at his back and nipped his earlobe and neck, all the while James continued to swirl himself around my needy cleft, dipping in the head and pulling out again, making me groan and whimper in shameless need. I tried to push myself down and move my hips so he would slide in, but he read my body language and pulled away smiling, taking one of my nipples into his mouth again and lashing at it with his tongue.

"Uh-uh, not yet, we don't want to rush this now do we?"

"Oh God, please," I whined. "Don't make me beg. I thought you said you couldn't go slow..."

He did it again before reaching beneath me to cup my butt and pull my hips tighter against his torturous grinding. My eyes rolled into the back of my head, and I let out an impatient moan.

"Ah, well, I want to savor you. Prolong the feeling as long as I can. Because once I'm inside you, I won't last long." He smiled against my neck, nipping that sensitive spot right below my ear. "Am I torturing you?"

"Yes," I growled, pushing my hips up again, hoping he wouldn't be paying attention and I could slip him in without notice.

Fat chance of that.

I grabbed his ass and pushed down. But the man was all muscle; I couldn't make him do anything he didn't want to. Lifting his head, he looked me square in the eyes, raised his hips away from where they were nestled between my legs and then slammed into me.

"HOLY FUCK!" I cried.

A look of panic took over his face. "Oh fuck, a-are you okay?"

"Yeah... just... just be gentle for a bit, it's been a while for me, and you're fucking massive. You just punched me in the cervix with your monster cock."

"Oh shit, sorry." A soft laugh rumbled in his chest. "You're just so snug."

"It's okay. I groaned, wriggling my butt on the bed to try to get more acclimatized to the invader inside my body. "Just be gentle for a second, give me time to get used to it. You need to stretch me out, then you can go harder."

He slowed right down, and it felt unbelievable. Smooth, languid movements, as he filled me. A gigantic force of nature inside my body, pulling all the way out to my ultra-sensitive entrance and then pushing in again to the hilt. I shifted slightly to accommodate the heavy surge of his cock and lifted my hips off the bed so he could go deeper; his moan let me know that he felt it too.

"Jesus Christ, you're so fucking tight. Your pussy is so beautiful, so pink and soft."

"S-stop talking! Harder!"

He sped up and started hammering into me with measured and deliberate thrusts. I was past that brief bit of awkwardness now and everything felt good. Better than good. Everything felt fucking incredible. Our bodies raged at each other. James thundered into me, and I bucked my hips to meet each powerful lunge, pounding my body against his, stimulating myself with the force of my own movements as much as with the fervor of his.

I closed my eyes and focused on the connection between us, envisioning his thick cock, roped in veins, as it split me open and rammed into my aching core. I dug my nails into his muscular back and wrapped my legs around his hips resting my heels on his taut ass cheeks, feeling them flex and release with each thrust.

He kissed me again, hard, his tongue mimicking the pace of his hips, fucking my mouth as thoroughly as he was fucking my pussy. I could feel my climax building, and I was having a difficult time holding on. My need for release was causing my legs to fatigue, and I found it difficult to match his power. The swift and deep pulls of his cock echoed the clenching within my pussy.

I tightened myself around his rod like a fist and let go.

"Oh, God, oh God, ah... ah, oh... God." In a glorious wave of pleasure, my release rippled through me, and I came apart at the seams. Pressing my heels harder into his ass in an attempt to push him deeper into me and biting his shoulder at the intensity of it all as he continued to nail me into the mattress.

He stilled for a moment and grunted loudly, "Oh fuck… ah," before giving one final hard thrust, and poured himself into me, finding his own climax.

I continued to squeeze my muscles, milking his cock for all that it was worth.

He's a big, muscular piece of man and was getting a little heavy resting all of his body weight on me, but at the same time, I loved it. I didn't want to move from my spot beneath him; I felt so safe and satiated. Limp and boneless. And yet already my body thrummed and asked for more. This man was a drug.

As if reading my mind, he murmured in my ear, "I'm probably getting too heavy for you, maybe we should move."

"Mhmm," I murmured, my brain not completely back on earth yet. James gently rolled over and sat up on the edge of the bed pulling the condom off and tying it at the end. I sat up and stuffed my breasts back into my bra and then went on the hunt for my underwear. Grabbing my thong off the floor, I headed for the en suite bathroom.

"Where are you going?" he asked rhetorically as I closed the door behind me.

"To pee," I called back.

What else was I going to do in the bathroom after sex?

Even if I didn't have to pee, I *needed* to pee. One thing I'll never understand is the number of women who don't know that you need to pee after sex.

As I sat there doing my thing, I couldn't control the girly giggle that bubbled up my throat. That had been incredible—world rocking, mind-boggling, coma-inducing, incredible. I knew from the moment I saw him that the man would be a beast in the sack, and his mouth would be pure magic, but Jesus Christ, he'd surpassed any and all expectations.

Much like any first time between a couple, there were awkward moments of fumbling and the squelching sounds of our skin when the air got trapped between us, and a few times he had to adjust his position as it felt like he was going to crush me. But all that aside, it had been amazing, and I was already eager and excited to do it again... and again and again. I only hoped James was just as eager and I hadn't disappointed him. Had it been as world-rocking and coma-inducing for him as well? I certainly hoped so.

I found him fully dressed when I returned to the bedroom. He had gathered the rest of my clothes and placed them on the bed for me, neatly folded. Smiling shyly, I began dressing. I was sitting on the bed zipping up my boots when he came over and sat next to me tilting my chin up with his finger, so I had to look him in the eye.

"Not that I'm complaining in the least," he said softly, "but what was that about? Why did we have to have sex *now* and not tonight?"

I grabbed my shirt and pulled it over my head turning back to face him, sighing and shifting slightly in embarrassment.

"I just felt like there was so much pressure riding on tonight. And I was worried that I was going to over-think the whole thing and be terrible or drunk and stupid. I just thought that if we did it in the middle of the day as our sober, normal selves, with no expectations or preconceived ideas, it would be easier and better. I'm not saying we can't do it again tonight, because please, let's, but this way if we do it tonight there just won't be any first time pressure. I know it's stupid, but I just... I dunno." I shrugged. "Now just seemed right."

"Okay." He leaned over and kissed me.

Was it really that easy with this man?

"And for what it's worth, you were unbelievable. I would not even consider using *terrible* or *stupid* to describe your skills. That mouth..." He smiled, cupping my chin and running the pad of his thumb over my bruised bottom lip, smiling salaciously and shaking his head as if he couldn't believe what I had done to him with my mouth.

I nipped at his thumb and grinned as he jerked it away and chuckled before tackling me to the bed, growling against my lips.

"I fucking love this mouth," he said, as he lay back on top of me and nibbled on my lips and jawline, tracing his tongue along the sensitive vein in my neck. I grinned widely, pleased that I had managed to bring so much pleasure to this vastly experienced man.

"Do you know what happened to my hair elastic?" I asked as we sat back up and straightened our clothes. "You pulled it out at one point, and my hair is a bit of rat's nest now, where did it end up?"

"I broke it."

"Oh."

"And I don't think your hair looks like a rat's nest. I think it looks beautiful... *you* are beautiful. You have that content *just-fucked* look. A soft flush of pink on your skin and wild jungle woman hair. I'm getting hard again just looking at you."

I blushed at his compliment and at the fact that he was already getting hard again. Holy shit! I needed to get myself together so took a swig from the water bottle James had left by the side of the bed.

My hair was quite long; it fell just below my ribcage. I had sported a curly bob style for a significant portion of my adolescence, but when I entered high school, I'd decided to grow it out. As a child I was obsessed with the movie *Splash,* starring Tom Hanks and Daryl Hannah. I loved how long and wild the mermaid Madison's hair was. I'd made it my mission when I entered the tenth grade, to grow my hair as long as was necessary to cover my breasts completely. So if I went into the water and gracefully emerged like a mermaid who had just been granted legs, you couldn't see my boobs. I told my grandma of my plan one time, and she had laughed, asking for a picture when I reached my goal length. I obliged, with a bathing suit on, though, of course. To this day, she keeps the photo on her fridge and tells anyone and everyone the story.

"Will you wear your hair down tonight, all wavy and wild?" He asked. "I love this look. You look like a mermaid."

What was it with this man? When he mentioned mermaid hair, I spat the contents of my mouth out and all over myself and the bed, and this time a little on James.

"Did you just say mermaid hair?"

"Yeah, why? And why do you have such difficulty keeping liquid in your mouth?" He used his sleeve to wipe the droplets off my face and his own and then proceeded to blot the bedspread, but it was just water, so he didn't seem too concerned.

I explained my mermaid hair story, and he burst out laughing, reaching behind me and lifting my hair from behind my back and resting in front of my shoulders, so it covered my breasts; fingering a curl that twirled right at my temple and skimming his knuckles against my cheek. I closed my eyes at the soft touch, my body thrumming with need. I needed him like I needed water, food, and shelter, he was becoming one of life's necessities. When I finally opened my eyes, he was staring at me, eyes dark and seductive with a twinkle of delight right on the surface.

"You're way hotter than Daryl Hannah," he said bending forward and kissing my nose.

6

I left James' house shortly after, pleased that I'd seduced him and successfully diffused the pressure of the upcoming night. I ran a few errands and picked up some groceries before heading home to grade some papers. James was picking me up at six o'clock, and I figured I needed to give myself a solid two hours to get ready. I'd shower again before heading out, even though I loved how I smelled after being with him, traces of his aftershave and manly scent were still on my skin, and I became aroused and felt my face get sore from how big my smile was, every time I caught a whiff.

As Alyssa had suggested, I wore the cobalt blue satin floor length gown I had bought for her sister's wedding in June. It was a simple wide strapped tank top style shift dress with a twist at the bust, a crisscross lattice back and a high slit halfway up the thigh. The fabric glided over my body like quicksilver, clinging where I needed it to cling, enhancing what I needed it to enhance, while hiding all those problem areas that I needed it to hide.

I'd noticed it in a shop window around Christmas and had to have it. It was a bit out of my price range, but when I tried it on, I felt regal and beautiful. I even managed to make the shop girl gush and say that the fit was perfect. She worked on commission so she probably would have said I looked fabulous in a burlap sack, but I bought it anyway and periodically tried it on when I was feeling frumpy or having a dark day.

I had recently bought a pair of five-inch silver snakeskin print peep toe stilettos, and the two were a lethal combination. I tried the ensemble with my hair down and thought it looked a little weird, so going against James' request I loosely pinned it up at the nape of my neck and let a few pieces fall around to frame my face. I was sure there would be more pieces falling by the time I had to leave because my hair rarely cooperated.

I kept my makeup minimal, as I can't for the life of me execute a smoky eye—it just winds up looking like I got punched in the face—and I was busy scrutinizing my pores in my bathroom mirror when there was a knock at the door, causing me to jump.

How is he getting into the building without buzzing me?

I walked with care in my heels to the door, the butterflies back in my belly and flitting about with unprecedented fervor. I opened the door and stumbled backward a half step. Holy Mother of God, he looked amazing, beyond amazing, this man was the epitome of sex appeal. How was I going to go the whole night without jumping his bones? One hand was shoved casually in his pocket, while the other was holding a bottle of champagne and bouquet of gerbera daisies in the other. My favorite. Had I told him that?

He looked up from where he was studying his feet, and the smile that grew on his face made me feel like the most beautiful woman in the world. It took him half a stride to enter my foyer and pin me against the wall, flowers, and champagne still in hand. He didn't kiss me, he just held me there with his vaguely menacing gladiator body, running his free hand down my cheek, neck, and arm, sending shivers through my entire body.

The air around him pulsed and the heat between us was intoxicating and a tad overwhelming. I closed my eyes and bit my lip as his body pressed me against the wall. He inhaled deeply and nuzzled his face against my neck. I could feel his erection through his pants, as he continued to push against me, expertly rotating his hips ever so slightly, letting me know just how he felt.

My breathing grew ragged, and my chest heaved against the strain of my dress. My breasts became heavy with desire and my core tightened with need. I couldn't figure out what to do with my hands, and my palms were sweaty, so I decided to be playful and reached around to grab his butt, squeezing it, appreciating how firm and full it was while inconspicuously wiping the sweat off on his pants. He chuckled softly and flexed beneath my palms. I laughed and gripped him tighter. So many men have flat asses; but not my man, my man had an ass, a taut, full, delicious ass. Like two well-done steaks. He growled in my ear and nipped my lobe. Were we even going to get to the gala? Did I care? I'd be cool with spending the rest of the night in bed.

"You look stunning," he purred, fingering a loose curl near my temple. "I'm glad you didn't listen to me and you pinned your hair up. I love your long neck." He ran his nose up and down the side of my neck and then peppered kisses around my collarbone and up the other side.

I took the flowers from him when he finally pulled away, adjusting the front of his pants with a grunt, and went in search of a vase.

"Thank you for the flowers. They're lovely, how did you know that gerberas are my favorite? I don't remember mentioning it." I filled a simple cylinder glass vase with water and cut the paper away from the daisies.

"I didn't know. I just saw them and bought them because they were bright and cheery, and reminded me of you." Warm arms wrapped around my waist and he began biting my shoulder and neck as I put each flower in the vase. "You smell good, like spiced oranges." He kissed my shoulder and then moved away to start opening cupboards, hunting for wine glasses or champagne flutes.

"They're in the far cupboard on top, they may need to be washed. I haven't used them in a while, so they probably have a healthy coat of dust on them."

He washed two flutes in the sink, and I put my beautiful bouquet on the bar, admiring how they enlivened the kitchen. He deployed the cork like a pro and filled our glasses.

"For the lady."

"Thank you."

"To firsts. May all our firsts be as memorable and mind-blowing."

I laughed. "To firsts." We clinked glasses and sipped our champagne, locking eyes and having a complete and perfectly understandable conversation without uttering a word.

I loved James' car. It was a sleek charcoal gray almost black BMW M3; and just like the man who drove it, it wasn't ostentatious or over the top, just sexy and oh so powerful. He helped me into my seat and tucked my dress in by my feet for me. We pulled out onto the road, and my gaze drifted down to his pants and the beautiful organ that was hidden within. I needed it inside me again. Soon. Now. In some way. He had awakened a beast. I'd only had a few tastes of him, but already, I needed more. I was becoming an addict, and my hunger was real.

James controlled the car the way he controlled everything, with calm, calculated movements and impenetrable concentration. I licked my lips, and watched his shoulder and arm flex beneath his suit jacket as he changed gears and pulled the car out onto the main road. His mouth was set in a thin line of focus and determination. My eyes fell back to the impressive package between his legs, and I felt my mouth start to water. I'd always wanted to try to give road head, but Tom said it was a dirty idea and I needed to act more like a lady. Tom was an asshole.

"How far to the golf club?"

"About twenty minutes. Dinner is at eight, so we'll be there just after seven. Time for a bit of mingling and champagne and then we'll sit down to eat. Are you hungry?"

"Not for food." I bit my lip and eyed him coyly beneath my lashes.

He turned his head quickly with a flash of surprise, his blue eyes flaring in the shadows of the intermittent street lights as a smile the size of Jupiter took over his features.

I loosened my seatbelt and leaned over the center console searching for the zipper on his pants. He was already getting hard, his cock like an iron bar as I pulled him out of his trousers and began gently kissing the tip. He moaned and adjusted himself in the seat so that I could get easier access. I took him in my mouth and immediately started to deep throat.

"Oh fuck, yeah." He growled.

There wasn't a lot of room between his lap and the steering wheel for me to get my head and arm in there, so I couldn't use my hand effectively to help pump, I was forced to rely entirely on my mouth to do the job. Swirling my tongue around his shaft, I bobbed my head up and down in his lap, hollowing out my cheeks and sucking. I grazed him with my teeth, and he inhaled quickly. I paused.

"No, I like the teeth."

He couldn't really thrust into my mouth and establish a pattern because of his seatbelt, leaving him completely at my mercy. I had all the power, and I loved it. He tried to put his hand on my head and push me to take him deeper, but the car was manual, and he had to change gears. But, I took the hint and started to deep throat again; ramming him all the way into my mouth until I could feel him knocking my tonsils.

"That's right, baby, suck it, suck it hard. God, you give great head. Oh fuck," he panted. "I'm going to come."

"Mmmmm," I hummed, picking up my pace and sucking him harder, letting the rumble of my hum travel through him, tingling his sensitive crown.

James exploded inside my mouth seconds later, shooting semen into the back of my throat in thick warm spurts. I swallowed as fast as I could, knowing that the sensation of swallowing heightened the pleasure of his release. I licked him clean and dotted kisses along his length and around the head as he trembled with the aftershocks before tucking himself back into his pants. I sat up and adjusted my seatbelt and dress, avoiding his gaze and trying to hide how pleased with myself I was.

"H-holy Fuck... holy... Holy Fuck... where...where did that come from?" He ran his hand through his hair and over his face shaking his head. He was short of breath and clearly lacking adequate blood flow to his brain because his speech was broken and his demeanor frazzled.

Did I actually manage to rattle Mr. Cool-as-a-Cucumber-Firm-Handshake-Sexy-Mouth?

"You've awakened a beast, Mr. Shaw." I opened my purse and fished out my lipstick, flicking the visor down for the mirror so I could reapply. "A beast that didn't even know she was starving until she tasted you, but now it's all she can think about, all she wants." I shrugged. "Besides...what else can a girl do when you look so damn fine in that tux?" I feigned innocence and attempted to appear as blasé as possible, as if it was a simple matter of fact thing that just had to be done.

His grin was almost boyish. "No one has ever done that for me before."

"Really? Well, that was my first time doing it too. To firsts." I raised a pretend glass of champagne.

"You just keep surprising me, Miss Everly. You're not at all like I thought you were when we first met at the pub. And I love that I was wrong. Tom was a fucking fool. But his loss is my gain. Holy Fuck. You just blew my mind, and my cock."

I laughed, delighted because I had managed to make him lose all composure. I'd given him his first road head. One hundred and twenty-six women before me and he'd never gotten a blow job while driving? That's nuts.

Wait... what kind of a woman did he think I was when we met?

"You managed to combine two of my favorite things, sex, and driving. Well, that's going to have to become a regular road trip activity, you know that don't you? I might have to take some time off work so we can *go* on a road trip so that you can do more of that."

I smiled like an idiot and smoothed out my dress.

"I owe you," he said with a purr, reaching over and playfully pulling on one of my rogue curls. "I promise to have you home, on your back and screaming my name by midnight."

I flashed him a big grin. "I can hardly wait."

7

"Have you ever been to Vegas?" James asked as he grabbed each of us a glass of champagne from a passing waiter and steered me toward a table where a relatively large crowd was gathering. The gala's theme was Las Vegas, with various gaming tables and iconic landmarks.

I shook my head. "No. You?"

He made a disinterested face and quickly looked down at his phone before shoving it back into his pocket. "A few times. It's nothing special. I prefer to earn my money the old fashion way. But the shows are all right, and I got to see the Blue Man Group last time I was there for a bachelor party."

"Tom was big into online poker. He paid for the majority of his schooling with his winnings. But he spent so much time online." My eyes scanned the room while my fingers toyed with the stem of my glass. "Sometimes he'd be up until four or five in the morning playing. And whenever he lost a lot of cash, he'd be in a foul mood for days. Truthfully, his gambling bothered me."

I placed my complimentary chips into his hand and wandered away from the table, preferring to admire the decorations and people watch. I wasn't into gambling at all. I didn't see what James did with the chips, but when he joined me again, draping his arm around my shoulder as I stood in front of the ice sculpture of three dice, he no longer had them in his hands.

We wandered around the ballroom checking out the silent auction items and making small talk with people. James seemed to know everyone, and they were all eager to pick his brain and shake his hand.

"Well, Jim, how goes it?"

We were standing beneath the Eiffel Tower when an elderly man with a black handlebar mustache and comb-over walked up to James and patted his back before shaking his hand. Looking closer, I noticed that he had hair coming out of his ears and nose making it look as if there were mice stuck in there, trying to get out, whiskers first. He seemed friendly enough if a little loud and abrupt.

"And who is this glorious vision beside you?" Mr. Mustache offered me his hand, and I shook it—it was limp and clammy. I'm sure he thought I was trying to crush his septuagenarian bones with the force I put in on my end.

James placed his hand on the small of my back. "Stanley Fletcher, this is Emma Everly. Emma, Stanley."

"Emma, nice to meet you." He made no attempt to hide his appreciation for my appearance; his eyes traveled up and down my body with blatant approval, lingering an exceptionally long time on my breasts and widening before his milky dove-gray stare finally made its way back to my face. I watched James, and his gaze followed Stanley's with cautious humor.

"And you, Mr. Fletcher. How do you know James?" I leaned into my man, and he caressed my waist affectionately, before moving it lower to shamelessly cup my butt for anyone and everyone behind us to see.

"Oh, honey, call me Stan," he said, and jovially nudged my elbow with his own. "Jim and I work together. I own a masonry company, and he employs my boys in a lot of his projects, don'tcha, Jimmy?"

"Stan's men are some of the best bricklayers in town," James said stoically with a quick nod. "They earn every contract and every penny. They actually did all the brick and rock work on my house. That's how much I respect their work."

"Oh Jimmy, you're going to make me blush, ha-ha-ha-ha." Stanley smacked James on the back and laughed a deep thunderous roar, causing heads to turn.

"Can I get you a drink?" James asked, he drained his champagne quickly and placed it on a passing waiter's tray. "What are you having? Emma, champagne, or a vodka?" He tickled the nape of my neck as he waited for my order.

"Champagne please, I can't mix."

"I'm drinking scotch, single malt, mah boy. Here let's go to the bar together I've got a story for you." And with that, the men were off to the bar slapping shoulders and laughing.

I turned and looked up at the large Eiffel Tower copy. It was an impressive paper-mache masterpiece and the tiny white twinkly lights running up and down the legs made the silver spray paint sparkle. I'd been to the top of the original in France, and it was magnificent. This one was cool and very well done, but there is nothing like the original.

My mind drifted back to my two weeks in France. I'd spent the first fortnight of my four-month Euro-trip in England and then headed to France for two weeks. I'd met a very cute, very young nineteen-year-old boy, named Ronan, from Scotland while at a hostel in Paris. We hung out for a few days while our stays overlapped, visiting the Eiffel Tower, The Seine, Louvre and all the other things that Lonely Planet suggested we do. He was hot, really hot, like Calvin Klein underwear model hot, but also a lot of fun and easy to be around.

We made out a few times on his bed in the hostel, but because we were both staying in shared single-sex dorms with a plethora of other roommates, and I had just split up with Tom, I was reluctant to go any further than second base. Maybe a slight lead off to third? I never played baseball as a kid.

But he'd understood and willingly and enthusiastically accepted the hand-job I offered him, sliding his fingers into my panties in return but not really knowing what do once they were there. He'd confessed later that he was a virgin. And although he'd put in a solid and valiant effort, I wound up faking an orgasm so he wouldn't feel bad.

Despite his lack of sexual prowess—because who are we kidding? I didn't have any either—he was a breath of fresh air after the stifling smog that was Tom. And even though he was just a puppy, taking a gap year to travel before he started uni, we had a sweet, innocuous fling that made me feel happy and sexy. He was fun as a travel companion, much like Max and Alex had been, and best of all I didn't have to sightsee alone.

"Emma?"

I spun around at the sound of my name, shaking my head to dislodge my nostalgic flashback. I already knew James' voice so well, I was surprised that someone else at the gala knew me. It was Arthur Simmons, one of the partners at Tom's accounting firm, *Simmons, Patterson, and Hall*. Mr. Simmons had always been very kind to me anytime our paths crossed, and I shouldn't have been surprised to see him here; he was a very philanthropic man, constantly fundraising for something and often encouraging his employees and co-workers to donate. Arthur's expectations that his employees contribute to his causes used to drive Tom nuts. But of course, Tom, Mr. Negativity, never bothered to add that Mr. Simmons matched every donation—from his own pocket no less.

"Mr. Simmons, hello. How are you?" He leaned in and kissed my cheek lightly.

"I'm wonderful, Emma, and yourself?"

"Doing quite well, sir. Thank you."

"What brings you here this evening?" He teetered back and forth on his orthopedic loafers. "Don't tell me you've joined the stuffy corporate white collar world of ass-kissers, not sweet little Emma? I mean, I know it's a fundraiser, but you have to have money to give it away."

He was very grandfatherly, with short thinning white hair, wispy bushy eyebrows, a bit of a hunch, and a soft, calm and inviting manner. I'd liked him the moment I met him about four years ago when Tom started working at their firm while still attending school. I hadn't seen Mr. Simmons very often, once in a while when I would stop in to visit Tom and at Christmas parties, but he always made time to talk to me. I'm no gambler, but I'd bet that he had scotch mints in his pocket, most grandpas do.

"Oh no." I chuckled. "I'm here with someone who is in the stuffy corporate world, though I'm not sure how much ass-kissing he does. Do you know James Shaw?

His eyes twinkled. "You're here with James? Oh, darling that is a step-up indeed, good for you. I always thought you were too good, too kind for that Tom. He's good at his job, I'll give him that much. But between you and me..." He brought his voice down to a yelling whisper and leaned in close to my ear. "He's a bit of douche-bag if you know what I mean?"

I couldn't stop myself, I burst out laughing and gave Mr. Simmons a peck on the cheek. He started laughing as well, but it soon turned into a cough, and I wound up whacking him on the back as he reached for a handkerchief from his inside breast pocket.

"Thank you, my dear."

"No, Mr. Simmons, thank *you*, that was not at all what I expected you to say, but it was perfect. Tom is a *douche-bag*."

He dabbed at his mouth and then tucked his handkerchief back into his pocket before looking up at me with sympathetic eyes. "I know the breakup was hard, dear, what with *Jennifer* ruining things, swooping in weeks if not days after you left. But believe me, honey, you're much better off. James is a good man. We have him as a client."

"Oh really?" My mind was reeling. I didn't hear much else after Mr. Simmons had said that Jennifer had "swooped" in on Tom weeks if not days after I left for China. So, he'd been cheating on me the whole time I was away? It hadn't just happened when his grandmother died, and he was grieving? Not that he'd truly mourned her. He'd never spoken fondly of her, none of the family had. The only reason Tom ever had anything to do with his father's mother was that she had been loaded. She hadn't been a nice person; to that, I can attest. A lot like Tom now that I think about it.

But Tom, seeing the advantage of cozying up to his ailing grandmother, believed that because no one else in the family gave her a moment's thought, she'd leave her fortune to him—which she had.

But that fucker! He'd been cheating on me the whole time! Not that it matters anymore, I guess. But still, that fucker!

I continued to nod as Mr. Simmons chatted away, picking up on bits and pieces, something about his grandson Marcus joining the firm in the fall. A warm, strong hand landed on my back, and a flute of cold bubbly came into my line of vision.

"James!"

"Arthur. Good to see you." James extended his empty hand and gripped Mr. Simmons' hand with firm but casual familiarity.

"You've hit the jackpot with this girl here, m'boy. Hold onto her, marry her, don't be stupid and piss your life away with work, it doesn't keep you warm at night."

The two men chuckled. I took a sip of my champagne and kept my eyes hooded, secretly watching the exchange they were having.

James' laugh seemed a tad forced, but his smile never wavered. "I'll keep that in mind, thank you." He pulled me close and squeezed my waist, drawing soft circles on my hip bone. "And I certainly plan to hold onto her."

8

By the time the second course came around, I was thoroughly enjoying myself. I hadn't spoken to a soul at our table, but the food alone was enough to keep me content and entertained. The jazz band on stage played smooth dinner tunes, and the hum of all the conversations mixed with the tinkling of silverware around the room made the place sound like a beehive full of blacksmiths. The most exquisite and generous piece of halibut over a cauliflower mash, grilled asparagus, and roasted potatoes with a citrus glaze followed the previous courses. I felt like I had died and gone to heaven. Only angels should eat so well. Do angels eat?

"Are you enjoying your meal so far?" James asked, watching my eyes bulge as the halibut was placed in front of me.

"Oh, my God." I gushed, letting my eyes roll into the back of my head for just a moment. "It's all so incredible. I'm going to have a giant food baby by the time we're done. You'll have to help me waddle out to the car."

"Food baby?" He cocked his head like a curious puppy. I could have jumped him right then and there he looked so adorable.

"You know, when you eat so much that you look like you're about five months pregnant, but it's not a baby, it's food—a food baby. Men can have them too."

"Never heard that term before."

"That's because you live under a rock."

He raised his eyebrows in mock surprise. "Do I now? And what makes you say that?" He was playing with me, goading me to tease him. I really liked this playful side of him.

"Well, I've made some pop-culture references and used some words and terms that have either flown right over your head, or I've had to explain to you. Remember when I made a comment last Saturday at your place about the hashtag and how I hated that everyone hash-tagged their daily lives. And then I proceeded to hashtag the next five minutes as a joke? I had to explain what a hashtag was."

"I know it as the pound key or the number sign. When did it start becoming the *hash*?" he asked with a shrug. "I'm old. What can I say? And I like my rock home. It's comfy. And hard. And we know *you* like things *hard*." He picked up a piece of asparagus with his fingers and took a bite, flashing me a mischievous closed mouth grin.

I pouted slightly. "You're not old."

"I'm twelve years older than you," he corrected, lifting one thick eyebrow to drive home the point. "That's a whole generation between us. I'm Generation-X, and you're a millennial. I'm not saying I mind or that it bothers me, on the contrary, I love it. I'm just pointing out a fact. We grew up watching different Saturday morning cartoons."

We were having this conversation as though we were sitting at home eating a private dinner together; I'd forgotten that there were eight other pairs of eyes and ears at the table, so I lowered my voice and leaned in toward him. "It doesn't bother me either, as long as you're not old enough to be my dad I'm cool with the age difference. In fact, I like that you're older and more mature. It's hot."

He smiled again and reached under the table to squeeze my knee. Only he didn't stop there; he found the slit that ran high up my leg and worked his hand under the fabric trailing it softly, but deftly north until he reached the juncture of my thighs. My eyes bulged at him, but I was afraid to show any more emotion on my face that might give away what was going on under the table.

I tried to keep my expression as neutral as possible, but I'm a terrible liar, so I put my head down and stared at my halibut. James had started talking to the man on his left about permits and licensing, but I couldn't really follow what they were saying. I was too focused on the hand and fingers that were busy pushing my panties to the side and brushing my clit in hypnotizing concentric circles.

"Do you not like the halibut, dear?"

"W-what... huh?" It was the older woman sitting on my left. She was probably close to eighty-five or ninety and wearing enough jewels they could probably see her from space. Her dress was black and designed to look like a 1920s flapper. She even had the headband with a feather to match, and her butter blonde hair was short and in tight curls; I'm sure she had it set that afternoon at the beauty parlor. She was charming. I'm surprised I hadn't noticed her sitting next to me earlier, but I guess I'd been too focused on other *things*.

"Oh, uh, no I love the halibut, it's wonderful. I'm... I'm just trying to pace myself. I ate the soup and salad rather quickly because it was so good, but I'm not sure how many courses there are to go, and I want to try them all... so, so, uh, I'm slowing down a bit."

By this time James had slipped one finger inside me and was slowly sliding it in and out while caressing my clit with his thumb. I was so wet and probably making a damp spot on my dress and in turn the fabric seat cover.

What was his angle? Where the hell did he intend to go with this? Surely he didn't expect me to come—not here!

When dessert came, he was still fiddling beneath the table, relentlessly tormenting me. I tried my damnedest to have a chat with Edith, sitting beside me, but I couldn't form a coherent sentence.

I shifted and ground my pelvis into his hand, muffling moans of delight with my napkin. But the perpetrator in my panties didn't seem fazed in the least and was still deep in discussion with the man on his right. I didn't know what to do. It felt so good, but I was going to come if he didn't stop. There were people all around us, yet at the same time I felt shrouded in a kinky cocoon of loveliness, solitary denizens caught up in our own delicious devices.

How could I orgasm at the table without anyone knowing? Thank God for the long fabric table cloths, no one was the wiser, or so I hoped.

Dessert was a continuation of the excellence before, and between the sensations, I was experiencing in my mouth and the sensations beneath the table, I was a bundle of tightly wound dynamite ready to explode. I sincerely hoped the man had a plan.

Once again as if reading my mind, he leaned over and whispered, "When everyone claps, I want you to come for me."

What? When was that going to happen?

"Ladies and gentlemen, may I have your attention please," a big voice bellowed from the stage. I looked up to see a man in a white-tailed tux, tapping the microphone. "I'd like to announce that thanks to your generous donations tonight, and throughout the last few months we've managed to raise over twelve million dollars toward the renovations of the new cancer clinic."

And then the applause erupted. James' fingers increased their speed and force beneath the table, and in moments I couldn't take it anymore, I closed my eyes and let go. Gripping the edge of the table, I leaned forward slightly, so any expression of ecstasy was masked by my fallen tendrils of hair. It was such an incredible feeling; to be doing something so intimate, so personal, so dirty—in public. And no one was the wiser.

The exhibitionism of it only added to the pleasure and excitement. I joined in the applause at the end when I had regained enough composure to let go of the table. Watching in fascination and insatiable hunger as James licked his fingers clean of my wetness; his eyes speaking wicked and wild promises while his mouth foreshadowed the debauchery of the evening to come.

As the applause died down, he leaned back over and murmured in my ear, his warm breath stirring the embers of arousal inside me, "I told you I owed you. Good job." He pecked me on the cheek and then turned back to answer the question of the man beside him.

The remainder of the evening at the gala went by without any problems or anymore under the table shenanigans. James modestly accepted an award on stage for his philanthropy and for spearheading the new oncology wing at the children's hospital, as well as his tireless efforts in making sure that all the *I's were dotted, and T's were crossed* in the permits and development of the new world-class cancer treatment center. He gave a small speech that focused on the need for donors of money, time and tissue and how he appreciated all that his fellow colleagues and associates had contributed; urging people to sign up with OneMatch and get their names on the donor list. Not once did he thank anyone for the award or bring the attention to himself. He concentrated on the benefit and why everyone was there. I found myself getting more and more inspired with each word.

It was a cold, clear night, but ominous clouds loomed off in the distance, threatening rain… or perhaps snow. It smelled like snow. The golf club was quite a distance from the city, so the stars twinkled and danced with extra brilliance, their luster uninhibited by the city lights. James opened the car door for me, gently tucked in my dress before closing it and went around to the driver's side.

"Did you enjoy yourself this evening?" he asked as we made our way down the long tree-lined driveway and out onto the main road.

"Yeah." I nodded. "It wasn't so bad. The food on the table was unbelievable, and the fingers under the table were pretty unbelievable too. Do you think we got away with it?"

A smirk tugged at the corner of his mouth. "I don't think anyone was aware of you coming during dessert, and if they were, who cares?"

"Well, Edith probably figured something was up. It took me five minutes to tell her where I worked and what I did. I couldn't form a complete sentence. Thanks."

His grin grew wider. "You're very welcome."

"That was sarcasm."

"I'll still take it." He was smiling his gorgeous leg-spreading grin that I'd fell for only eight days ago. "You look radiant tonight," he said matter-of-factly. "Absolutely breathtaking. By far the most gorgeous woman there. I had a quite a few colleagues and associates asking me where I'd found you."

"And what did you tell them?"

He was quiet for a moment, and I found myself sitting on pins and needles waiting for his answer.

"I told them you fell out of the sky and landed next to me on a barstool on one of my darker days, making it bright again."

I was speechless. *Darker days?* I struggled between laughing at such a corny line and kissing him over how sweet and confusing it was.

What does he mean by darker days? Did he actually say that to people?

"Wow... uh, thank you. That's so sweet. But... um... what do you mean darker days?"

"Well, I didn't really say all *that*, exactly." He shrugged. "But I did tell them that we met on a shitty day, and you helped make it better."

"Oh, okay." I wanted to know what "darker days" meant, but I was afraid to push. Would he shut down or think I was a nag? Tom had called me a nag all the time, even when I'd merely asked him how his day had been.

"My twin brother died of leukemia when we were thirteen," he said softly. "I wasn't able to save him. We weren't a match. And last Friday was the anniversary of his death. It's always a really bad day for me, despite the fact that it's been twenty-five years. I usually just hide in my office and work and drink until I'm too drunk to work. And then I cab home and pass out. Only this time I'd run out of scotch in my office before I was sufficiently plastered, so I decided to go to a pub. I was actually pretty intoxicated when you met me."

I just stared at him. He'd opened up. The words tumbled out of his mouth so fast I hardly had time to think. Reaching out tentatively, as if not wanting to frighten a wounded animal, I put my hand on his arm. He pulled the car over to the side of the road and put it into park.

"I couldn't tell," I whispered, "that you were drunk."

"I'm very good at hiding my inebriation," he said with a snort. "It comes from years of experience as a teenager sneaking in after parties and getting past my parents. Not that it was hard." He rolled his eyes.

"My mom pretty much checked out as a parent for a significant portion of my teenage years. Andrew's death nearly destroyed my family."

I stared out the window into the darkness and wracked my brain for something meaningful and non-cliché to say. "I-I'm sorry about your brother. So, is that one of the reasons why you're so involved with the cancer center?"

"Yeah, one of the reasons." He shifted in his seat to face me. "I want you to know that I don't have a lot of dark days, and I don't drink that heavily, normally. I just allow myself one day a year to wallow in grief and pity. I'm back to normal the next day. Well, hungover as hell but back to normal." Deep in thought, he hesitated and made his lips all pouty and cute. "I mean a lot of people might tell you that I'm miserable all the time, and they're probably right. Hell, I'll tell you, I'm a miserable fucker, but I don't have a lot of days like I did on Friday."

I shook my head. "I wouldn't hold it against you if you took a whole week to wallow. He was your brother. I know if I lost either of my brothers I'd be a mess. Probably forever."

A small smile touched his lips, but it didn't reach his eyes. I could tell he wasn't comfortable talking about his feelings, but I appreciated that he was trying. I unbuckled my seatbelt and climbed across the center console into his lap. He undid his belt and wrapped his arms around me burying his face in my neck, slowly moving it down to settle and nuzzle between my breasts.

"God, you smell good."

My hands traveled up his body and wended their way into his silky soft hair. "We don't have to talk about it anymore if you don't want to. I don't want to push. It's late we can just go home to bed."

"I'm so lucky to have found you. You're perfect. Perfect for me," James murmured. I turned in his lap and straddled him, bending my knees and putting them on either side of his legs. I had to hike my dress up around my thighs to sit comfortably, but my high slit made it work. He ran his free hand up my side and neck gently caressing my cheek before brushing his lips against mine.

"You promised to have me home on my back and screaming your name by midnight," I reminded him. "You're running out of time."

"*Hmmm*," he hummed. "Did I? Well, I don't know about your back, but I bet I can still have you screaming my name before midnight."

I drew my tongue around the shell of his ear. "You think so, do you?

"*Mhmm*." He moved a hand between us, ruffling up my dress and sliding his fingers beneath my thong to where I was already quite wet and ready. He began drawing large lazy circles around my clit with the palm of his hand as magic fingers explored my swollen entrance.

I reached down and unzipped his pants, freeing his length, then I started to work him with my hand, gently pumping up and down. He grabbed the back of my neck and pulled me in for a very deep and driven kiss, plunging his tongue into my mouth and grazing his teeth against my lips. His need was becoming evident. Only it felt like more than just need. It felt like sudden, almost fearful desperation. He was holding onto me for dear life as if he let go for a moment I would disappear. Our sweet and gentle love-making quickly turned into an inherent need for connection, a wild and reckless craving to fuck. To live. To feel alive. To relinquish the control that life had on us and just feel.

He reached into his pants pocket and pulled out a condom, tearing the package open behind my back so as not to break our kiss. We came apart for a second so he could roll it on and then in one swift movement he lifted me up, pulled my thong to the side and positioned me onto his waiting cock. A breathless cry escaped me as I took him to the root. We were both panting and out of breath as we pawed and groped at each other, clawing to be closer, desperate for more skin to skin.

He was nipping at my shoulders and collarbone, pushing his hands into the top of my dress to caress my breasts and pinch my nipples. Sucking hard on one of the swollen buds and then biting down at just the right moment, forcing a thready cry to burst from my lips as the pain quickly transformed into pleasure, spreading through me, building and seeping into every corner of my aroused body.

His hips churned impatiently with greed while my need for release continued to grow. If I lifted up one more time and plunged down, I knew I would come. I was hoping James was close too; I didn't want to go without him.

Lifting up again I circled my hips over the tip of him; he put both of his hands on my shoulders urging me to take him deeper. Crazy for him, I smiled and leaned forward, sliding my tongue along the sweat beaded curve of his upper lip, lapping up his saltiness with a hum of joy. He lunged with his teeth and caught my bottom lip, growling as I continued to tease him.

"Jesus, Emma," he swore, through clenched teeth. "I'm going to come, stop playing!"

At that moment I sank back down slowly, tightening my internal muscles, squeezing his cock like a fist. Drawing him deep inside me, never wanting to let go. And then I lost my mind. The primitive driving urge to fuck took over. I threw my head forward against the headrest and rode him until the building tension burst and released me from its confines.

"Oh, God, James! Holy fuck, oh God, oh, ohhhh."

And as I came undone so did James.

"Ah, ah, oh... fuck, ah," he grunted with a beast-like sound of ecstasy that ricocheted through me and around the car. Yanking my hips down to meet his punishing thrusts he battered the end of me with every deep and luscious plunge, shaking as it tore through him. His eyes were wild with the need to claim me.

He cupped my face and gently grazed his lips across mine as our gasping breaths and heaving chests fought for equanimity.

"Emma," he mumbled, continuing to brush his lips over my face and neck. "Emma..."

We sat there for a little while, content in our post-orgasmic comas as he traced soft circles on my back with his fingers. My legs were threatening to fall asleep, and I needed to jump out and pee, so I lifted my head up to see how awake he was. His face was shred, emotions raw and out in plain sight. Stripped, laid bare. But only for a fleeting second. When our eyes met, he reclaimed his mask of indifference and then transformed his expression again into playful James, smirking softly as he pressed the indiglo on his watch.

"12:06, and I do believe I heard my name. So, besides the fact that you weren't on your back, I'd say I kept my promise."

"Mmmmm." I smiled, my eyelids heavy and every muscle in my body begging me for sleep. "I need to pee."

"Ha-ha, can you wait until we get home?"

"No," I moaned as he helped me climb off him. Lacking any kind of grace or fluidity as I clambered back into my seat, with my dress hiked up around my waist. "I really shouldn't."

"Okay, should I go find a gas station?" He tied off the condom and put it back in his pocket,

"No, no, this looks like a secluded enough place. And if I open both doors on this side, I should be hidden from traffic. It's just bushes."

"You're going to pee on the side of the road, like a like a..."

I gave him a wry look. "Like a man? Yes, I need to pee."

I got out of the car on my side and opened the back door as well. Situating myself between the two and trying to hide from his view.

"You couldn't hold it?" he asked after I'd climbed back in and he put the car back into drive, pulling out onto the highway.

"No, that's bad. Women need to pee as soon as they can after sex. Otherwise, they run the risk of contracting a UTI or yeast infection."

His brows scrunched into a Deep-V. "How?"

"Because you're busy jamming bacteria and shit up my urethra with all of your pounding and thrusting. It's just best to flush the system when it's all over. Push it all out."

"Really?"

And so I started my tirade. "It seriously cuts down on the likelihood of contracting a UTI or a yeast infection. All those naughty whip and flogger erotica books where the couple is fucking twelve times a day and then just lay and cuddle after, but the girl never gets up to pee are so unrealistic. In real life you know she would have been on medication like a week into the relationship because it started to burn when she went to the washroom."

"I uh... I don't really read *those* kind of books." He chuckled.

"Well, either way, you can't have that much sex without peeing afterward and not get a bladder infection, it's virtually impossible. I learned that the hard way with Max and Alex. I didn't know you needed to pee after sex, and I'd just finished a filthy erotic trilogy right before I met them. Needless to say, it started to burn when I sat down to pee within a week of when we started being *more than just friends*. But maybe they just choose not to include bathroom time in the books as it's kind of mundane. But they really should, for educational purposes. Not enough women know."

His lip turned up in a smirk as he shot me a curious side-eye.

Did he think I was a weirdo?

"Huh, I never knew that."

I let out a small exhale of relief and turned on my biggest mega-watt playful smile. "Learn something new every day. Stick with me, kid. I'll educate your ass off."

He laughed again and rubbed my knee. "Have you ever had anal sex?"

My eyes went wide. "Wow. Well, hello there, Mr. Random. Yes, I have."

"You have?" He turned and looked at me, mildly shocked at my answer. But as always, he quickly recovered. "With Tom or Max and Alex?"

"Max and Alex. Tom wasn't interested in that at all. He caught me masturbating with a shower head once and wouldn't speak to me for a week and denied me sex for a month. So, anal sex was definitely off the table. He was beyond vanilla. The man was plain yogurt."

"Tom sounds like a giant douche-bag. I mean I know he's a fuck-head for letting you get away and cheating on you, but he just sounds like a douche-bag."

"Funny you should say that, that's what Mr. Simmons called him tonight."

"Arthur's awesome! So, did you like it?"

"What? Anal? Yeah, it was all right. I'm totally down for a finger or two in the ass during oral or sex, but I just couldn't really find the orgasmic enjoyment with anal sex. I tried it a few times with just Max, and it was better with him, he was the gentler lover of the two. I actually managed to get off once when he and I were doing it. But when I tried with Alex it just hurt, but he is also bigger. Not as big as you though. I definitely need to be really, really relaxed and turned on, lots of lube, and it's best if I have a vibrator on my clit at the time or some kind of stimulation."

He shifted up as we hit the highway. "Would you be willing to try it again with me?"

"Yeah, if it's something you want to do. I'm not saying I'll like it and want it to become a regular addition to our sex life." I lifted one shoulder casually. "But if it's something you want, then sure."

"Not right away, we'll work up to it. We've only had sex twice, so we've got lots of other things to try to do before we move to the back door."

I laughed softly. "That's good. What about you? Do you like a finger on the prostate?"

He grinned but didn't take his eyes off the road. "I won't say no if you're willing. But I'm not one of those guys that make a woman do it. I could take it or leave it, but if you're willing, then hell yeah."

"All right then, good to know. Hey, quick question. You mentioned on the drive here that I'm not at all what you thought I was when we first met, and that you're glad you were wrong. What kind of woman did you think I was?"

He turned off the highway, a flash of another grin transforming his profile.

"Innocent and naïve. I didn't think you were a virgin, but you came across as very reserved when we first met. You were chatty enough and funny as hell. I don't think any woman has ever made me laugh as much as you do. But I certainly didn't think you were the type who has had a threesome with two men, or who gives road-head. And I love that I was wrong. I knew there was more to you when we met which is why I called you the next day. I never do that. I love that you're sexually adventurous, but at the same time still sweet and pure. You've perfected the paradox."

I bit my lip, searching my brain for something witty to say. "I'm not as callow as you might think, Mr. Shaw. Just you wait and see."

"What does callow mean? Why do you use such big words?"

"It means inexperienced or immature. And I use big words because I like big words. I'm an English teacher. I read a lot, and I feel that since

I've adopted the vernacular of a truck driver and am prone to dropping quite a few F-bombs, I need to make up for my trash mouth by having a sophisticated vocabulary the rest of the time."

"Ah." He nodded. "Fair enough, that makes sense. Maybe I should start doing that. I swear a lot."

"You sure fucking do."

9

The next morning found us staring out the window at one and a half feet of lily white snow, relentlessly falling and piling up high around the house; creating a cozy soundproof cocoon for the two lustful inhabitants. We slept in and lazily made love. Exploring one another's bodies and massaging aching muscles from our workouts the day before. James brought me tea and fruit salad, and we watched cartoons in bed until almost noon. I didn't bother taking my pajamas off, and when I caught a chill, he was quick to drape me in his thick burgundy housecoat.

We made a delicious lunch together of roasted butternut squash soup and cheesy garlic bread that we enjoyed in his home theater where we watched old movies and cuddled. Around five o'clock James found me in his office checking my emails. He had a bottle of amaretto and two stemless glasses in his hand.

"Come with me," he ordered, eyes glittering with mischief.

Without hesitation or question, I got up and took his hand. He led me outside onto the patio through a path he'd cleared of snow to a bubbling, steaming hot tub surrounded by burning votive candles. We disrobed and quickly slid in, relishing the delicious burning sensation that hits as you initially submerge yourself into the 103-degree water. It was bliss. James jumped out of the water and ran over to the railing scooping some of the fresh powder into his hand and hopping back into the tub with a splash. Making two snowballs with his hands, he placed them in the stemless glasses and poured the amaretto over the top.

We sat in companionable silence, content to just be together, sipping the sweet almond liquor and enjoying the quiet peace that comes after a heavy snowfall. James' hands traveled around my body, caressing and tickling behind joints, stroking my inner thighs and torso, kneading my swollen and buoyant breasts. I soaked up the attention and nuzzled his neck, softly nipping and licking along the thick pulsing vein.

His hands grazed up and down my stomach, settling them to rest on the small swell of my lower abs, my *fat,* and I began to grow self-conscious knowing that his fingers were lightly brushing over my *pudge*. I shifted in his lap, but he just pulled me tighter, digging his digits into my self-perceived *plump* belly.

"Can, you uh move your hands?" I asked softly, wriggling and trying to get him to loosen his vice grip.

"Sure, but why?" He slid them up and cupped my breasts squeezing them affectionately and gently tugging on my nipples causing me to squeak and then sigh in delight.

"Because you were grabbing my fat, and it makes me uncomfortable."

"What fat? Emma, you're not fat." He lifted my chin with a finger so that our faces were mere inches from each other, his cerulean eyes searching for reason and understanding.

"I know I'm not *fat* per se, but I *have* fat. I have problem areas and my lower abs or lack thereof, is one of them. Not to mention my triceps, my love-handles and my lack of a thigh-gap, etcetera, etcetera."

He shook his head, a slight tick of negative emotion building in his jaw.

"You're beautiful. And you're not *fat*, and you don't have *fat*." He slid his hands back down to my stomach. "I love your soft feminine curves. And your curves aren't *fat*. And for the record even if you did have fat I wouldn't care. I think your body is sexy as hell. I'd rather you have a little meat on your bones than be rail thin. I'd be afraid of snapping you in two. Meat is what gives you tits and ass, and I can't get enough of either of those." He gave my breast another affectionate squeeze, his eyes softening and his jaw unclenching. "Please don't deny me the pleasure of running my hands over every gorgeous inch of your perfect body."

"I can't help it." I shrugged. "I'm insecure about my body." Moving my arms, I pushed them beneath his hands, crossing them in front of my lower stomach.

"You shouldn't be. You're stunning. And you *definitely* don't need to have insecurities about your body around me. I've seen you naked, I'm seeing you naked now, and I really, really like what I see. Can't you tell?" He thrust his always impressive hard-on up between my legs, making me giggle and squirm; grinding my body into his.

I reached between my legs and started pumping my hand up and down his length, but he stopped me with his hand.

"No, baby, not right now. Let's just relax, let me run my hands over your body. That's what I want. Don't deny me an inch... please." He pulled my other hand away, the one that was still resting on my stomach, replacing it with his adoring caress.

I let out another sigh and rested my head against his chest. "Okay."

It was hard not to let his hands worship my body the way they wanted to; the man knew exactly what to say to get his way, no wonder he was so good in the business world. But his words had hit me in the heart, lifting it up and making it light. My mind traveled back in time to the twelve-year-old who was called fat in gym class, the fourteen-year-old who was never asked to dance and the twenty-two-year-old who ran for two hours on the treadmill and then threw up her lunch before she got home and her boyfriend weighed her.

James' words and his hands made all those girls feel a little less heavy, and a whole lot more beautiful. Unshed tears stung my eyes as my horrible memories came and went, dissolving in the warm water as the silence and steam wrapped us in its impenetrable mantle of safety. No one could hurt me here. Here, I was safe. Here, I was beautiful.

"Em?" I wasn't sure if I'd fallen asleep or just dozed off, but when I opened my eyes twilight had given way to the darkness and steam enveloped us like a blanket.

"Mmmm." I sat up, feeling groggy from the heat and liquor. Suddenly, I was reminded of what we used to do as kids in my parent's hot tub when it snowed, and I jumped up off James' lap, downed the rest of my drink, and climbed out of the tub, running down the steps out into the frigid black of the back yard.

"What the hell?" I heard him call out behind me.

Giggling at my nostalgic childishness, I fell backward into the pillowy soft snow, naked as the day I was born, and started making snow angels. But it wasn't overly deep, and soon the grass tickled my butt. I sat up, thoroughly pleased with myself and unable to feel my ass, only to see a naked James making his own snow angel next to me. I shuffled over and straddled him, kissing his blue lips. He laughed softly and reached up to pinch my pert nipples causing me to yelp and pinch his in return.

We didn't last much longer in the snow; the shivers claimed us and James scooped me up in a front piggyback and bounded back to the hot tub. We laughed and screamed as the heat penetrated our numb skin, causing that all too familiar tingling and stinging sensation.

"I need to tell you something," he said softly. I was sitting in the adjacent seat as James massaged my feet; his features were difficult to make out through the mist and darkness. "I have to go away for business tomorrow. We've just acquired a new, very large contract to rebuild an old abandoned shopping center into an outlet mall in Grand Prairie, so I'll be gone for ten days or more. It's one of the reasons why I wanted to jump right into a relationship with you. I couldn't imagine periodic dating and *getting to know each other*, especially if I'm going to be gone for so long."

"Oh... Okay."

"That's it? You're not mad?"

"It's your job." I shrugged, even though a harsh and painful unexpected sadness began to settle like a dense fog around my heart. "Of course I'm disappointed, but I'm not going to get mad. And you made it very clear last Saturday that you wouldn't always be a hands-on, always home kind of boyfriend. Now I know what that means. You also said you're not a good guy, but so far, I just can't see it."

"Trust me," he whispered, "I'm not."

I chose to ignore him and continued, "But don't you have associates who you could send? I mean you're the big boss, why do you have to go?"

"This is a huge project, one that will take well over a year possibly two and involves a lot of major investors. I prefer to start projects of this size myself as I am the face of the company. Once all the major kinks have been worked out, then I will send one of my trusted associates." His smooth chuckle rumbled through him and into his big strong hands as they kneaded the pads of my feet into jelly. "But you're not mad?"

"No, of course not. I'm just going to have to make sure I send you off with something to remember me by."

We got out of the hot tub, and James wrapped a bath sheet from the nearby warming rack around me, squeezing each of my boobs in the process with a satisfied grin. I shook my head and smiled as I headed inside to the shower while he blew out the candles and closed the hot tub cover. His shower was something out of an architectural magazine: three sides of the room were made up of large frosted glass cubes stacked to make a wall, and they extended almost up to the ceiling while four powerful showerheads inside beat down on aching and tired bodies. A tiled bench in the middle served as a seat or bench to shave your legs on; or in our case, for me to sit on and take James in my mouth.

I'd packed enough clothes in my bag, just in case, so that come Monday morning I could head right to work. James said he'd drive me to work and have his assistant take him to the airport as he didn't want me driving in the snow with my old, beat-up Nissan Sentra, even though my parents had just bought me new winter tires for my birthday last year. I wasn't looking forward to almost two weeks without him, but he had warned me he'd be away a lot so I chose to use our snowed in predicament and my second night's stay as an opportunity to soak up as much of him as I could.

I had a thing about sleeping naked. I just couldn't do it. I'm still traumatized, and probably always will be, by a fire at our neighbor's house across the street from where I grew up. The unattended flame of an aromatherapy candle set the Sullivan's bedroom drapes on fire and torched half their house in the middle of the night. All I remember is the image of Mr. Sullivan sitting on our front lawn with his son's Slip n' Slide wrapped around his waist talking to the firemen. And Mrs. Sullivan, who wasn't much better off—she'd managed to find a small towel outside and wrap it around herself—was holding their singed cat, Leroy, and crying on my mother's shoulder. Thankfully, their kids had been away at camp that week. But I never want to be caught in such a predicament. When I was a kid, I just thought that they were the nut jobs next door that slept naked, it never occurred to me until years later that they were probably having sex.

James and I climbed into bed together so naturally, as if we had been doing it for ages, and thankfully James slept on the left because I always sleep on the right. We made love again, slowly and quietly, I'm not sure who we were afraid of waking up, but the lack of conversation and sound made it feel all the more intimate. We couldn't see each other in the dark, so it was all just breathing and body movement with the occasional nose bump and eye kiss. It was perfectly wonderful, and as I slipped off to sleep, I couldn't halt the sudden rush of feelings that flooded me. No-strings-attached or not, the sex was incredible, and James was a nice guy, despite what he believed. He was a great guy, in fact, he was exactly the kind of guy I could fall in love with—if he'd let me.

Later that night I woke suddenly, not sure where I was, it took a second to sort out the sleepy fog. But what was more alarming than not knowing where I was, was how aroused I was. Panting heavily, my nipples were tight and achy against my tank top and my face and neck were warm and flushed. The clock on the nightstand said it was close to three. I could hear his heavy, even breathing beside me—he was out. Gently, I reached under the covers and below. I know men get random erections during the night, and I was just wondering, hoping, that perhaps he had one.

He did, and he was naked.

Ducking my head beneath the covers and slowly making my way over to his waist I took him in my hands and guided him into my mouth. I was careful not to touch him anywhere else. I wasn't sure if I wanted him to wake up or not, but I was excited and turned on by what I was doing. I pumped him with my hand and swirled my tongue around the head slowly taking him deeper and deeper into my mouth until he hit the back of my throat.

"Emma?" Came a groggy voice from above the covers.

I ignored him and continued my task, using my hand to work him as I took one of his smooth testicles into my mouth gently sucking it and applying only enough pressure and pull to earn a moan from above. I gave the same attention to the other ball before returning to his shaft and taking it in my mouth again, immediately deep throating.

Big, warm hands moved beneath my arms, and he motioned for me to move up from under the covers. He had a condom out of the wrapper and quickly slid it onto himself. Then without a word, he encouraged me to scoot up and over his head until I straddled his face. From there he began to lick and suck where I was already swollen and needy. Straightening his tongue so that it was long and firm he then proceeded to fuck my pussy with it, darting in and out quickly, all the while using his nose to massage my clit until I was a bundle of nerves ready to implode.

I planted my hands on the cold wall in front of me, pressing my breasts into it and leaning forward until my nipples pearled. I reached up and started pinching and pulling them, heightening my pleasure, riding James' face shamelessly, greedily taking the pleasure he offered. I was close, so close, and it seemed that James already knew my body well and could tell how ready I was, because seconds later he grabbed my hips and pulled me back down, slowly sliding me onto his waiting hardness.

Monday morning greeted me with feather-light kisses on my neck and collarbone, with the delicious scent of James awakening my senses better than any morning coffee ever could. My eyes fluttered open, and there he was, sitting on the edge of the bed dressed in two scrumptious pieces of a charcoal three-piece suit, with a steaming cup of Earl Grey for yours truly. His hair was wet from his morning shower and his face freshly shaven. He had let his beard grow yesterday, I found the five o'clock shadow rough and gritty look such a turn-on, but I also loved the clean-shaved look as well. Who am I kidding? He looked good no matter what.

"My flight is at eleven o'clock," he said softly, leaning over to tuck a strand of hair behind my ear. "It's six forty-five now, so we've got some time before we have to leave. You start work at eight thirty, right?

"Yeah. *Mmmm*, thank you," I hummed, taking a sip of my tea. It was perfect. Just the right amount of milk and honey.

When I walked into the kitchen, James had half a grapefruit and a hard-boiled egg sitting on a plate for me with another cup of tea and a glass of orange juice. He was taking care of me, just as he'd promised.

"Would you like me to put something together for your lunch or will you just go buy something?" he asked, taking a sip of his coffee and walking over to grab my boob.

I rolled my eyes at his newly forming habit. He just smiled.

"I'll just go pick up a salad or soup from the deli next door, but thanks for offering. You spoil me."

"And you just keep surprising me." He grinned over his coffee mug. "My 3 a.m. wake-up call was incredible. Thank you."

"You're welcome. I'm glad I was able to catch you when you were *up* for it." I took a bite of my egg. "Did you treat your other *girlfriends* like this?"

"Like what?" He bit into a piece of peanut butter toast and leaned his hip into the counter. God, he even made eating toast look sexy.

"You know, spoiling them with candlelit hot tubs, making them breakfast, offering to make their lunch, just being so attentive and wonderful. Were you like this with all the women you've dated? I won't be mad if you say yes."

One shoulder casually lifted up as he slowly chewed. "I haven't had a lot of girlfriends. It's been a while since I've been in any *real* relationship with a woman besides a strictly physical one. And there was a time when I was trying to get the business back on its feet where I was having a lot of one-night stands. I like to make a woman feel special, but I've never been as attentive as I am with you." He shrugged again and grabbed his second piece of toast. "And I don't usually invite women to my home. You're only the second woman I've had over here. I dunno, you just make me want to do nice things for you. You seem so strong, but at the same time so fragile, and I just want to take care of you."

He gave me a shy half smile, attempting to defuse the magnitude of his statement. But I felt like I had been punched in the gut; winded by his sweet words. This man was something else. I didn't want to make him any more uncomfortable than he already was, expressing more of his deep hidden feelings, so I decided to let the subject drop.

I got up to put my grapefruit rind in the compost and dishes in the sink, but not before rising up on my tiptoes and kissing away a speck of peanut butter stuck at the corner of his mouth. "I'm going to miss you."

He took my dishes from me, putting them on the counter, and then wrapped his arms around me kissing my forehead. "I'm going to miss you so much."

10

I could still feel his goodbye kiss on my lips an hour into my class, which made me reluctant to sip my tea and wash it away. It'd be almost two weeks before I'd have those lips on me again.

We had agreed that if it were still snowing when I finished work, I would bus home and continue to bus around town until the weather let up. James didn't want me driving anymore in the snow than was necessary, and I didn't feel like arguing with him; however, his controlling and bossy nature was starting to niggle at me, resurrecting old demons. I don't like being told what to do, especially by a man. But this man made me feel safe and protected if a little pushed around.

It was going to be a long ten days. My body had gotten used to the days of endless orgasms again; going cold turkey was going to be a nightmare. So, instead of tottering around in a melancholic funk, I began to pour myself into work and exercise over the next week. I upped my workouts at the gym, choosing to channel all my sexual frustration into two hours of aerobics, doing a one-hour class and running thirty to forty-five minutes, followed by fifteen minutes of abs and arms. I was feeling really good, exhausted, but really good.

James and I spoke almost every night on the phone which was unexpected since he had stated from the beginning that he wasn't going to be a hands-on, always-around boyfriend. I'd expected that meant phone calls too, so when he started ringing, I was elated beyond words, but also surprised.

He was working long hours and troubleshooting non-stop, though, and each time we spoke, he sounded more exhausted and increasingly frustrated by the people he was dealing with. More than anything, I wished I could be there to massage his broad shoulders in the evening before bed, if not to help him but to help myself. I missed the feeling of his body beneath my fingers. I was starting to go through James withdrawals, and it wasn't pretty.

Alyssa and I grabbed dinner at a bistro after the gym on Friday where I caught her up on the events of the weekend—the gala, our snowed in love-nest and the earth-shattering sex that just kept getting better. She invited me to a party on Saturday night that her law office was throwing; it was instead of a Christmas party which they had somehow forgotten to throw late last year. Seeing as it was just over a week before Mardi Gras, we were all supposed to dress in a masquerade theme, preferably in green, purple and gold.

I wasn't too keen on going, but I figured it would take my mind off James, and I did need to socialize more. After Tom and I split, all of our couple friends fell off the radar. Maybe they chose to befriend Jennifer and forsake me, or maybe they just thought I'd constantly feel like the third wheel. Either way, I didn't hang out with many people besides Alyssa. I had made it one of this year's resolutions to put myself out there more and meet new people. Ordinarily, I never would have accepted the offer of a drink from a stranger, handsome or otherwise, but thanks to my resolution I was in the most wonderful relationship of my life.

Sticking with the Mardi Gras theme, I decided to go with a plain tight black mini skirt with black fishnets, and a gold sequined loose fitting tank top. I found some green stone chunky costume jewelry, which I paired with four-inch black stilettos and a sparkly purple eye mask on a stick with gold and purple feathers that I had fashioned myself earlier that day using supplies I picked up at the craft supply store. I was quite proud of my outfit, and though I'm not at all the type of person to take a selfie, I took one with my phone and sent it to James with the caption *"wishing you were here so that I could collect some beads the old fashioned way."* We hadn't had a chance to talk since Thursday night, and although I'd texted him and let him know I was going to a party with Alyssa, I just really wanted to talk to him before I went.

And, again, as if he were in my head, I got a call from his number while I was getting into the taxi and on my way to Alyssa's house.

"Hi," I said.

"Hi. Are you heading out to your party?"

"Yeah, just in the cab now."

"You look hot. I especially like the fishnets and the mask."

"Thanks. I made the mask myself."

"You did? It looks really good. I'm sure you'll have fun."

"I'd rather be with you. What are you up to tonight?"

"I'd *definitely* rather be with you. Rather be inside you." Oh God, my nipples instantly grew diamond-hard. "I'm busy pouring over contracts in my hotel room. My brain is almost numb from the monotony. How was your day?"

"Same old, same old. Gym, errands, work. Yours?"

"Ah, spending money, building shit, it's a job." He sighed deeply. I could almost picture him rolling his eyes and pouting.

"How much longer until you're home." I tapped the cab driver on the shoulder and whispered where to turn onto Alyssa's street.

"Probably at least another three days, I'm afraid."

"Tuesday? That sucks." I handed the driver enough money to include the tip and climbed out of the cab. Alyssa lived in a townhouse not too far from me, but I wasn't going to drive if I was drinking and it was certainly too far to walk in my shoes.

"Yeah, I know. I'm sorry I didn't call you last night. We had a late dinner with some contractors, and it went on and on. I was tempted to call you when I got in at 2 a.m., but I figured you'd be sleeping."

"I was, but you could still call. But I get that you're busy working. It's okay. Call me tomorrow though?"

I heard him yawn and imagined him stretching like a proud male lion. "You bet. I miss you."

"I miss you too."

"Have fun at your party."

"Thanks. Try not to die of boredom."

"It'll be tough, but I'll try. Good night, *Emma*." I loved how he said my name, he growled it with such feral promise it made my core tighten and a tingle run up my spine, settling in the parts of my body that were missing him most.

"'Night, James." I was at Alyssa's front door at this time. She had seen me walking up the path, so the door was open and I was ushered in by my very purple best friend.

"Hey!" She grinned, waiting for me to take off my shoes and then quickly motioning for me to follow her upstairs. "You look great. I love your top. And your mask. Did you make it like you said you were going to?"

"Thanks. Yeah, I got my craft on today. It didn't turn out too bad, eh?"

"Looks great."

I gave her the once over and tried to hide my face of disgust. "Uh, that's a lot of purples."

Oblivious to my scrutiny she twirled and laughed. "Haha, thanks. I raided my closet and pulled out everything purple I had. I don't have a lot of green or gold, so I figured I go with purple and then accessorize with the other two colors. Kind of like what you did with the green jewelry and purple mask."

Alyssa, bless her heart, has never had the best fashion sense. She usually just goes with a dark pantsuit and blouse, which she buys in multiples whenever there is a sale on at The Bay. Since having made partner her style had most definitely improved, but I'm still often called over at the eleventh hour to help sort out one clothing crisis or another. I wasn't sure if tonight was a night to interfere, or if she should just be left to her own devices, though. She was head to toe in varying shades of purple. Bright purple leggings, a plum pencil skirt and a mauve blouse with fuchsia suede pumps. Her only contrasting shade so far was a gold mask she had that was sitting next to her purse on the table by the door.

We'd met in a first-year anthropology class. A few of years older than me, Alyssa had been in her third year, taking Anthro 100 as a lower level elective for an "easy A" as she called it. My "easy A" was Theater Appreciation 102 and only because the African Drumming class didn't fit into my timetable, but to each her own.

She'd powered through her undergrad. Took six classes when she could and went to school year-round, all through the summer, and graduated in record time with honors, well before the customary four years. Then she got early acceptance to law school and was hired by the firm she's with now after receiving job offers from half the firms in town. And although the firm is on the small side, they're known around town for being good at what they do.

Alyssa did her articling with them and moved up to Associate, proving her loyalty and dedication, which combined with her keen eye for detail and overwhelming tenacity, earned her the coveted title of Full Partner well before her thirtieth birthday; a true accomplishment for someone her age. I was always in awe of how she managed to do it all. The woman was a machine. So, if I'm honest I kind of loved that her fashion sense was severely lacking, it made her seem more real and less like a robot that might malfunction one day and try to eliminate the human race.

I decided that because this was a work party, she needed to go with all her guns loaded, including her wardrobe bazooka. As her best friend I believed that her current fashion atrocity needed to be tackled and as much as I loved her inability to accessorize and dress, I wasn't going to be mean by throwing her to the wolves at the party looking like a delicious, juicy purple... thing.

"Uh, honey. Can I make a couple of suggestions?" I asked as I slipped off my cardigan and draped it over the banister.

She handed me a glass of vodka and soda with a lemon wedge and smiled. "I look ridiculous don't I?"

I took a sip. "Yep, a little bit. I'm glad you said it because I wasn't sure if I should. We've got time. Let's go back to the closet."

Laughing at her own ineptitude, she started unzipping her skirt and headed in the direction of her bedroom.

I fell into bed later that night with all my clothes and makeup at around 2 a.m. I was quite drunk and couldn't be bothered to take anything off; sleep was more appealing to me than pajamas or a clean face. The last thing I remember is staring at a picture of James on my phone and telling it/him how sexy he was.

11

I woke to my phone ringing and my head pounding. Fortunately, even in my inebriated wisdom, although I'd forsaken changing clothes and brushing my teeth, I had managed to draw the blinds in my room, so at least it was dark when I unglued my eyes. I would probably have cried if it was light out. I couldn't find my phone, and I tore my bed apart looking for it. It turns out I'd put it on the nightstand, the logical place for such a thing. It was James. It was also 11:02 a.m., a reasonable time to call... for people who hadn't imbibed the night before in one too many vodka sodas.

"Hello?" Oh dear God, did I really sound like that? He was probably wondering how an eighty-five-year-old chain smoker got a hold of my phone.

"Ma'am," he drawled.

"Shut up. You woke me up."

"Did I? It's lunch time."

"Maybe for you, you're an hour ahead. It's still morning here."

"Late night I take it?"

"You could say that."

"Well, I'm glad you got home safe." He paused. "You are home, aren't you?"

"Yeah, I'm home. Steve didn't drink, so he dropped me off on their way home."

"Oh, good. I'll let you go. We'll talk tonight when you're awake and don't sound like my grandmother after a Metallica concert."

"Okay, thanks. Wait, your grandma goes to Metallica concerts? Cool."

"Go have a shower, wake up."

"Okay, okay. Bye."

"Bye."

I had every intention of going to the gym on Sunday and getting a decent run in on the treadmill. But my brain and guts had other ideas. So, instead, I spent the majority of the day in my pajamas on the couch drinking coconut water and eating plain rice cakes while watching the Home and Garden channel. It wasn't until around six thirty that night that I started to feel normal.

I brought out my yoga mat, not wanting to let the entire day escape me without at least *trying* to exercise, and did some stretches and crunches. There was only a light pounding in my head when I put it down for Downward Dog. My phone started to vibrate while I was in Pigeon Stretch and I scrambled to grab it off the coffee table, knowing that it'd be James. I'd spoken to my parents and Alyssa earlier in the day, and no one else besides my brother's on the blue moon called me.

"Hi," I said, trying to sound as chipper as I could and as little like an octogenarian chain smoker as possible.

"You sound better."

"I am better. Only a slight pounding in my head now as opposed to the bongo drums that were in there earlier."

"That's good. What are you wearing?"

I looked down at my lap. "My flannel penguin pajamas, why?" And then it dawned on me. "Oh, uh, no wait, I'm not wearing anything, of course, nothing but whip cream and a smile. You?"

"Ha-ha, well yes, that had been my intention, but you caught on a little late. Good recovery, though."

I pouted. "Let's start over."

I could hear him trying to suppress a laugh. "All right. What are you wearing?" That dark and dangerous voice set jolts of warmth zinging through my body until they settled deep in my belly and spread into a growing and tantalizing heat between my legs.

"Oh, you know... I'm just sitting here doing some paperwork in my plaid mini skirt and white knee-highs. I was wearing my white blouse, but it got so hot in here that I had to take it off. Now I'm just in my lacy black bra."

"School girl route, eh? Okay then. Well, why don't you take your skirt off as well, cool off?"

I grinned. "Okay."

"Are you stressed over all the *homework* you have to do? May I suggest a stress release?"

"So stressed," I hummed. "Are you offering to help me out, Mr. Shaw?"

"Yes, I am." He was all business.

"Oh, please, Mr. Shaw, I neeeeeed your help," I cooed.

"All right, baby, first I want you to lie back and bend your legs. I need you to close your eyes and pretend your hand is me."

"Okay." I'd never had phone sex before, but I was rather excited to try. It was another thing that I had suggested to Tom only to be shut down and called a pervert.

"It's been so long since I've tasted you, can you remind me of what I'm missing?"

I wasn't surprised that I had started to get wet. His voice was enough to make me cream even without the dirty talk. I reached down and touched myself, sliding one finger inside and pumping it in and out while lightly brushing my clit. I brought it to my mouth and sucked my fingers.

"I'm so wet, James, wet for you. I taste... I taste salty and a little sweet and sour. My body is craving your touch. I need you inside me."

"Slide your hand back down and pretend you're me. You're going to need to talk to me and tell me what you're doing, so I can be right there with you. I want to dip my head between your thighs and nip at your inner lips. Would you like that?"

"Oh, God yes. Don't stop. I need your tongue on me. And your fingers inside me." I slid my fingers back down beneath my pajamas and started massaging lazy circles around my clit. "I'm touching myself, making circles around my clit, and it feels so... so good."

"Good, baby, good. I'm stroking myself too. I miss your mouth. You give the best head. You're able to take me in so deep. I love being able to feel the back of your throat with the head of my cock. It's such a huge turn on. Suck my cock now."

"I love having your cock in my mouth," I sighed. "You're so big, and it turns me on too. I need you to put your fingers inside me, suck my clit, and use your beautiful tongue to tease me. I need to come."

"Oh, baby, I need you to come too." My eyes were closed, and I was picturing everything he was saying. In my mind we were in the sixty-nine position, fucking each other with our mouths. I slipped another finger inside myself and started working the two in and out, scissoring them back and forth as I used the fingers of my other hand to circle my clit. "I want you to suck my balls baby. I loved it when you did that before, your tongue is so soft and your mouth so warm. Suck my balls."

"Oh, God yes. I'm going to take one in my mouth slowly while I continue to work your cock with my hand. I love the sounds you make when I'm sucking you off, the moans and the grunts, it lets me know I'm doing it right. You taste so good. I take your other ball in my mouth and gently pull and massage it. They're so big."

"Your pussy is dripping wet. I'm having a hard time licking up all your sweetness. It tastes so good. I love your soft, bare pink pussy."

"I need to deep throat you. Feel your big, thick cock hitting the back of my throat... it makes me wet."

"Oh, baby, yeah, talk dirty to me."

"I'm close, James." It hadn't taken long for my orgasm to start pounding on the door, screaming to be let free. His voice, his words, knowing that he was touching himself while I touched myself, it was hot and dirty and so damn sexy that it took every ounce of self-control for me to not just go off like a rocket.

"Me too, baby. Just finish yourself off, but be sure to make lots of noise. I need to hear you come."

"Okay." I was breathless; I'd put the phone on speaker and laid it next to my head on the floor seeing as both my hands were occupied.

"How many fingers do you have inside, baby?"

"Two."

"Add a third."

"Okay." I continued to make circles around my clit with two of my fingers on my right hand as I slid a third finger inside from my left. I pumped furiously. My release was only seconds away. I needed another hand to pinch my nipples; I needed James. I gently pulled on my clit with my thumb and forefinger, and my climax erupted. "Oh, oh, ah, oh God, oh God, oh fuck James, yes, oh, oh."

"That's it, baby, yes... take it all, all the way in... fuck. Swallow everything. I give you. Yes, Emma, yeah, oh God, *ahh*, *err*, ah, ah, FUCK!"

I'm not sure how phone sex is supposed to go, but I thought it was hot as hell.

"Emma?"

I was panting. "Yeah?"

"That was..."

"Hot?"

"Yeah, hot. Amazing. Fucking awesome. Pick one."

My chest was heaving. "Oh, good. I was worried I wasn't going to do it right."

"Oh no, you did... fine. Just fine indeed." He was breathing heavy into the phone as well. "Next time we'll have to role play and use the video chat."

"That sounds fun."

"I miss you."

"I miss you too. Hey, what do you say we give up sex for Lent? Spend the next forty days *really* getting to know one another, on a... on a spiritual level, not just a physical one." There were crickets on the other end of the line. "Hello? James?"

"You're... you're kidding, right? I'd rather give up oxygen than give up fucking you. Both would be murder."

"Yeaaaaaah, I'm kidding." I giggled. "I just wanted to see what you would say. I like your answer."

"Jesus, woman you nearly gave me a heart attack. Give up sex? Give up sex with you? For forty days? This past week has been a bloody nightmare. Give your head a shake."

I continued to laugh at him, enjoying his playful side. We talked a bit more. I filled him in on the gong show party of last night, and he described his days to me. Even though I didn't understand everything he was talking about, it sounded important, and I just enjoyed hearing his voice.

We agreed to make time to talk Monday and then get together on Tuesday when he was due back. Even though I had to work until nine o'clock that night, I was going to go straight to James' house to spend the night. His flight got in at seven, so he'd be there waiting for me.

12

I had a new intake of five students from Mexico, all young adult women here for a year on a work experience and exchange program. Their spoken English was fairly understandable, but their written language would need some work. I was excited to start teaching them as their energy and enthusiasm were contagious, but by two thirty, Tuesday afternoon, I could hardly contain myself. I was all nerves and having difficulty sitting still, yet there wasn't anything else to do but sit as my students were taking a test. Images of my reunion with James were dancing through my head, and I was getting aroused at the thought. The minutes seemed to tick by at an extra slow pace and I felt like getting up and turning the hands of the clock forward when no one was looking but realized that that wouldn't make his jet fly any faster, I'd just have more time to sit around. The wait was torturous.

When nine o'clock rolled around, I ran out the office at lightning speed. Thankful that none of my Conversational English students wanted to go for a drink or stand around and talk, as was often the case, and even more thankful that Wendell didn't stop me and ask if my dishsoap was environmentally friendly. I'd decided just to drive James' truck rather than bus around town today, even though it hadn't snowed again since the weekend before. Up until Monday night, it had been freezing pretty hard in the evening, and the roads were slick, but it had started to warm up, and the snow was melting.

I pulled into his driveway giddy as a school girl, deciding that I should get myself a schoolgirl outfit since he seemed to like that idea during our phone call.

Odd… His house was in darkness. Perhaps he had candles lit, ready for our romantic reunion? I opened the door and immediately knew that he wasn't home. I couldn't feel his presence. It was cold and dark inside, and his signature smell wasn't fresh and new. It was barely there—two weeks old. Something was wrong.

I tried his cell phone, which went to voicemail after countless rings. I sent a text but got nothing. I rang Alyssa in a mild panic. She was real with me and told me to "calm the fuck down" and go online or call the airline to see if the flight had been delayed or canceled—solid advice. I called and was told that all the flights had departed and arrived on time but that Mr. Shaw had not been on his flight. After wracking my brain for an explanation and turning up empty, I crawled into bed one his side, smelling his pillow. I couldn't sleep though. I was saturated with worry, busy trying to figure out what to do next. It was too late to call his office and I couldn't find any contact information for his family or friends anywhere in his house.

Where the hell was he? What had happened?

Wednesday morning arrived slowly. I hoped to open my eyes to James lying next to me in bed, but seeing as I hadn't slept, I was just fooling myself. I knew he hadn't come home. I drove to work in a fog, determined to call his office at nine o'clock and ask his secretary, Brandy, to tell me where he was. Only when I did so, she was less than helpful, telling me she didn't know where he was and even if she did she couldn't tell me as I wasn't family or on his emergency call list. I explained that I was James' girlfriend and was worried because he hadn't been on his scheduled flight. Still aloof, she "informed" me that she'd call around and try to find out what was going on in Grand

Prairie. Though she made no promise of calling me if she found out anything—the bitch!

I walked around like a zombie all day Wednesday, bumping into desks and chairs, as well as my co-workers, and spacing out while one of my students asked me the definition of, "frank." I'd replied with, "I don't know anyone named Frank." I just couldn't stop thinking about James and if he were okay. He consumed my every thought.

"Whoa, Emma," Wendell said over lunch in the staff room. I was sitting at the table and mindlessly picking at my salad, the same fork of lettuce poised in front of my lips for minutes, hovering but not moving. "What's going on? You seem like you're in a trance... Emma? Emma? Emma!"

"W-what?" I shook my head. "Sorry, Wendell. What did you ask me?"

"What's going on? You seem like you're in a trance."

"Oh, uh, it's nothing..." My eyes welled up, and I put my fork down and started packing up my lunch, unable to eat anything.

"Is it your boyfriend? Did he hurt you?"

"No." I avoided his serpentine stare. "He didn't hurt me."

"Well, he obviously did something for you to be this upset."

"Wendell, drop it. Don't upset her," Allan, another one of my co-workers and a friend, cautioned.

"What?" Wendell spun around and sneered at Allan. "She seems upset. And I'm concerned. Am I not allowed to be *concerned*?"

"It's nothing. Just drop it, please." I sniffed and then stood up to go and put my lunch kit back in the fridge. "I'm just having a bad day." And then I put my head down and walked out of the lunchroom.

"Wait up," Wendell hollered, following me down the hallway.

He stopped only inches away. This guy just didn't understand the concept of personal space; he was forever *popping my bubble*.

My shoulders slumped, and I let out an exasperated sigh. "It's nothing. I appreciate your concern, but I have to get some photocopying done before my students arrive." I motioned that I wanted to leave, but he put his arm out against the wall, blocking me.

"He's hurt you, hasn't he? I would never hurt you, you know."

My back was to the wall; I had nowhere to go. He'd boxed me in again, his arms on either side of my body. The same burnt toast and onion odor on his breath.

"I wouldn't make you cry."

Well, your onion breath might...

"No, you would just criticize me for *showering* and make me sell my car. Leave me be, please." I choked. "I just need to work." I pushed his arm, but he didn't budge, his sympathetic eyes darkened with anger behind his white-framed hipster glasses.

"You know what I think?" His top lip curled up into a snarl. "I don't even think you *have* a boyfriend. I think you made up the whole thing so you wouldn't have to go out with me."

So, what if I had? He's real now.

A woman shouldn't have to make up a boyfriend just to turn down a date. A simple "no, thank you" should always suffice. Wendell was such an ass.

I sighed again and looked him in the eye, my own eyes blurry with unshed tears. "I don't have to justify anything to you. Please, just let me pass. I'm sorry for the shower and car comment. I didn't mean it."

"Wendell!" Allan boomed down the hallway. "Let her go!" He stalked toward us, eyes flaring, ready to jump to my defense. "Are you okay, honey?"

Wendell rolled his eyes and moved his arms, letting me pass. He turned to Allan, and the two started having an argument. They'd never really gotten along; Wendell was homophobic and patronizing toward Allan at every opportunity, and Allan couldn't handle Wendell's holier-than-thou mentality. I mouthed a small "thank-you" to Allan and disappeared down the hall. I didn't feel like sticking around and smelling burnt toast and onions anymore than I had to.

At four o'clock I called Brandy again, asking if she'd heard anything, or managed to find out where he was. Again she was tight-lipped and bitchy but eventually disclosed that she had spoken with James' mother, who had since flown out to Edmonton as he had been admitted to hospital. Whether she knew why he was in the hospital or not, she wouldn't say, and she wouldn't even give me his mother's phone number. I hoped Brandy was a decent secretary because she was a shit person. When I finished work at five thirty, I called his cell phone again letting it ring until the voicemail kicked in and then I left another long-winded, worrisome message. I didn't know what else to do. I knew from watching enough television and movies that the hospital wouldn't give me any information if I tried, and furthermore, I didn't even know *which* hospital he was at. I was at a loss.

I was barely present in my kickboxing class, so much so that I walked out halfway through; grabbing my bag and heading home in a funk. I didn't feel like eating, so I just showered and crawled into bed, clutching one of James' shirts that I'd grabbed out of his laundry hamper and closing my eyes. I managed to get maybe two hours of sleep that night, better than the night before but still not nearly enough.

On Thursday I kept trying his cell phone until his mailbox was full. It wasn't until lunchtime when I was sitting at the café next to the school, drinking a cup of tea and not touching my salad that someone picked up on James' end. It was a woman's voice.

"Hello?"

"Hello. Is this James' phone?" Of course, it was his phone, what a stupid question.

"Yes. Who's this?" It was a bit of a rhetorical question considering that my name and face popped up on the screen of his phone when I called, but then I'd asked a rhetorical question, so I couldn't fault the woman too much.

"Um, Emma, Emma Everly. His girlfriend. Is... is James okay?"

"His girlfriend? Well, this is news. So, you're the pretty blonde dressed up and ready for Mardi Gras on the wallpaper of his phone? Yes, he's fine. His appendix burst Tuesday morning, and he was rushed to the hospital. They had to airlift him to Edmonton for surgery."

I gasped and choked on a sob as tears filled my eyes. In a way I was relieved, appendicitis is bad but usually not fatal. It's bad when it bursts, but it's still better than a heart attack or a car crash which had been my first thought.

"But he's okay?"

"Yes, he's fine. He's sleeping now." James hadn't told me much about his mother. Just that she had gone back to school after his brother Andrew had died. She'd gotten her master's degree in Public Administration, and although retired now, she had worked in the Mayor's Office for many years. She didn't come across as an overly warm and gentle woman, but that could have been fear. Another child in the hospital, it had to bring back horrible memories.

"Um, could you, if he's able, have him call me when he's awake, please? I've been so worried. His secretary wouldn't tell me anything, and he was supposed to be back on Tuesday and... oh, God... I'm sorry, I'm just really relieved."

I hoped she didn't think I was some blubbering idiot. I was sniffling a lot, and my voice does this high pitched whiny thing when I'm trying to talk while crying. I find it annoying, so I can only imagine how others must find it.

"He's awake now. Here."

"Thank you."

"Emma?"

"James! Oh God, James, I've been so worried." I was bawling by this time, barely understandable. And I was still in the café drawing quite a bit of attention. I left my salad and walked out finding a vacant and private bench to sit on.

"Hey, hey, it's okay. I'm okay. It was just my appendix, didn't need it, anyway. It'll be all right."

"I know," I mewled. "It's just... it's just that when you didn't come home on Tuesday and then I didn't hear anything Wednesday either, I feared the worst. That your plane had crashed, you were in a car accident or that you'd had a heart attack. And your secretary was so secretive. She wouldn't tell me anything. All I got out of her was that you were in the hospital in Edmonton and that your mum had flown up to be with you. So, then my imagination went wild."

"Brandy wouldn't tell you anything? Really? That's strange."

"I'm not family or an emergency contact. And I don't have any of your family or staff numbers. I had no way to get in touch with you besides your phone, which was off." I had calmed down a little, still sniffing a bit, but no longer blubbering.

"Well, I'll have to make you an emergency contact."

"When are you coming home?"

"I told the doctors that I'm leaving tomorrow. I'm flying home with my mother on an afternoon flight at 5:10. Will you come to the house after work? I need to see you."

"Of course. I'm off early tomorrow, anyway. I can come get you from the airport if you'd like."

"That'd be nice. You can meet my mum. The flight gets in at five forty-five. Bring my truck."

"Okay, I'll be there." I had started crying again.

"Hey, hey, listen," he said, his voice all low and soft, trying to comfort me even though he was the one sitting in the hospital bed. "I'm fine. The doctors say I'm going to make a full recovery and be back to normal in no time. But for a while, I'm going to need someone to be my nursemaid and help bathe me. See to my *every* need. Do you know of anyone qualified?"

I laughed. "Qualified? No. Willing? Yes. I think I have just the nurse in mind."

"Do you now?"

"*Mhmm.*"

"Well, send her over after you leave tomorrow." He laughed again. "Listen, babe—the doctor's here to talk to me, so I have to go. Everything is going to be okay. I'm alive and not going anywhere, besides back to you. So, get back to work and stop fretting, okay? I'll see you tomorrow."

"Okay," I sighed, my chest no longer feeling like it was lying under a stack of bricks. "See you tomorrow."

I finished work at two o'clock the following day and ran to the grocery store, buying loads of fresh produce, some meat, and cheese. I hadn't really taken a solid inventory of what James had in his kitchen, but from what I remember it wasn't much. I went to his house and put away the groceries; turning on some lights and the heat. I wanted him to be comfortable and worry free when he got home. I wasn't sure where he would want to set up—the couch or his bed—so I didn't take any liberties setting up blankets and pillows, but I'd build him a nest wherever he wanted once we were home. I drove back to my house to shower and pack an overnight bag. We wouldn't be having sex anytime soon, but I wanted to be there for him if he needed anything, and I also just wanted to be with him.

On my way to the airport, I swung into an adult novelty store to see if they had something I wanted, something for James to enjoy while he was laid up. I arrived at the airport early, just in case his jet landed ahead of schedule.

As I had assumed because of his condition James was first to exit the jet. With the help of his mother he slowly made his way down the stairs to the tarmac where a wheelchair was waiting for him. I could see the exchange between mother and son. He didn't want to use the wheelchair, but she was insisting. James was defeated and reluctantly took a seat.

From the window I watched them approach. Mrs. Shaw was a very comely woman; in her early sixty's from the look of it, with short black-brown hair that she styled in the ever popular messy spiked look. She wore simple small diamond studs in her ears, and a black down North Face winter jacket with a white scarf and dark wash jeans. And just judging by her appearance and body language, and our quick phone conversation, she seemed like a no-nonsense kind of woman.

I watched them approach from the doorway and when James looked up and saw me his face lit up with a giant smile though I'm sure it wasn't as big as my own. His mother, on the other hand, seemed very cautious and stand-offish when her eyes locked on me. I could tell she was going to be a difficult one to win over, but at the moment she wasn't my concern.

"Hey, you." He grinned as he rolled to a stop in front of me.

I was speechless, struggling to keep the tears at bay. He tried to stand up, but his mother put a hand on his shoulder urging him to remain seated. He grumbled something I couldn't quite hear, but then rolled his eyes at her and reached for me.

I leaned in and let him wrap his big arms around, hugging him just as tight, only to then hear him whisper so only I could hear, "Ignore my mother, she's a hard-ass and has been worried. She'll be fine once we're home. God, I missed you. You smell good."

I fought to wipe the tears away with my sleeve before lifting my head to look at his mother. Only before I could, James grabbed my hand and pulled me back down to him, kissing me softly on the lips.

"So, Emma. I'm Patricia, or Pat, James' mother." She extended her hand, and I took it, receiving the same firm handshake that James' had delivered just a couple of weeks ago. I offered the same strength in return, not wanting her to find me weak or passive. "Thank you for meeting us at the airport. I'm going to go wait for our bags on the belt, James." She rested her hand on her son's shoulder and smiled coldly at me before heading off in the direction of the conveyor belt.

I walked behind the wheelchair and started pushing James in the direction Patricia had gone.

"You're awfully quiet," he said reaching up and patting my hand.

It felt so good to feel his hands on me again. I closed my eyes briefly, and choked back another sob, soaking up his presence. He was fine; home safe and sound, minus one useless organ.

"Hey, it's okay, stop for a second, come here," he said, grabbing my hand and pulling me around to stand in front of him again.

I knelt down, so we were on the same level. My eyes were blurry with unshed tears, and I wiped my nose with the back of my hand.

He shook his head. "I'm okay. It was just an appendix, and the hospital in Grand Prairie would have been fine, only there had been a major multi-car pile-up an hour before I was brought in and all the doctors were in surgery. I'm okay." Reaching up he used his thumb to wipe away a straying tear, cupping my face with his hand. I leaned into it and closed my eyes. He was okay. He was home. It would be okay.

"I know." My voice sounded so whiny and foreign that I scrunched my nose up in confusion.

Was that really how I sounded?

"I was just really worried when you didn't come home on Tuesday. It scared me. I'm sorry. I don't mean to be crying." I flapped my hands. "Ignore me."

I stood up and walked back behind his wheelchair. When I looked up, I saw Patricia standing by the baggage carousel watching us. Her expression was blank.

13

"Really, Mother I'm fine," James protested, once we'd gotten him home and onto the couch. "You can go now. Emma will be here. And I'd like to rest. Thank you for everything. But I'm sure Dad misses you. Go. I'll call you tomorrow."

"Are you sure, honey?" Her eyes flitted to me, questioning whether her son was going to be in capable hands or not. "I could stay in the guestroom if you'd like. I don't mind."

"Go home, Mum, please. I'll be fine. Your cab is waiting." When we'd arrived back at James' house, Patricia had been surprised that I had thought ahead and turned up the heat and bought groceries, but she didn't show any appreciation and certainly didn't offer me any thanks. She just continued to be shocked that I'd managed to think ahead. Why did I get the feeling that this woman disliked me?

"All right fine, but you call me if you need anything, okay? Bye, honey." She leaned down and kissed him on the forehead. "Goodbye, Emma. Thank you for your help."

"Of course, Mrs. Shaw. Um, you're welcome. It was nice to meet you."

"All right then. Goodbye, James."

"Bye, Mum."

I flopped down on the couch next to James where he had chosen to set up temporary camp when I heard the front door close. "Why does your mother dislike me?"

"She doesn't. She is just very judgmental and over protective. The family therapist determined that she is overcompensating for the years she was virtually non-existent as a parent—she pretty much forgot about her other two children when she lost one."

He swallowed hard, his own anguish and guilt over his brother's death passing across his face like a moving shadow. But he gave his head a quick shake and blinked a couple of times before giving me a small smile. It didn't reach his eyes though.

"And, well this appendicitis scare was hard on her. It brought up a lot of old memories about Andrew. Don't worry about her though. She'll warm up to you. Well, as warm as Patricia Shaw can get. She's never been big on the warm and fuzzies."

"All right, if you say so." I snuggled up to him as much as I could, being careful not to touch his abdomen.

He reached over and grabbed my boob. "Ah, I missed these," he mumbled. "Are you just going to sit there, woman? Or are you going to kiss me properly and welcome me home like a good girlfriend, now that my mother is gone?"

"I... I didn't think we could do *that* so soon after surgery."

"We can't have sex, no," he said with a dirty twinkle in his eye. "But we can do *other* things." He gingerly moved, so we were sitting on the couch facing each other and then grabbing my ponytail, pulled me into a deep and devouring kiss.

When we came up for air, I excused myself saying that I had a surprise. I returned five minutes later wearing what I'd bought at the adult novelty store earlier that day—a sexy nurse outfit. With sheer white thigh highs, garters, a very tight, very short, pleated, white mini skirt and an indecently low-cut white crop top with red crosses over each of the nipples. The outfit came with an old fashioned nurse's hat and a faux stethoscope as well, and I'd brought my own shiny, cherry red fuck-me stiletto pumps to complete the look.

I cleared my throat. "Mr. Shaw, I do believe it may be time for your sponge bath. Would you like me to help you undress?" I walked back into the living room and stood in front of him, twirling the stethoscope around in my hand.

"Emma? Oh!" A wily grin spread across his face, and his pupils dilated to near dinner plates.

"It's *Nurse* Emma, Mr. Shaw. Now, where would you like your sponge bath? Here or are you able to make it to the bathroom?"

"Oh, sorry, *Nurse* Emma. I'm... I'm so weak," he moaned, closing his eyes and draping his hand over his forehead. "I-I think you may have to do it here. If you don't mind?"

"As you wish, sir, I'll be right back." I left the room to go and find a small basin and washcloth. I returned moments later to find that James had repositioned himself on the couch, so he was lying flat with his head propped up on the armrest.

"All right, Mr. Shaw. Let's get that shirt off first." I knelt down next to him and slowly unfastened it, kissing a trail down his exposed flesh as I released each button. He sat up for a moment so I could remove the shirt and then I picked up the washcloth from the warm water in the basin, wrung it out and gently lifted his left arm.

His biceps were chiseled and rock hard. I love nice arms, they spoke of such power, dedication and strength. And if there was anything that defined James besides *sexy*, it was strength and power. You didn't even have to speak to him, know him or who he was, not to recognize the power and strength he wielded. It oozed from him and captivated the room, letting everyone within a one-mile radius know he wasn't a man to trifle with.

Suddenly I was bombarded with the urge to remove my panties and ride his bulging arm muscle, rub my aching clit against his toned bicep until I screamed out his name, but I refrained and washed it instead. This was about James; maybe once he healed, I could indulge in my depraved little fantasy. He moaned in delight as I delivered the same attention to the other arm before washing his abdomen and back; taking care not to apply too much pressure to his incision area or get the bandage wet.

"Now, Mr. Shaw I think we should get you out of those pants."

"*Mmmm*, whatever you think is best, *Nurse* Emma." His eyes were closed, and a small content smile spread across his lips.

I moved his sweats down his legs, removing his socks in the process. I left his boxers on and washed his lower legs and feet. God, even this man's feet were sexy. Big and powerful with perfectly trimmed toenails and a high arch. I massaged his strong calves working my hands up his thighs. His hard-on was obvious, straining against his black boxer briefs. I pulled the elastic down and removed his shorts, allowing his erection to spring free in all its masculine glory.

"Did I say you could point that thing at me?" I playfully chided. "Awfully rude, don't you think?"

"I'm sorry, *Nurse* Emma." He grinned. "It has a mind of its own. But please don't take it as anything but a compliment. Your attention and uniform are much, *much* appreciated."

"Oh." I shrugged. "Well, in that case, I'll continue."

He smiled again and reached down with his hand, grasping his cock and pointing it in my direction, bobbing it up and down in a come-hither motion. I burst out laughing and leaned forward, brushing a soft kiss on the tip. He let out a content sigh.

"Mr. Shaw, I suggest you stop playing around and let me get back to my job."

"Sorry, *Nurse* Emma." He pouted, doing a crap job of looking shamed.

With a stern look, I put the cloth in the water and wrung it out, gently cupping his balls and washing them, well, more like massaging them. Moving onto his shaft, I ran the warm cloth up his length slowly, and when I reached the head and got it damp, I leaned forward and gently blew cold air onto it.

"Oh, *Nurse* Emma, you are so naughty."

I put the washcloth back in the basin and moved it out of the way, undoing the buttons on my crop top to release my breasts. James reached forward to grab at my nipple, but I swatted his hand away. "Uh-uh, Mr. Shaw, no touching."

His grin grew wider, but he pulled his hand away and put his head back down, closing his eyes.

I leaned forward and took his cock between my breasts, sliding it back and forth, fucking him with my tits, using the soapy water as lubrication. He moaned and arched his hips up, thrusting into my chest. A small drop of pre-cum appeared on the tip and I took my finger and rubbed the dewy bead around the head, making the plum crown glow, before sucking off the salty sweetness. I closed my eyes and savored the taste of him.

When my lashes fluttered open, James was staring at me in awe. I smiled confidently, rinsed him off and then bowed my head taking him in my mouth, running my tongue up and down him in circles. He inhaled as I pushed him deep into my mouth, so he hit the back of my throat. It'd been a while since our phone sex fun, and I wasn't sure if he'd masturbated since, and he certainly hadn't while he was in the hospital, so I was pretty sure he wasn't going to last long.

I worked him hard and fast, pumping and twisting my fist around, sucking on the head before ramming him back to my tonsils. He moved a hand to my cheek, caressing my face softly, feeling himself inside my mouth with his thumb. I pushed him to the back of my throat again, and he came in thick, warm spurts.

"Oh God, Emma, I... I mean *Nurse* Emma," he said a few moments later. His arm draped over his eyes while his chest bobbed quickly as if he'd just finished a run.

I stood up and took his clothes and the basin to the laundry room; returning with a new pair of boxers for him and his plush burgundy house coat, the same one he'd draped over me two weekends before. I helped him dress and made him a cup of tea so he could take his medication. His doctors had prescribed painkillers plus an antibiotic because they were concerned about infection, especially since James had discharged himself early and was flying so soon after his operation.

"Are you hungry?" I asked after I made sure he was comfortable and had what he needed. "Can I make you something for supper? I picked up a bunch of groceries to stock your fridge because there wasn't much to work with when I checked."

"I'm not too hungry." He shook his head. "But you need to eat, so make yourself something, and I'll have a few bites."

"Okay." I had buttoned up my crop-top while I was busy getting his clothes, but decided it was warm enough in the house with the fire going and the heat on that I would continue wearing it. It was fun.

I settled on childhood comfort food—grilled cheese, tomato soup and dill pickles. And even though James said he wasn't hungry, I was famished, and not overly keen on sharing, so I made enough for both of us. Good decision on my part because as it turned out, James was pretty hungry too, finishing his entire meal and then stealing one of my pickles. Ordinarily an act of such treachery would have resulted in a war; or at the very least a fork to the back of the hand—I love my pickles—but he was injured, and I'd just bought a giant jar, so I decided to let the devious act slide, though not without a stern warning.

I was jabbering away about work and the Mardi Gras party while dunking my sandwich into my soup when James grabbed my hands and put my sandwich down. For a split second I thought he was about to steal my grilled cheese too, but when he put it down and not in his mouth, I relaxed. I turned to face him; he was serious, more so than I ever remember seeing him. His eyes narrowed in concentration and his lips were pursed tightly with an adorable wrinkle creasing his forehead.

"I um... I can't thank you enough f-for dinner," he stammered, his eyes suddenly dropping from my face to his empty soup bowl.

I cocked my head to the side and raised one of my eyebrows.

He stopped me from eating my dinner so he could thank me for making it? Huh?

Slowly he lifted his head to look me in the eyes again. "Sorry, that didn't come out right. I'm not good at this kind of thing."

He took a deep breath and shook his head a couple of times. "What I meant to say was... thank you for being here. For making dinner, for buying groceries, for picking my mother and I up from the airport, for caring so much, for the nurse's outfit, for the mind-blowing blowjob, for being so open minded when I proposed this... this arrangement... for... for everything. I feel like I've asked so much of you and you've given me so much of yourself in such a short time. And..."

He looked down at his lap and let out a weighty sigh.

"And for the first time in a long time, I'm re-thinking my whole plan, and what it is I find important. I'm re-thinking everything and what I want out of life. I'm re-evaluating my priorities and my goals, so, please... please continue to be patient with me."

He looked at me again, somber, urging me with his eyes to say something. But what could I say? It wasn't one of those awkward T.V. moments where one person says "I love you" and the other person doesn't say it back, or says "thank-you." James never said "I love you," he said something even more profound, how do I respond to that? Do I say, "Me too."? I mean I'm crazy about him, but...

"James, I... I..." But he didn't let me say anything. Instead, he grabbed my face between his hands and kissed me.

Yeah... I'm pretty sure I love this man.

14

I walked into the house and through the laundry room after a quick grocery shop and a stint at the gym Saturday morning. Planning to do a load of laundry after my shower, I stripped down to my sports bra and thong and threw my sweaty stuff on top of the dryer then headed into the kitchen.

But when I looked up from where I'd plunked my groceries on the counter, and into the living room, there were two pairs of eyes staring at me. One pair belonged to James; the other rather bugged out pair were rimmed by thick black-framed glasses that were attached to a young redheaded man. His mouth hung open and then he quickly turned around, showing me his back. I ran back into the laundry room and grabbed a giant bath towel, wrapping it around myself. Choosing to feign indifference rather than mortification, I walked back into the living room to meet our guest, whose car I had failed to notice in the driveway.

"Emma. This is Zac, my executive assistant," James said. "He's just here to catch me up on what I missed while I was under the knife." There was a hint of a smile on James' face. Clearly, he found my half-naked entrance comical. At least he wasn't pissed, if it were Tom I would have been in big shit.

"Hello." I walked over and carefully extended my hand to Zac, being sure to tuck the end of the towel tightly under my arm.

"Hi." He had a nice smile, and it seemed genuine, albeit a little sheepish. And the pink hue of embarrassment that crept up his neck made his rust-colored beard appear as though it traveled down into the top of his shirt. "I'm almost done with Mr. Shaw, and then I'll be out of your hair. Sorry, Miss Everly."

"Oh, don't worry about it," I scoffed. "I was a fool for not seeing your car in the driveway. I just assumed James was home alone."

"My car isn't in the driveway, Miss." His head was shaking like a bobble-headed doll. "It's in the shop. I took a cab."

"Oh. Well, that makes me feel better. I thought I was going crazy and missed an entire vehicle. Anyway, don't worry about it. It's not like I was naked." I moved to stand next to James who was sitting on the couch. Bending down to kiss his head, I whispered that I was going to have a shower and went upstairs to the en suite leaving them to their business.

I was washing my hair with my eyes closed and my back to the door, humming some Katy Perry song, when two big, strong hands wrapped around my waist from behind. I carefully opened my eyes and looked back to find a naked and smiling James.

"What are you doing?"

"Having a shower, same as you." He squirted some shampoo into his hand and started lathering his hair. His movements were slow. I could tell he was in a bit of pain, especially since he decided that last night he had taken his final painkiller.

"Are you sure this is okay?" I was concerned that he was going to overdo it too soon and end up injured or with an infection.

"Yep." His eyes closed while he rinsed his head under one of the high-powered nozzles. "I just need to take it easy. I hate being so helpless. And as wonderful as my sponge bath last night was, I need a real shower." He opened one eye and peered down at me. "You certainly gave Zac quite a show. I don't think I've ever seen that boy turn that shade of red before. I thought he was going to faint."

He grinned and reached up to knead my soap covered breasts, tweaking my nipples until he got the squeak and gasp he wanted. I rolled my eyes and playfully swatted his hard chest with the back of my hand.

"Do you want to sit down? I can scrub your back for you."

"No, baby." He shook his head. "You've already done enough. It's time for me to take care of you..."

He grabbed my hand and led me over to the tiled bench, helping me lie back, positioning my butt on the edge before moving around to where my feet dangled over. Crouching down he lifted my legs over his shoulders and with a salacious smile buried his face between my thighs.

Anytime I've ever reached my own G-spot or even when Max or Alex found it I couldn't bring myself to orgasm. The feeling of having to pee was just too strong, and I was so worried I would pee in their mouth or all over my bed sheets that I didn't allow myself to get there. But James was so skilled and patient, treating it almost like a quest, a quest he was determined to fulfill. He massaged my most tender area until I was supple and pliant; putty in his mouth and hands. Working me into a heated frenzy, until my head thrashed side to side, and my hair stuck to my face and neck and I had no other choice but to let go. I could feel the cosmic release building in my belly, my legs trembled with each suck from his lips while my hips bucked like mad. It was inevitable, I was going to come, and I was going to come so fucking hard.

I gripped his wet hair in my hands and pulled his face deeper into my pussy. He slipped in another finger, pressing on my anterior wall and that magic little spot—I came undone. The waves of pleasure ripped through me as he continued to stroke my clit and plunge and scissor his fingers inside. He pressed hard on my G-spot and I screamed, my whole body shaking. It felt like I just kept climaxing, surge after surge of pure ecstasy, while the heat and steam from the water around us lulled me into a dreamy state of bliss.

Finally, after what felt like hours I opened my eyes, post-orgasm delirium still in full-swing and causing me to see spots. I pushed away from the delightful torture and gently urged James to come up for air. His gaze was hooded and drowsy—drunk on lust. When he stood up his beautiful cock lay elegantly feral against his belly, I reached for it and without hesitation, hungrily slid him into my mouth.

The remainder of our Saturday was lazy and thoroughly enjoyable. I spent a significant portion of the day in the kitchen, whipping up a big batch of turkey chili and extra gooey cinnamon buns. I was busy drizzling icing on the cinnamon buns when I heard a familiar voice.

"James? James, where are you, dear? How are you feeling?" It was Patricia; she obviously had a key to her son's house.

No more naughty nurse outfits then I guess if we could be interrupted at any time. She came around the corner into the kitchen and looked surprised to see me.

"Oh, Emma. Hello. I didn't think you'd still be here." That's a weird thing so say. Why wouldn't I be here?

"Hi, Mrs. Shaw. Nice to see you again." I decided my first approach to thawing her icy exterior was to kill her with kindness. Actually, that was my only approach; I had no second. So, all my eggs were in the killing with kindness basket. "Um... yes, James and I are spending the weekend together. I wanted to be here in case he needed anything. Would you like a cinnamon bun?"

"What? Oh... ah, sure, I guess... thank you." She accepted my peace offering of gooey goodness and walked off toward the office in search of her son, without so much as a smile or a glance back.

Shaking my head at the jigsaw puzzle that was Patricia, I went back to my baking and chili. I like to load my chili with lots of vegetables and legumes, not exactly a traditional recipe but it's hearty, delicious and packed with plenty of healthy goodness—the perfect comfort food for such a cold and blustery winter day. Not sure how long Patricia would stay with James I decided to keep myself busy and make a batch of ginger snap cookies as well. Next thing I knew it was five thirty; the day was closing in, and if James and I were going to watch a movie as planned, we needed to get a move on.

I dished up our bowls, setting them on the counter and wandered off to find him. I hadn't seen Patricia leave but if she were still here, would I have to extend a dinner invitation to her? How awkward would that meal be? I walked into the office and found the cinnamon bun I'd given her sitting on James' desk, untouched, and Patricia sitting across from her son reading a book, while James was busy typing away on his laptop.

What the fuck was going on?

I sidled up to James and put my arm around his shoulder leaning in and giving him an affectionate squeeze. He reached behind me and caressed my butt; a gesture, fortunately, lost from view of his mother's hawk-like stare.

"Dinner's ready when you are. Patricia, are you interested in joining us? I made a big pot of turkey chili."

One eyebrow slowly ascended her forehead in judgment. "Turkey chili? Uh... no. I should be heading home." She walked over to the other side of James as if marking her territory or staking a claim and then bent down and kissed him on the cheek. "Goodbye, sweetheart, I'll call you tomorrow." She nodded at me. "Emma." And then turned and walked out of the office, again, without a smile or a glance back.

What the actual *fuck?*

"Bye, Mum," James mumbled with a half-hearted wave, his eyes still glued to the screen of his laptop. He peeled his gaze off the spreadsheet and finally looked up at me. "Mmmm turkey chili sounds great. I'm all done. Shall I meet you in the theater room? You get the food, and I'll sort out the movie? Emma? Emma?" He lightly tapped my butt, and I sprang back to reality.

"What? Oh... ah, yeah, sure, sounds good." I'd been staring at the open door that Patricia had just walked through, willing her to come back and apologize for how she was treating me. Still stunned, I walked out of the office to fetch our dinner, picking up the untouched cinnamon bun as I left.

We were halfway through the second movie, dinner was long gone and so were a few cinnamon buns, when my stomach started to grumble, and I began shifting awkwardly in my seat next to James on the couch.

"You okay?" he asked as I shifted again for the third time in less than five minutes.

"Oh yeah, I'm okay. Just a little... a little indigestion."

"Do you need to fart?" he asked bluntly. As calmly it as if he were asking me if I wanted sugar in my tea. There was a hint of a smile on his face, but it wasn't teasing, it was one of genuine concern.

"What? No!"

"Don't lie." His mouth pinched into a warning scowl. "We just ate a ton of beans and turkey, and the two are notorious for causing gas. Let alone combining the two, it's practically atomic. I know I've needed to let a few go. Why do you think I've gotten up to stoke the fire, top up our wine glasses and take the dishes to the sink?"

I looked away from his face. "I... um... this is a rather uncomfortable topic, James."

He rolled his eyes. "Emma. You fart, I fart, we *all* fart. If we're going to do this thing, you and me, we have, to be honest with each other and come to terms with the bodily functions of the other. I'm not any less attracted to you because you're gassy. Are you any less attracted to me?

"No," I said sheepishly, still unable to look him in the eye.

"Look at me." He tilted my chin up with a lone finger. "I don't care if you fart. Or if it smells. It means you're human. Hell, I can fart on command." And he leaned to the side and let one rip right then and there, with that irresistible smile taking over his face.

I sat there gobsmacked. And then he burst out laughing and pulled me on top of him, well more to the side of him, so I wasn't lying on his incision.

"Oh, baby, before the night is through, you will fart in front of me."

"No." I shook my head. "I won't. I will not." I looked him square in the eye and tried to keep a serious face.

"We'll see about that." He started tickling me on my sides and under my arms. Giggling and squirming I tried to tickle him back, taking care not to touch his abdomen. But he was too strong and grabbed both my arms in one hand holding them above my head and then proceeded to tickle me with the other as I writhed to get out of his grasp.

And then it happened...

"Oh, God." I buried my face in his chest to hide my mortification.

"See I told you. Good job, baby. And..." He sniffed the air and wrinkled his nose. "Oh my, that's a potent one too. Good work!" Smiling he kissed my forehead, grabbed my boob and took the movie off pause.

Sunday brought forth a feeling of déjà vu. We had gone to bed lulled by the sound of the wind drumming tree branches on the roof and rain plummetting in torrents, but when we woke up, there was a thick layer of snow covering the ground and house. It was as if the last two weeks had never happened and we'd just got home from the gala at the golf club. I hoped that the sneak appearance of snow would deter Patricia from coming by again so soon.

"James?"

"*Mmmm?*" he muffled from behind my ear as we spooned and dozed in our post morning-coital stupors. We hadn't really made love, as James still wasn't quite back to one hundred percent, but I had described my envisioned sixty-nine scenario when we'd had phone sex, and he'd decided we needed to make good and do it for real.

"I don't think your mum likes me."

"Yeah," he sighed, breathing warm air on my shoulder, "she doesn't."

"What?" I pried myself out of his arms and sat up looking at him in disbelief, waiting for him to explain why his mother, who hardly knew me, disliked me so much. "Why? What have I done?"

He moaned and slowly sat up, wincing slightly when he bent his torso the wrong way and pulled at his incision.

"My mum is a bit of a bitch. She's my mother, and I love her, but she's always been a bit of a hard-ass and isn't the most affectionate or welcoming person. She was always this way. Andrew's death didn't make her this way. It just made here worse. My dad was the one who played with us and hugged us and cuddled with us. My mum was raised by very strict English parents, even though she was born and raised in Canada. She was sent away to boarding school at the age of ten, only going home for winter and summer breaks. My grandparents are very much the same way, not big on the affection, but big on the judgment."

He shook his head.

"It's not you. She's never really liked anyone I've dated. Which is why I stopped introducing her to the few women I've had relationships with. After she made Casey Chapman cry and cancel our date to the prom, I stopped letting women meet my mother. But for some reason, she is particularly nasty to you, and it's really starting to piss me off."

"Prom? You haven't introduced a woman to your mother in twenty years?"

He rolled his eyes. "Okay, well maybe Casey Chapman was a bit of an exaggeration, but it wasn't too many years after that that I stopped letting my mother meet my girlfriends. I think the last one was my college girlfriend."

"But why?" My brain hurt from the effort of trying to process why my new boyfriend's mother despised me. "What does she think I've done?"

"She just thinks that I belong to her. Or something like that." His tone was a combination of boredom and irritation. But I couldn't quite tell if he was bored and irritated with *me* for wanting to talk about it, with his mother for being the cause of it, or the entire topic in general. But I didn't care; I needed to know.

"Belong to her? You're a grown man."

"I know," he sighed. "But she's convinced that no woman is good enough for me, that they're all after my money and family name. It's weird and oedipal and believe me Freud could write a book, but I've learned how to keep my personal life and my family separate." He scratched his head and yawned. "But I guess now that I'm starting to think about possibly making the two one and the same I'm going to have to deal with my mother and her bitch-issues. I'm going to talk to her, see what's up. She never really, truly got over Andy's death, so if we ever want anything from her, we need to approach with kid-gloves. Otherwise, she just shuts down."

He reached for the glass of water that was on his nightstand and took a sip.

Meanwhile, I just sat there stupefied. My mind reeling.

"Making the two one and the same" what the heck did that mean? It's only been a couple of weeks, and he's already thinking about making me a member of his family? Where was this coming from? What happened to Mr. I'm-too-busy-for-a-conventional-relationship?

I pinched the bridge of my nose and closed my eyes letting it all sink in but trying to get back to the topic at hand. When I opened my eyes, he was staring at me with his head cocked like a kitten.

I took a deep breath and reached for his hand, for some reason I loved running my fingers over the rough calluses. "I don't want you to damage your relationship with your mother over me."

"No." He shook his head. "This has been a long time coming, and I've been running from the confrontation because it's just easier to give in to her and keep the peace. But I need to man up and deal with my mother. I just have to be sure to do it the right way. But, you're a permanent fixture in my life, so she needs to accept that. I'm just sorry for how she's treated you thus far."

"It's okay." I shrugged, pulling my hand from his and playing with a loose thread on the duvet.

"No, it's not. But on the bright side, I'm pretty sure my dad is going to love you. And my sister, Amy, wants to come over in the next few weeks and meet you as well. She's excited, in fact, she might be able to help us with my mother."

"Oh. You've mentioned me to your sister?"

What was it like to have a sister? What was James like as an older brother?

I bet he was super protective and doting.

My brothers are certainly wonderful men. Peter is thirty-one and in his second year of his surgical residency at a hospital in Saskatoon. He has his bachelor's in Biochemistry a Ph.D. in Biology, and as if two stacks of letters behind his name are not enough he now has M.D. as well. Needless to say, he left some impossibly large shoes to fill when it came to academia. He keeps saying he'll start dating once he's finished his residency and has a fellowship, but at the moment he doesn't have time. I guess everyone's priorities are different. I just hope for his sake that he's banging nurses in the on-call room to relieve the stress; otherwise, that man is going to have a stroke.

Then there's Lewis. Lew is twenty-three and a party boy. He's in his third year as an electrician's apprentice and lives in Calgary in a house with five other guys. I love Lew; he's spontaneous, charismatic and has a heart of gold. He was the first person I called after Tom kicked me out. I called him even before I called my parents, because unfortunately, Tom's parents and my parents had become good friends during our eight-and-a-half-year relationship, so I wasn't sure how to tell them.

Lewis flew out to Victoria immediately and helped me move the rest of my stuff into storage and to Alyssa's. He hadn't been able to stay with me for more than one night because he had to get back to work, but it meant the world that my little brother was there for me. I wasn't sure what was going on in Lew's love life, but if his past relationships were any indication, the man was giving his heart away too hard and too fast to a girl that just wasn't worthy of him.

"Yeah. Ames is great," James went on. "You'll love her. I think she wants to come over for the St. Paddy's Day weekend. She's going to bring her fiancé, Garret, as well. Hey, that reminds me, they're getting married in July. I think the third weekend, you'll come with me."

I'd had this idea of James' sister in my head, thinking she was this young early twenties little thing, but she wasn't, she was thirty-two and a very successful curator and framer at an extremely prestigious art gallery in Vancouver, and Garret was an architect.

"Um, I think so. Alyssa's sister's wedding is in June, so as far as I know, I'm free... four and a half months from now." I smiled sassily, fishing around through the sheets for my pajamas and underwear.

"Okay, great. I'll come to Alyssa's sister's wedding with you in June, and you'll come with me to Ames' wedding in July. Cool." And he climbed out of bed and headed for the shower.

He's so bossy. He'd just invited himself to Melanie's wedding. How did that happen?

15

"Do you have any holiday time coming up in the spring?" James asked as we made our way back up the trail toward the house. We decided to go for a walk in the snow after another *lengthy* shower because as much as I loved being cooped up in the house with James, we were both going a little stir crazy and feeling the onset of cabin fever. So, we bundled up and headed out, down a nearby trail and onto the beach

"Um," I hummed, biting my lip in thought, "I don't know. I usually have to give two weeks notice if I plan to take any significant amount of time off. I have sick days, but I prefer not to use them. I could probably get away for a week or two in late March or April. Why?"

"Well, because I want to take you away. My buddy, Justin, and his wife have chartered a live-aboard yacht for four months and are sailing it all through the Caribbean, stopping at different ports to go diving. And they've invited me to join them at any point in the trip."

"Seriously?"

A yacht? The Caribbean? James without a shirt in the sunshine? Yes, please!

"Do you dive?"

"Yeah, I do." He nodded. "Do you?"

"I took the course when I was twenty-one in Mexico when my family all went to Ixtapa for Christmas. And then I went with Max and Alex a few times in Spain and Greece."

"Do you want to do it again?" He held the door to the garage open for me, and we walked in and unbundled ourselves of our winter layers.

I toed off my boots. "Definitely."

"Should I look into some flights and a port to fly into to meet up with Justin and Kendra?"

I took his coat from him and hung it up next to mine on the hooks. "Yes, please, and the sooner, the better. I'm sick of the cold."

"All right then," he chuckled. "March it is. Let's go have a hot tub, warm up."

"Can you go in the hot tub with your incision?" I put my palms on my cheeks; my face was freezing.

"Oh shit! No, I can't. Let's go have another long shower to warm up then."

We had yet another long and sexy shower together and then wrapped up in flannel pajamas and blankets to eat leftover chili and watch a movie on HBO. I cherished how easy things were with James. He took everything in his stride and never got upset or shaken, so much so that I found myself looking for a fault in the man, so I would know that he was human and not some sexy figment of my imagination. Though, I'm pretty sure the mother of my manifestation would like me, so maybe Patricia was his fault.

"So, I'm going to go into the office tomorrow. Do you have enough clothes here so that we can go to work together?" He asked as we sat snuggled up under the blanket, a plate of cinnamon buns between us.

I looked at him in surprise. "You're going to work? Shouldn't you take a few more days to recuperate?"

"I work at a desk most of the day," he snapped. "I'm not lifting cinder blocks or arresting gigantic tattooed bikers. I'll be fine. I wish you and my mother would stop fussing over me. I'm not a child!" I watched his jaw clench as he rhythmically drummed his fingers on the armrest.

Was he mad? Had Mr. Perfect finally cracked?

"Okaaaay. Sorry. I do have enough clothes here, but I was hoping to go to the gym tomorrow, so we'll need to take separate vehicles. Maybe we can swing by my place on the way into town tomorrow, and I can take my car to work."

"No." He shook his head definitively. "I don't want you driving in this weather. We'll go to work together, and I'll drop you off at the gym and come get you. End of story."

I sat up and shot him an indignant look. "You're being awfully controlling." Where the hell was this attitude of his coming from? "And although I appreciate your concern," I continued, making sure my tone was as pleasant but authoritative as possible so that he knew I meant business, "please don't speak to me like that." I pulled away from his grasp and moved to the other end of the couch, so I didn't get hypnotized by his smell and the heat of his hard body.

His eyebrows furrowed. "Emma. I'm not controlling you. I'm just telling you what I think is best for your safety. And I don't think your car is as safe on the road as my truck. Stop being a child, use your head. What I'm saying just makes sense."

"Stop. Being. A. *Child*?" I gaped at him. Stunned at the way this man I'd grown so quickly to care for was talking to me, treating me as if I were some petulant toddler.

Regardless of whether he was right or not, and I didn't believe he was, the way he was speaking to me was completely disrespectful.

"Excuse me?"

Rolling his eyes, he gave me a chastising look; I suddenly felt as small as a cockroach.

"It's simple common sense," he said, appearing to be both bored and irritated with the conversation. "Now stop being so immature and needing to get your way and let's finish the movie." And he turned back to the television and took the film off pause.

I had spent over eight years living under the thumb of a controlling and manipulative man, and so two days before I left for Europe I made a solemn vow to myself, with my therapist as my witness, that I would never let a man push me around anymore or call the shots in my life. For too long I had done what someone else wanted me to do, forsaking my own needs and interests and I wasn't about to do it any longer.

I got up off the couch and walked out of the room. James didn't seem to understand the magnitude of his words or behavior and how it affected me, so I quietly packed my things upstairs and called for a taxi. It was waiting outside by the time I'd grabbed my wet gym clothes from the washing machine; I'd dry them at home. I left without saying "goodbye" because frankly, I couldn't look at him, and I knew that he would try to convince me to stay... and probably succeed.

It didn't take him too long to realize I wasn't coming back to the couch. I had been in the cab less than five minutes when his name came up on my phone. I canceled the call. I didn't feel like talking. It wasn't the fact that he was technically right, yes his truck was safer to drive, it was the way he was telling me what to do and when I questioned it, he called me a child. A text message popped up.

J: WHAT THE FUCK!? WHY DID YOU LEAVE?

I put my phone back in my purse. I had wished for my perfect man to have a fault and he'd shown me a big one, one that I couldn't deal with. And this fault just might be a deal breaker.

When I got home, my place was freezing. I put my wet laundry in the dryer and then started unpacking my bag. Totally at a loss, I put my pajamas back on and cranked the heat; then huddled under a blanket on my couch intermittently sobbing and staring blankly out my living room window at nothing in particular. I dozed off, my eyes heavy and exhausted from the tears. I wasn't long before I was jarred awake by heavy pounding on my door. I knew who it was. James was a smart man, and really, where else would I go?

How did he keep getting into the building without buzzing me?

"Emma? Emma! Open up."

He was mad. How could he be mad? He was the one who was acting like a complete and total asshole. I was the one who was mad. I took my time getting up from the couch and walking to the door. James could wait. When I finally turned the knob, he pushed himself inside, grabbing me by the shoulders and shaking me until my teeth rattled.

"Why did you leave? What the fuck?"

I pushed him away and backed up into my living room; I needed space to keep my head clear and focused. I needed to stand my ground and keep my promise to myself.

"Don't 'what the fuck' me." I kept my voice low and controlled, unlike Mr. Not-So-Perfect. "If we're going to have an adult conversation and discuss the reasons as to why I left, then you need to calm down and lower your voice."

Genuine surprise replaced his indignant look. He moved his lips as if ready to retaliate but thought better of it and walked to my armchair and sat down, snorting in derision.

"Fine," he sneered. "Let's discuss. Let's discuss why you refused to do what I said and then continued to question me. And then when you didn't get your way, you ran away. If that's not childish, I don't know what is."

Oh, this man. I was vibrating with rage, but I wrangled it in and clenched my jaw, determined not to let him break me. I'd come too far, grown too much to let anyone treat me that way again. I moved to sit down as far away from him as I could, reclaiming my seat on the couch and squaring off, ready to confront this gorgeous jerk.

"That's how *you* see it. Fine. You're entitled to *your* opinion. Now here's mine. And I'd appreciate it if you would remain silent until I'm finished." I swallowed, took a deep breath and then started. "James. The fact that your truck is better in the snow then my car is axiomatic." I saw him mouth the word *axiomatic*, rolling it around on his tongue, trying to figure out what it meant. He looked adorable. I glanced down at my lap so as not to be distracted by his cuteness. I went on, "It means irrelevant. Of course, it is, it's a truck. However, when we had that massive snowfall just after the new year before we'd even met, I managed to make it back and forth in my car on my brand new snow tires."

He discretely rolled his eyes but didn't say anything.

"But again, this point is indubitable." At this point, I was using big words just to fuck with him. "I've told you a lot about my relationship with Tom and how oppressive he was. I made a promise to myself after all of that that I would never let a man control me again. I gave up so much of myself for so many years—all my needs, my interests, and my passions—for someone else who never appreciated what I did or who I was. And I promised that I would never allow myself to give in to pressure and control by a man again. Regardless of how inane or pedantic the issue was because in my case it could be a slippery slope.

"And I like the strong woman I've become. I am independent and self-sufficient. I don't make a lot of money, but it's enough to pay my bills, fill my fridge and put a little bit away each month into my savings. I'm debt free, besides my mortgage. I'm educated, and I'm proud of who I am, of who I've become. So, when you *told* me what I was going to do and then called me a child, so many red flags went up that I could no longer see anything else. I needed to get out. And I ran. I shouldn't have run, I should have stood my ground and stayed, but I'm still a work in progress."

I took a deep breath. "Okay… I'm finished."

I looked down at my fingers, they were sweaty, and I continued to knot them pensively in my lap.

"Emma… I…" He was up off his chair and cradling me in his lap before I could blink, let alone protest. "I'm sorry. I had no idea how I was coming across or making you feel. I was just thinking about your safety. You're not a child, you're a beautiful, smart, sexy woman and I'm crazy about you." He grabbed both my hands and kissed the insides of my wrists. "Baby, I'm *really* sorry. I wasn't hearing myself or what I was saying. I'm used to being in control at work, and I have a hard time not ordering people around and expecting obedience. Please say you forgive me, be patient with me, I'm not good at this relationship thing. I'm a work in progress too."

I let out a weighty sigh and nodded, wanting desperately to forgive him and move forward, even though inside I was still a confused and distraught mess.

We trod lightly around each other for the next little while. James had wanted to take me back to his house to spend the night, but I refused. I needed some space after what had happened. He accepted my refusal, albeit reluctantly, and then changed tactics and hinted at wanting to stay over at my place, but again, I needed my space. We had slow and gentle make-up sex, where he poured his apology and heart out to me through his body. But as hard as I tried I wasn't able to get off, which he took as a personal failure, even though I assured him that it wasn't his fault. There was just too much on my mind; I still needed some time *and* space to think.

I had gone from my parent's house where I'd lived for my entire childhood, to Tom's house. I'd never had the opportunity to live on my own and grow as an individual. I'd hoped that my time in China would have helped, but that notion had been blown to smithereens after five measly months. So, I took the opportunity of my time in Europe and now living alone, to grow as a woman, to grow as a whole "me" rather than as a half of a "we."

I tried explaining this to James, and he seemed to understand, though he still made noise about spending the night and getting me to orgasm. And part of me felt guilty for leaving him on his own so soon after his surgery, but the man had managed to walk on the beach and give me mind-blowing orgasms since he'd been cut open, so he wasn't a failure by any stretch of the imagination, I figured he'd be okay. Plus, there was enough leftover chili in the fridge to feed a football team and loads of cookies and cinnamon buns on the counter, he certainly wasn't going to starve.

I went to bed as soon as James left and was unable to get warm. I put on socks, a sweatshirt, and my housecoat and climbed under the covers. My sheets still smelled like him; all man with a hint of woods and spice. I put my head down and hugged the pillow he'd used, crying softly for reasons unknown. The hurricane of emotions over the last week had left me exhausted and confused.

I had fallen so hard for this man, given so much of myself so quickly, but I was beginning to wonder if I was emotionally ready for another serious relationship. I wanted this, wanted him, but was I ready? He had said that if at any time I wanted out of our *arrangement,* then I just had to say the word. I had been very content in my pre-James life. My world was predictable and routine. I had work, the gym, and Alyssa—things were good. So, the question was, excluding today's fiasco, was I happier in my James-filled life?

16

We spoke on Monday and Tuesday, but we didn't see each other, at my request. James had wanted to come over, but I'd said no. We needed a night apart, and I still needed my space. He'd argued passionately that we'd only spent two nights together and had been apart for twelve, but when I said I needed to be alone, he'd dropped it, but not without a heavy sigh and an audible grumble.

After spin class on Wednesday, Alyssa and I went for a late dinner, and I filled her in on the weekend and how my glorious reunion with James had abruptly turned south. She seemed to understand where I was coming from; however, she made some keen observations that only an astute lady lawyer such as herself would be able to discern.

"I get where you're coming from," she said, "and I think James was out of line when he spoke to you that way, especially knowing how Tom had treated you. However, have you told him the *whole* story about Tom? The dieting, the jealousy? Is James even half aware of how fucked up Tom made you? Because if not, he may not understand how traumatic it is when someone speaks to you like that."

She shoveled a pita wedge with hummus into her mouth.

"Because honestly, the topic of your argument is pretty trivial. Yes, he could have used nicer words, and been a little more tactful, but he was looking out for your safety and wanted to spend as much time with you as possible. Your car's a piece of shit compared to his truck, and he wasn't telling you to get your ass into the kitchen to make him a sandwich. Does he know the *whole* story?"

Leave it to Alyssa to tell me how it really is. I loved her blatant honesty.

I gnawed on a carrot stick. "No."

"How much have you told him?"

"A fair bit. It's embarrassing to talk about how horrible Tom treated me because when you lay it all out on the table, I was a complete and total moron to have ever been with him in the first place, let alone stayed with him for almost nine years. I'm embarrassed for having made such a terrible mistake. What does that say about the type of person *I* am? About my self-respect, or lack thereof?"

"Oh, honey." She shook her head. "Tom was a master manipulator. He had us all fooled." She handed me a napkin when I hastily went to wipe away a rogue tear. "It will be hard, but you need to tell him everything. If you ever want it to work out, he has to know what your triggers are."

I sniffed. "I know."

It was almost nine thirty by the time I left Alyssa. I popped home quickly and then drove to James' house, not knowing if he'd be home or what to expect if he was. We hadn't spoken since Monday evening when he'd called me after the gym, and even then that call had been awkward and short. The nerves that coursed through me were very different from the ones that were tingling the last time I showed up unannounced to his house, and the butterflies in my belly seemed to be getting ready to vomit instead of throwing a righteous dance party.

I parked in the driveway and then walked along the path that I had shoveled clear of snow for him on Sunday—most had already melted away with the rain—and knocked on the door. I took a deep breath, not that it helped to calm my nerves, the pit that had settled in my stomach was the size of a bowling ball.

"Emma?" His face was a mosaic of expressions. He probably thought I'd come over to end it.

"I've made a big mistake," I whispered, licking my lips and then taking a deep breath. "A-and I need to fix it. Can we talk?"

"Yes, of course, come in." His Adam's apple bobbed in his throat. Was he nervous? "I'm glad you're here. I've missed you." He leaned in hesitantly and kissed me on the cheek.

"I've missed you too," I said softly, taking great care not to get too close, his wonderful smell and the electricity that charged between us was mesmerizing and often left me flummoxed.

We sat down in the living room on the big couch. James had the fire going, and his laptop was out with airline and flight information to The Bahamas.

Oh yeah, our trip.

"So, I don't feel like I've been very fair to you," I started. "I wigged out on Sunday because of how you spoke to me and how it made me feel. And when I sit back and think about it all, the topic was really, very trivial. You were just being you, albeit a bossy dink, but I should have taken into consideration your lack of painkillers, fatigue from our walk and general irritability over not being able to do normal things. I guess it wasn't easy to let me shovel the path and driveway."

He shrugged, smiled sheepishly and nodded.

"I've told you bits and pieces about my relationship with Tom and what he did to me, but the truth is he was much, *much* worse. Tom essentially destroyed who I was as a person. And I've spent the last year trying to rebuild that person up again and make her stronger, along with finding out who I am and what I want out of life."

He blinked at me and nodded, encouraging me to continue and letting me know he had no intention of interrupting me.

I took another deep breath and started. "Tom and I met in high school. I had just lost a bunch of weight and jumped at the chance to date the first boy who had ever shown me any attention. We went to prom, then immediately moved in together after high school. Tom was aware of my insecurities about my weight and used that to control me. He would weigh me and my food every day. He said he was *helping* me avoid the freshman fifteen. But I don't think putting locks on the cupboards, and negative post-it notes that said 'STOP, FATTY' on food in the fridge was helpful. I became bulimic and would purge my meals before I got home from school or work before Tom weighed me. Even though he eventually found out and encouraged me to continue, saying that the vomiting was a good idea to keep my weight down.

"Nobody else knew. I hid it very well. I wouldn't always purge, only when I was sure I wouldn't get caught, and I didn't really binge eat, I've always eaten pretty healthy. So, maybe I didn't have bulimia, just an eating disorder. But I threw up a lot, and if I couldn't vomit, then I would just go crazy hard at the gym. But either way going to China saved me. I was forced to eat and was too busy to exercise regularly or purge. And Max and Alex were so complimentary that I never felt the need to change my body for them."

I swallowed hard, my throat suddenly dry from all the talking. James noticed and jumped up to grab me a glass of water. I took a sip and thanked him before continuing.

"Tom was insanely jealous too. And he took his jealousy out on me. If he ever caught me talking to another guy, other girls present or not, Tom would be livid. And his form of punishment was to put me down. He'd call me fat, a child, a dumb blonde, an idiot, a whore, you name it. He went so far one time as to lock me out of our apartment overnight one time. He'd noticed me talking to a male lab TA in the university library one afternoon. I was having issues with an assignment and was asking him a question. The guy was married with a kid, but Tom thought I was cheating on him with the TA, and he put the chain lock on the door and refused to let me into our apartment. I ended up having to sleep in my car that night.

"We'd started having sex in high school, but from the get-go, it was always all about Tom. I didn't have an orgasm for three years and maybe had all of fifteen or twenty orgasms from Tom during our entire relationship. And he wasn't a fan of giving oral sex, even though it was his preferred way of reaching climax himself. Max was the first guy to ever go down on me. My therapist used the term 'misogynist.' Through the years when the topic of marriage would come up, Tom would say he still wasn't sure if I were worthy—he would even say this in front of our friends.

"I was a fool for staying as long as I did. But whenever I made noise about leaving him, he would say that I would never find another person to love me that he was doing me a favor. I never told my parents any of this, couldn't because over the years they became close with Tom's parents, who are actually very nice people. But after Tom dumped me I told them almost everything. Only Alyssa and now you know everything though. Alex and Max know a bit, and my brother Lewis knows a lot too. None of the sexual things, but he knows pretty much everything else."

I took another sip of water; my heart felt as though it was going to leap out of my chest at any moment it was beating so fast.

You're almost done, you're doing great!

"I guess part of the reason why I was reluctant to disclose everything to you is that I was afraid of what you would think of me. I'm embarrassed and ashamed. I was so weak, and I apparently thought so little of myself to not have gotten out sooner. I just... I just want you to know everything, so you know my triggers and how what you say, although it may not be that bad in reality, to me it sounds a whole lot worse. I saw a counselor twice a week when he first dumped me, and then twice a month when I got back from Europe. I only just stopped going a few months ago because I was feeling really good about myself and my life."

I took a deep breath and pushed it out, flopping back against the headrest of the couch and closing my eyes. I hadn't been looking at James during the retelling of my painful past. I opened one eye and peered at him out of my peripheral, hoping to catch a glimmer of where his thoughts were. He sat forward with his arms resting on his knees and his head in his hands looking at his feet.

"James?"

He lifted his head to look at me, and in his stormy almost black eyes was pure, unadulterated hatred. Rage and loathing took over the beautiful features of his face as he ran his hands through his hair pulling at the ends in frustration.

"Are you mad?"

"Mad? Oh no, I'm beyond mad. I'm... I'm furious. I'm... words don't even begin to describe how I feel. I want to hit something. I *need* to hit something."

His fists bunched, and he pounded the armrest of the couch, grinding his teeth and flexing his jaw as the anger coursed through him causing the veins in his neck and forehead to pulse and pop out as his face grew a frightening shade of red.

I tucked my knees up to my chest and wrapped my arms around them. Shit, I never should have told him. Now he was mad at how stupid I was and how stupid he was for ever getting involved with me. It was over between us. I knew it.

"Okay... I'm... I'm so sorry. I should never have told you. I understand if you want me to go." I started to get up, reaching for my coat on the back of the couch.

Wild eyes swiveled to look at me. "Wait. What? Oh God, no!" He shook his head, knocking his current thoughts free. The features of his face morphing into ones of compassion mixed with confusion. "I'm not mad at you. Not at all. Oh God, never. I'm mad at myself for not considering how my actions would affect you, and I'm *furious* about Tom. I want to hunt down and kill this fucker who ruined you."

He grabbed my shoulders and pulled me into his arms, pressing my body to his and my head to his shoulder. "Jesus, Emma, I could never be mad at you. He is a manipulative bastard who mentally and emotionally abused you." Pushing me away again he grabbed my shoulders, shaking me gently. "Did he *ever* hit you? Because so help me, I will hunt that fucker down and kill him myself."

I swallowed the lump that had caught in my throat and barely nodded. "Once... he slapped me, but he apologized immediately, and I thought he meant it. Another time he tried to punch me. I ducked *and* was strong enough to tell him that if he ever raised a hand to me again, I would leave and tell my brothers—Lewis is an amateur cage fighter with a temper—but I should have gotten out then. I was an idiot to stay as long as I did."

Pulling me back to his chest and squeezing me even tighter, he kissed the top of my head. I decided to go on talking, hoping to stave off the flow of tears.

"Lew eventually did hit him—only it wasn't until he'd dumped me and kicked me out. I wish I could have seen Tom's face afterward. It would have made a great picture if Lew's badly bruised and cut up hand was anything to go by."

"So, you haven't seen Tom since he kicked you out?" His voice was a calming and reassuring rumble next to my ear.

"No. I've been so afraid that I'd run into him and Jennifer one day, pushing a baby stroller, acting like a happy little family. I honestly don't know what I'd do."

"Em?" He tilted my chin up to look at him. "Thank you for telling me everything. I know it couldn't have been easy. I am going to try very, *very* hard to rein in my controlling tendencies and give you the space and independence you need. And please, if I'm pushing too hard tell me to back the fuck off. I don't want to lose you."

"Okay." I smiled.

"Would you spend the night with me? Please."

I shrugged. "Okay. My bag is in my car."

"You brought an overnight bag?" He was chuckling as he got up and retrieved my keys from my coat pocket.

"Yeah, just in case. Best to be prepared."

"I'll be right back."

I texted Alyssa while James ran out to my car.

E: He wants to kill Tom. It's all good. Spending the night. Thanks for the dose of reality. Xoxo

"So, are we okay?" He asked as he plunked himself back down on the couch next to me, throwing my bag on the coffee table and pulling me onto his lap.

"We're better than okay." I rolled the kinks out of my shoulders, my heart already feeling lighter and my chest less tight. "It feels like I just unloaded an elephant off my shoulders. You know everything now."

"Do I?" He wasn't challenging me; it was an honest question. I had to stop and think. Had I forgotten to mention anything else that could come up later?

"Ummm... well, Tom also said that if I got pregnant, he would force me to get an abortion, that I wouldn't have a choice. He didn't want kids, which should have been my first inclination to get out because I *do*. And yet, Jennifer had their baby, well at least I'm assuming she did. It's been over a year."

"I would never do that," he said softly. "Your body, your choice."

I bit my lip and played with the hem of his shirt. "*Well*, what would happen if I did get pregnant? We need to have that conversation. My STI test came back negative, and I'm assuming yours did too as they were done the same day."

"Yeah, it did." His hand was making its way up the back of my shirt to draw delightful little circles on the small of my back. "It came back negative. We don't have to use condoms anymore if you don't want to."

"Do you want to?"

"I hate condoms, but it's your choice. I'm not going to pressure you. I'll wear them if it's what you want. I'd rather fuck you wearing a rain jacket than not fuck you at all."

I snuggled into him. "I don't like them either. I want skin-to-skin."

"Did you use condoms with Max and Alex?"

"Yeah for the most part, even though I was on the pill, we got STI tests done, but they took forever to come back, and if I did get pregnant the whole 'who's the daddy?' game would have been ridiculous and embarrassing to explain to our parents.

"Yeah," he chuckled. "I never thought of that."

"We used them probably ninety percent of the time. I think there were a couple of drunken nights where we may have forgotten. Thank God for the pill. How are you feeling?" I lifted his black t-shirt and ran my hand over his abdomen, just inches away from his incision. "No unusual pain, inflammation, puss or redness?"

"No. Now that we're okay, I'm fine." He nuzzled his face between my breasts, inhaling deeply.

My hand rested on the top of his head. "I'm sorry for how I reacted."

"*Shh,*" he said softly. "Don't apologize again. It's over, you've told me everything, and we're stronger now because of it. Let's move on."

"Okay."

"I want you to know, though," he said as he lifted his head from my chest and looked me square in the eye, cobalt piercing my very soul. "I'm all in. This isn't just a sexual arrangement for me anymore. This is a relationship."

"I'm all in too," I whispered, kissing the top of his head and running my fingers lightly through his thick hair.

"Let's go to bed." He patted my butt, and I climbed off his lap.

"Okay." I reached for his hand as he grabbed my bag and led me upstairs, turning lights off on the way. "As long as you promise to fuck me until I pass out."

"It's a promise."

17

When I came down the stairs the next morning, my breath caught in my throat, and I nearly fell ass-over-tea-kettle on the last step. James was standing in front of the French doors that headed to the patio, his arms were braced against the wall while the daylight cast his muscular body into an almost biblical glow, and the two pieces of a three-piece suit hugged his body so damn perfectly.

I watched in quiet awe as his muscles flexed and rippled beneath his dress shirt and vest; he was exquisite. He knew I was watching him; he had a keen sense of awareness when it came to our proximity; the air seemed to sizzle and spark.

His back stiffened but he didn't turn around, he knew the effect he had on me, and he was acting coy, letting me take in his beauty. Eventually, after a few moments he gave his butt a playful shake, and I laughed out loud. He'd been deep in thought when I'd first noticed him, his reflection in the window had been pensive, but when he turned around, there was nothing but feral want in his eyes. He stalked toward me and in less than four strides I was in his arms, swallowing my gasp with his mouth he bent my body back and deepened the kiss, dipping me low and moaning erotically against my lips. I wrapped my arms around his neck and pulled him into me, relishing in his heat and hardness.

"Well, good morning to you too," I said when he finally released me, my lips swollen and bruised, but craving more.

He growled in the back of his throat and the sound sent a flurry of shivers up and down my spine as he nipped at my earlobe before setting me back down on my feet. We'd found our groove again last night; James had gotten me off a number of times and was clearly riding high on his success.

"You look beautiful today," he purred, taking in my business casual attire.

I was wearing a pair of tight-fitting, tapered red pants, black ballet flats, a black long sleeve cotton tailored blouse and a gray cardigan. My hair was in a ponytail at the back of my head, and I wore white pearl studs in my ears.

"Thanks, and you look good enough to eat." I rose up on my tippy toes and nipped at his jaw. He inhaled abruptly and then slapped my ass as he chased me into the kitchen.

"Oh, baby, don't start something you don't have time to finish." His voice pitched low and threatening as he prowled after me.

I opened the fridge to grab myself some orange juice, and he pinned my body between his menacing frame and the closed fridge door.

"I'll take you right here in the kitchen I want you so badly. Can't you tell?" His hips pushed into me, rubbing his ever-impressive hard-on into my pelvis.

I closed my eyes and bit my lip as the need to be dominated by his body surged through me, blood beginning to boil with lust, wetness pooling between my legs.

"You already took me this morning in the shower where do you find the stamina?"

He leaned his head into my neck, inhaling and running his nose along the vein that pulsed my hot-for-him blood. "It's all you, baby. You make me hard all the time. If I could fuck you every minute of every day, I would."

I giggled. "Well, we'll have to get up earlier in the morning then if we're going to work *morning glory* into our routine."

"Or you quit your job, I retire, and we stay home all day, every day, and fuck like rabbits. Just screw until we pass out or die. What a way to go, eh?"

He was all grins and playful teasing, continuing to grind his hips into me so I could feel his excitement. He pushed my legs apart with his knee and settled himself between them. I leaned into him, arching my back against the fridge and closing my eyes, enjoying the divine pressure of his hard length.

"Well, your insatiable appetite this morning has left me with a real appetite, let me eat my breakfast..." I pleaded as I gave him a gentle shove. He moaned, coming back up behind me as I poured my juice, pressing his pelvis into my butt while reaching around to fondle my breasts. I giggled again and pushed into him; his moan was louder this time as he reluctantly released me to go and pour himself some coffee.

"I seem to remember you were the one who asked me to fuck you last night until you passed out. I'm not the only one with an insatiable sexual appetite. You were a pretty horny little thing—you drained me, woman."

"It's all you, baby," I whispered softly, batting my eyelashes at him as I took my seat at the bar where Earl Grey tea, half a grapefruit, and a hard-boiled egg sat in front of me.

"So, Amy and Garret are going to come and stay with us for the St. Patrick's Day weekend, and you said your parents are coming down for a visit at some point too?" He asked, taking a bite out his token peanut butter toast.

"Yeah, I think the following weekend. I'll call my mum sometime this week and double check."

"Okay, that works out well, because we're set to fly out the last weekend of March to The Bahamas. Justin and Kendra will meet us in Nassau. I booked the tickets last night."

"Really? This is so exciting."

"Two weeks, baby. You and me with hardly any clothes on, in the sunny tropics. Just us and the fishes." He washed out his coffee mug and put it in the drying rack and then took my empty dishes and returned to the sink to wash them up. Man, even if Patricia was a cold woman, she didn't raise no slob of a son, I'll give her that.

"Well, you, me, the fishes, and Justin and Kendra. We can't exactly have sex on the bow of the boat."

"Why not?"

"Well, not in daylight anyway."

His eyebrows bounced up and down as he took another bite of toast. "Oh, Miss Everly, we're going to have all kinds of filthy adventures on this holiday of ours."

On Monday I was standing in line at the bank on my lunch break waiting for the ATM when a familiar voice jarred me out of my daydream.

I spun around to see Elliot, an old friend from university and mutual friend of Tom's and mine. He looked good, *really* good, with a dark, close shave beard and mustache, short straight dark brown hair, and those ever mystifying different color eyes. The right one was a pale blue almost gray while the left was copper and amber. He wasn't overly tall, perhaps five-foot-nine, and he was stocky with a rugby player's build, which made sense considering he played and was passionate about the game. He was a striking man, with a friendly smile and a genuineness that made you want to open up and tell him your life's story along with all your dirty little secrets.

Truth be told, I'd always had a tiny crush on him. He had forever been a bit flirty with me as well. But I'd convinced myself that he was just being nice, that he'd never actually fancied me at all, seeing as Tom had done a damn good job convincing me that I was ugly and unlovable. He and Tom had become friends in first-year calculus, and then Elliot introduced me to his girlfriend Leila, and we became fast friends. They were two people I'd mourned the loss of most when Tom dumped me, more than I mourned the loss of Tom himself. Was Elliot still in touch with him?

"Hey Elliot, how are you?" He walked toward me after having left the teller and immediately embraced me in a big bear hug, bridging the gap of any awkwardness that I might have felt.

"I'm great how are you? It's been forever."

"I'm really good, thanks. It has been a while. What are you up to?"

"I work here. I'm a mortgage broker for the bank. Are you on lunch? Do you want to go grab a bite and catch up?"

"Uh." I looked at my watch. "Sure, I only have forty-five minutes left on my break, though."

"Okay. Let's go to Gonzales' they're quick, cheap and delicious."

"That sounds great. I haven't been there in ages."

He waited for me to do my transaction at the ATM and then followed me outside, holding the door for me and falling in line on the road-side of the sidewalk. Another thing I'd always admired about Elliot; he was such a gentleman compared to Tom.

"So, what are you up to these days? Last I'd heard, you went to China and then came back and then…" he trailed off when he realized the end of the story. "Sorry… I… I forgot how that ended." He looked down at his plate and pinched at a couple of pieces of fallen rice and popped them into his mouth.

"It's okay." I shrugged. "I'm sure everyone knows what happened by now. I'm an ESL teacher here in town. I work for Global Language Academy."

"Oh, that sounds great…" he paused and scrunched up his face in regret. "Listen Em, I want you to know, we all know what really happened. We know Tom cheated and got Jennifer pregnant. No one thinks anything less of you. We all just feel sorry for you." His eyes were pleading with me. But he also looked at me with pity; pity that I neither deserved nor wanted.

I shook my head. "Hey, don't feel sorry for me. I'm way better off. Tom was an asshole. I'm happy now and in a much better place."

"Hello," came a husky voice behind me, while the all-too-familiar and arousing scent permeated my nostrils causing lust to ignite in my veins and rush between my legs.

Elliot's eyes went wide, and his face froze as he took in the man at my back. I spun around in my chair to see James standing six inches behind me; the crotch of his pants directly in front of my mouth.

"Hi." I smiled, my eyes lingering a second or two too long on his pants before drifting up to his face.

I expected to see the beautiful smile that always left me winded, but instead, I was met with a mask of indifference, his face devoid of emotion and almost recognition.

"James this is Elliot, an old friend. Elliot this is... this is James, my boyfriend."

"Oh hey, man, nice to meet you." Elliot stood up and extended his hand toward James. James took it and shook it, stiffly, his eyes traveling up and down Elliot's body, taking in his appearance, sizing him up. "We just finished lunch but would you care to join us?" Elliot asked, his own eyes darting back and forth between James and me, trying to get a read on the increasingly awkward situation.

"No, thank you," he said flatly. "I'll let you two finish your *date*. Emma."

He looked down into my eyes for no more than a second, nodded and then spun on his heel and headed toward the elevator. I watched his back disappear around the corner, a delicious ass working its magic and taunting me in perfectly tailored pants. A small but quickly growing craving ran rampant through my body, mixing with a whole lot of confusion and frustration that was compounding by the second.

What just happened? He'd barely acknowledged Elliot; he'd barely acknowledged me.

"Well, that was interesting," Elliot mumbled grabbing both of our trays and taking them to the garbage can.

"Yeah, I don't know what's up. He's normally a lot friendlier." I stood up, and we walked back out into the cold March afternoon.

"I think he was jealous."

"Of what, us? Having lunch? No! James isn't the jealous type," I said with a scoff, dismissing the idea entirely.

But then, maybe he was. We hadn't known each other that long, and he hadn't opened up about his other relationships at all. Sure, he'd told me he'd been with a lot of women, but I knew nothing about any of them. *Was* he the jealous type?

Elliot shook his head as he pulled his coat tighter around his body. "I know jealous Em. Tom was jealous, and *that* was jealous."

"Well, even if it was, he has nothing to worry about. I'm with him, and you're with Leila."

"Uh," he hummed, "I'm not with Leila anymore. We split up shortly after you and Tom."

I stopped on the sidewalk and stared at him. "What? Why?"

"We grew apart." He shrugged. "And to be honest, I'd always had a bit of a thing for you." He reached for my hand. "I'd thought, well hoped, that we could have given it a try when you and Tom broke up, and Leila and I ended, but you fell off the map. Changed your numbers and email. I couldn't find you."

He looked right at me, through me, down to my soul, his different color eyes glittering in the sun, beseeching and hopeful.

"But now that I've found you again..." he trailed off, cocking an eyebrow in question.

My mind began to spin, conflicting feelings and forgotten urges bashing around in my brain, cannoning off each other. I'd considered my affections for Elliot had only ever been one sided. Tom had diminished my self-esteem to infinitesimal pieces, so that I was incapable of believing that any man would ever find me attractive. But Elliot had. Elliot did. The harmless flirtations hadn't been one-sided. My ego did a back flip, but my conscience was quick to drag me back to reality. As much as I liked Elliot and found him kind and attractive, he wasn't James; and James was all I wanted, all I needed. Elliot's hand was soft and warm, no calluses or scars marred his office-boy palm. I let it go. Pulling away and smiling shyly, desperate not to offend him but also get my point across.

"I... I had no idea," I stammered. "But I'm with James now."

His face fell. "But, you're not serious yet are you? And he seems like a bit of a jealous ass. You don't deserve that again."

My lips twisted, and I nodded. "We are serious. It happened fast, but I'm really, really happy. And I don't know if it was jealousy or not.

But I'll deal with that later." I gave him a small smile. "And James knows all about Tom. He says he'd never treat me that way. Besides, I'm much stronger now."

"I could make you happy," he said reaching for my hand again, but I backed away.

"You probably could," I sighed. "But I'm with James now."

He let out his own deep sigh and forced a smile though it didn't reach his eyes.

"Be my friend, Elliot. I need more of those. I miss you and Leila. When Tom dumped me, I lost all of our friends." I tilted my head, suggesting that we ought to start walking again, lighten the mood and get me closer to work.

"I can try," he whispered. "But I won't stop wanting you."

I sighed. "We need to change the subject." Eager to move onto something less awkward and more neutral.

"Fine," he huffed. "So, what does James do?"

I looked at him out of the corner of my eye. Neutral ground my ass. He shrugged innocently and put his hands in his pockets.

"He owns J.P.S Developing Inc. here in town."

"He *owns*?"

"Yeah."

"Holy shit, the dude is loaded. They're building half or more of the new projects here in Victoria. Just won the bid for that strip mall plaza being built on the West Shore. Not to mention whatever other national and international projects they have their hands in. Wait is *he*, J.P.S?

I nodded. "Yeah, James Parker Shaw. How do you know so much about the company?"

"I'm a mortgage broker. I deal with money and finances all day long. It's my job to be aware of what's going on in this city, to know the upcoming and current residential and commercial developments."

I lifted one shoulder. "Fair enough. Well, uh, this is where I turn off, my school is that way," I said, pointing down the road toward the water.

"All right, well it was awesome to see you, Emma. You have my number, and I have yours. Call me if you need anything. I hope we can do this again sometime." He shuffled his feet and dug his hands deeper into his pockets. "And, uh, sorry about freaking you out when I poured my heart out back there."

I huffed out a laugh. "That's okay. I'm sorry I stomped all over it."

"I'll recover." He looked up at me from beneath his lashes. "But if things between you and Shaw go south, promise me you'll give me a call? I'd love to take you to dinner."

I smiled. "It was nice to see you. Thanks for lunch." He leaned in, going for the hug; I embraced him back but kept it quick and nothing but arms and upper body. After the awkwardness of earlier, I didn't want to lead him on.

As I walked back to work my phone vibrated in my pocket. It was a text from James.

J: **Care to tell me what the hell that was about?**

E: **Uh, I had lunch with an old friend. Exactly what I said it was when you saw us. Could you be any ruder?**

J: **Looked a lot cozier than just a LUNCH!**

E: **What is that supposed to mean?**

J: **Who is he? Why wasn't I made aware of your date?**

E: **Excuse me? He's an old friend who I haven't seen in a while. We ran into each other at the bank where he works and we decided to grab lunch. I wasn't aware I had to let you know my hour-by-hour plans. And it wasn't a DATE!**

Where the hell was this jealousy coming from? He was acting like Tom! A frisson of nerves prickled the back of my neck and then slid south like an icicle raking its way down my spine. This was the same dominating, possessive and skeptical behavior that Tom had exhibited; the signs were clear, the red flags were blazing. What had I gotten myself into with this man?

J: **Not hour-by-hour, but a heads-up would have been nice. I felt like an idiot seeing my girlfriend having a date with another man that I was unaware of. And then I see you two hug as I get into my car. What the hell was that about?**

E: **IT WASN'T A DATE!!! I can't do this. This is over. I have to go to work.**

My hands trembled as I typed my last text. I couldn't do it, not over text, it's so impersonal, and there's no way of knowing the tone of voice or context. It would have to wait for a face-to-face discussion. But I did know I couldn't handle a relationship if it were going to be like this; neither the lack of trust nor the prying jealousy. It was Tom all over again.

I turned off my phone and put my head down. I had to focus on work. Closing my eyes, I took three deep breaths and forcibly pushed my anger down and away. I locked up all my toiling emotions and concentrated on my job, on my students.

"Fuck you, James," I muttered as I threw my purse down on my desk with a loud thump, determined to bury myself in my work and plough through the remainder of the day.

I drove home after the gym that night, my mind a cacophony of discordant feelings and worries. I wasn't sure how or when I was going to address things with James, but I knew that I had to and better sooner than later. When I opened the door into my apartment, instantly I knew that I wasn't alone. I could smell him; feel the charge in the air from the presence of his warm, hard body. I'd given him a key over the weekend, and he was clearly making good use of it.

Hesitantly I walked down the hallway; my body was on high alert, nervous about what kind of state I would find him in. If he were Tom, I knew that I would be in for a barrage of insults, screaming, and threats. The lights were off. Okay, so he's going for ultra-dramatic—great!

I was tired, sweaty, and all I wanted to do was have a shower and throw on my flannel penguin pajamas; the last thing I wanted was a rehash of our texting war. But it had to happen. If it festered, like an infected wound, it would bubble and worsen and inevitably burst, tainting our whole relationship.

Get a grip, woman.

I strode into the living room, and there he was, dressed down in well-worn jeans, a black t-shirt, and gray socks. Jeez, why were his big, socked feet turning me on? I'm one perverted chick. He'd slung his jacket over the back of the bar stool in my kitchen, and his shoes were nestled neatly beneath it.

"Hello, James."

"So, we're over?" he growled, with barely a hint of inflection, causing me to pause and wonder if it was a question or a statement.

I opened my mouth and then closed it, choosing my words carefully and wisely. I could tell he was tightly wound, his fists flexed on the arm of the chair, and his jaw was set tight as he ground his teeth.

"Is that a question, or are you telling me that we're over?"

"You told me that we were over. You said that you couldn't do it and that it was over. What does that mean?"

He stood abruptly and stalked toward me. Instinctively I backed up, grabbing the second barstool to maneuver it between us. He paused, noticed what I was doing and stepped back. "Are you... are you afraid of me?"

"I don't know. Should I be?"

His head shook emphatically. "No! Never. I will *never* hurt you." He took a tentative step toward me again but stopped when he saw me flinch. I couldn't help it; it was an impulse I couldn't control.

"Why did you say it was over? What does that mean?" he asked again, holding his hands up in surrender and backing away a step.

"I didn't say *we* were over. I said that *it* was over," I sighed, relaxing slightly and moving the stool out from between us. "As in the texting war, we were having. I hate text messaging. It always messes things up. I couldn't do it anymore. I never broke up with you via text and never would. That's the coward's way out."

"So... so you're going to do it in person?" His Adam's apple jogged in his throat as he looked at me with deep-seated fear.

"No, I don't think so. But you have a lot of explaining to do. Your behavior and text messages today were atrocious and are not working in your favor right now. I've told you what Tom was like. I can't deal with possessive behavior. Elliot and I are *just* friends."

His jaw gritted, but he kept his tone civil. "The way he was looking at you is *not* how one friend looks at another. He wants you."

I paused, my eyes darted around the room and then fixated on a spot on the ceiling.

"He does, doesn't he? He said something to you. Don't lie." He ground his teeth again and flexed his jaw. The muscles on his forearms bulged as he clenched his hands into vein-popping fists.

I let my eyes slowly travel back to his face. "He may have mentioned that he has always had a bit of a thing for me and thought that we might get together when he and his girlfriend split up, and Tom and I ended. But I told him that I was with you. And regardless of the fact that I once had a crush on him, I'm *with* you. You're all I want and need. I'm not interested in anything but Elliot's friendship."

"You can't be friends with him if he wants to fuck you." He said bluntly with a dismissive shake of his head.

"Excuse me?" I roared, my hackles rising while I flailed my arms for emphasis. "Listen, Buster," I continued to holler at him, and then I poked his hard chest with my finger. "It's not my fault that you have some asinine idea about what it means to be in a relationship. We are two equals, who have chosen of our own volition to spend our free time together and engage in copious amounts of intercourse. But at no point in time did I submit my free will nor will I allow you to run roughshod over my life. Your views on what it means to be a boyfriend are heinously warped, and I suggest you re-evaluate. You have no right to tell me who I can and can't be friends with."

"Yes, I do," he countered, his voice rising a few octaves. I was beginning to worry about the neighbors hearing that they would think we were having a domestic dispute. Would they call the cops?

"I'm your boyfriend, and I don't feel comfortable with you going out for lunch with random guys I've never met who want to nail you."

"Too bad," I said flippantly. "Either deal with it or take a hike. I won't be dictated to, and we've already discussed this." I was fuming, the fear of experience replaced by an adrenaline rush of bitter tasting fury, a simmering pot of anger that was mere seconds from boiling over.

"So that's it?" The threads of his frustration were beginning to unravel.

"Maybe it is." I heard myself say before I knew what it was I was saying.

His face fell. "We're over?"

Shaking my head, I could manage no more than a whisper. "I don't know. I don't want to break up, but I need some space. I think you should go. I have a lot of thinking to do, and I'd prefer to do it alone." I looked down at the floor and toed at a non-existent piece of fluff on the carpet. I was a coward for not looking him in the eye.

He hesitated for a while, waiting for me to say something else, but I didn't, I couldn't.

"Fine!" He finally growled, grabbing his coat off the chair and shoving his feet in his shoes. I didn't look up until I heard the door slam.

I slumped to the shower and climbed in, clothes and all. The tears mixed with water and ran salty and warm into my mouth. Peeling off my gym clothes I let them form a dark puddle of fabric at my feet, but somehow the heat and steam couldn't stave off the shivers that came in waves, and I just stood there shaking. I don't even remember washing my hair or shaving my armpits, but I'm sure I did. After wrapping a towel around myself in a cloud of frustration and sadness, I shoveled some toast and an apple into my face and then crawled into bed, positively exhausted, but of course, unable to sleep.

I tossed and turned, hugging my pillow and pretending it was James. Why was he so jealous? The way he thought he could control who I went to lunch with, who I hung out with and which people I was and wasn't friends with wasn't acceptable. That sort of behavior was *so* Tom, and I wanted nothing to do with it.

It was late—or early Tuesday depending on how you want to look at it, around the three o'clock mark as the red glare from my alarm clock permeated the darkness—that I decided I wouldn't see or talk to James until Friday. I would take the rest of the week to think. I'd get Alyssa's opinion and then make a decision by Friday. Somehow coming to that conclusion set my mind at ease enough to drift off into a restless and unfulfilling sleep.

18

I woke up the following morning with elephant sized bags under my eyes and a giant zit on my cheek from where I had apparently not rinsed off the soap from my shower well enough. I dressed down in a pair of black pants and a gray sweater with no jewelry and dragged my hair into an unassuming ponytail at the base of my neck. I troweled on the concealer to cover-up the pustule of sadness on my face and then headed out the door to work.

Thankfully my day was very busy, and my ESL students were full of questions and conversation, so I had little time to worry. I'd texted Alyssa on my lunch hour, and the two of us were going to bail on the gym and get pedicures then Thai food instead and talk about how dumb boys could be.

"So, what do you think I should do?" I asked, scanning the never-ending wall of nail polishes at the beauty salon. I was in a dark mood and felt like I needed a dark color on my toes, maybe charcoal or chocolate plum.

"I don't know," she sighed, picking up a bright green bottle and reading the name. "It's a tough call. Ha, *Key to his Apartment Lime Pie*. Man, this would be the best job ever. Just sit in a room all day and name nail polishes. I bet they all get drunk or high. That's probably when their most creative names come out."

I nodded. "Should I end it with him before things get too serious, before I wind up getting hurt or losing all the independence and self-confidence I've gained over the last year?"

"Like I said, it's a tough call." She put the green bottle back and grabbed a peacock blue. "*More than Just a One-Night-Stand.* Seriously? At least the green one gave an indication of its shade. This one could be anything. How arbitrary is that?"

I picked out a muted matte burgundy and walked over to the counter, turning it over in my hand to read the name, *Broken Hearted.* Wow, how fitting!

"Em, what do you want from him? What do *you* want?" Lys asked, joining me at the counter with her color choice, a soft pearly pink.

"I want him to be trusting and not jealous."

We followed our estheticians to the chairs and sat down.

"I want him to be accepting of my friends, no matter who they are, and trust me not to sleep with any man that looks at me twice."

"Did you tell him this?"

"I can't remember what I said. It's all such a blur. I was so mad at how domineering he was and how he treated me. His possessiveness and... and how he thinks he can tell me who to be friends with. I don't remember what I said or what he said."

"So, do you want to change him?"

"No. Yes... I don't know. No..."

"Well, then you need to find out if he's all these things on his own or have him change... willingly... because *he* wants to, not because you're making him. If there is anything I've learned from past failed relationships, it's that people don't change unless they want to because it takes work. Otherwise, it's a temporary quick fix with a hugely disappointing rebound, laden with bitter resentment."

I let out a big sigh and closed my eyes nodding, enjoying the foot massage but hating that Alyssa was right. She was always right. My phone vibrated in my purse, and I reached for it. It was James, he'd been texting me all day, but I hadn't responded.

J: Please, talk to me.

I showed it to Alyssa. She rolled her eyes and smiled. "Are you going to talk to him or continue ignoring him?"

I huffed out an impatient sigh through my nose. "All I want to do is talk to him, but I don't know what to say."

"Say that you need more time and space and that you want to talk Friday. That's been your plan all along anyway, right?"

I nodded and then started to text.

E: I need more time and space. Please give me that. Let's talk Friday.

He texted back within seconds.

J: Okay. Where?

"Where should I say we meet? He wants to know."

"Go to the gym Friday, do your thing, don't make any compromises to see him and say you'll meet him afterward at your place. That way you don't have to leave and go home if things end badly, you're already there, and you can just kick him out."

E: My place. 8:00.

J: Okay. Thank you. I miss you.

I showed the text message to Alyssa again, and she shook her head, advising me not to respond.

By Friday I was a shadow, hungry and exhausted, while every muscle in my body ached from fatigue and tension. I managed to make it to the gym after work, but I spent the majority of the time staring off into space while pedaling slowly on the stationary bike, preoccupied with what was going to happen when I got home. I must have worked out harder than I thought, though, for when I grabbed my bag to go home and the cold air hit my skin the sweat chilled my body to the bone within seconds, my teeth chattering as I got into my car.

James was waiting outside my door when I got home. At least he had the decency not to let himself in this time, knowing full well he wasn't welcome unless I was there. We said small "hellos," and he followed me inside.

"Thank you, for finally agreeing to see me," he said, letting me walk ahead of him into the apartment. I removed my shoes and tossed them into the hall closet, standing in the kitchen I filled up my water bottle and chugged it, not sure what else to do and suddenly very thirsty.

"So, what have you decided?" he asked. "Are we over?" Wow, this guy really cut to the chase, no small talk or pleasantries.

Is he not going to apologize?

"I don't know. Are you ready to admit that the way you behaved was wrong, and you had no right to treat Elliot or me the way you did?"

"No."

I gaped at him. "No?" My voice rose along with my blood pressure; the anger tasted acrid on my tongue.

"No. I don't think that I'm wrong in how I reacted. I don't think it was appropriate for you to be out with a man I've never met, for lunch. Especially a man who clearly wants to fuck you."

Dumbfounded, I stared at him. Obviously, our time apart had not been a week of clarity and reflection for him; he didn't think the way he treated me was wrong at all. Wow!

I shook my head. "I... I can't believe you. I can have lunch with whoever I want. I can hang out with whoever I want, man or woman, and I certainly don't have to ask you for *permission* beforehand."

"You do when the guy wants to nail you," he countered, his voice going up in volume but somehow getting deeper and more gravely.

Realizing that the louder our words got, the less we would hear each other, I took a deep breath and spoke, slow and contained. "I told Elliot no when he insinuated that the two of us go out. I told him that I am with you and only you that you make me happy. I asked him to be my friend, and if he can't just be my friend, then that's his loss. But it's not up to *you* to decide whether I can be friends with him or not."

"But apparently at one point, you wanted to fuck him too. So, it's not a one-sided attraction." He took my cue and lowered his voice to a more reasonable decibel; now we could have a mature, adult conversation.

"At one point yes, I did, but that was a long time ago, and we never acted on it. I didn't even know he felt the same way. I don't want him now. I want you. But I don't want you when you're like *this*."

He made a challenging face. "How would you feel if you saw me out for lunch with another woman?"

"Fine, I'm sure. You're in the corporate world, and you must go out for lunch with plenty of women, work lunches, work dinners. I don't *need* to know your every move, and I'm okay with that. I trust you!"

"*Arghhhh!*" He raged, his voice rising again. He ran his hands through his hair and across his face, threw his arms in the air and started pacing the room. "For fuck's sake, woman, I trust *you*. It's every other fucking man out there that I don't trust."

"Then give *me* the benefit of the doubt, and trust *me* to fight them off on my own. You don't own me. You need to get your jealousy in check." I let out a frustrated huff. "Otherwise this will never work."

I was drained. Drained from our battle, drained from the gym, drained from work, and absolutely desperate for a shower, some dinner and sleep. I wanted to put this whole thing behind me. I closed my eyes, hanging onto the bar stool for support.

"I don't like it," he growled.

I sighed. "You don't have to like it. You just have to trust me to make the right choices."

I decided to meet him halfway, to compromise because I wasn't ready to call it quits with this man just yet. I cared too much for him, but he needed to know that everything I offered him was my choice, not his.

"Without being *told* to do it, James, I don't have a problem calling or texting you with a heads up about my plans to go out for lunch with someone. But I'm not going to ask for your permission. If I want to go, I will. And you can't order me to do something. If it's a compromise you're after, then I'm willing to do that. But you can't cut people out of my life because you think they want to sleep with me."

"Fine!" He threw his hands back up in the air.

"Fine?"

"Well, I'm not going to win this, and I don't want to lose you, so fine, whatever you say. You win." I couldn't be certain, but I'm pretty sure I heard him mutter as he turned his head away for a split second, "You've got me by the fucking balls, woman."

"That's not a compromise," I said softly, shaking my head. "I will call or text you the next time something like this happens, and I may even ask how you feel about it, but in the end, it's my choice. So, you may not get a heads up at all. It all depends on the circumstances. And my mood."

"I said, *fine*," he said again, snapping at me with a venomous tone.

I narrowed my eyes at him. "Who fucked you up? Did someone cheat on you? Why are you so jealous?"

"It's nothing. I said, *fine*. If you want to go out for lunch with Elliot, then go out for lunch. I won't stop you."

I let out another sigh. My shoulders ached, and a big lump in my throat was making it difficult to swallow. "I'm going for a shower." I was severely disappointed with the direction our conversation had gone. "This is exhausting. I'm exhausted."

I tossed my bag down onto the couch and walked past him toward the bathroom. If he wasn't going to add to the compromise and discussion any further, then I wasn't going to either. I was tired of standing around in my sweaty, smelly clothes and I was still freezing.

He didn't protest when I left him alone in the living room, he just moved out of my way and let me pass. I wasn't sure if he would be there when I got out, but a part of me didn't care. I was just so fatigued from the turmoil, and my stomach was grumbling.

I tilted my head back under the slightly too—hot shower and closed my eyes, captivated by its purging capabilities. I watched my problems circle the drain and disappear, feeling the massive weight lift off my soapy shoulders. I had offered up a compromise, which was more than the man in the living room had offered. No matter what happened between us, I felt good about my decision. I hadn't backed down, but I was flexible.

I leaned my head back again, the sensation quickly becoming addictive, running my hands over my face and down my hair and body. And once again, I felt him before I saw him. Smelled him before I heard him.

I opened my eyes and turned around to see James, his naked body hard and toned behind me, his face pleading and somber. He was such a big man that my standard bathtub felt like a closet with his frame occupying so much of it. He gulped, and blinked through the steam, nervous as to whether or not I would welcome him or ask him to leave.

"Please, be patient with me," he started. "I'm a jealous person, but I'll work on it, I promise. I trust you. You're free to see who you want and when you want. And you don't need to text or call me beforehand. Please... don't give up on me. I'm new at this. But I will get better." He blinked again as a few water droplets caught on his eyelashes. "I can't lose you."

"Who hurt you?" I asked. "Why are you so jealous?"

He shook his head. "Let it go. Just let me apologize. I fucked up, and that's it. Don't give up on me, on us."

Nodding slowly and continuing to look down at his big feet, I sighed, slumping

my shoulder forward in defeat, even though it would appear that I had won.

"I appreciate your effort and willingness to change. But change because you want to, not because I'm making you."

"I'll change anything and everything to keep you, Emma. And I'll do it willingly. Just be patient with me. Please."

He reached for me, hesitating, with his arms mid-air waiting for a sign. I moved into him, and his lips crushed mine. Desperation and apologies pouring out of his mouth, his soft tongue licking gently as his hands tangled in my hair. When we pulled apart, I was out of breath, blinking the water away and sighing with content. I looked up into his eyes. They were dark, the blue almost entirely gone.

"Let me apologize properly, baby," he growled, sliding his hands down my body, crouching and urging me to spread my legs.

He slipped a finger into my folds and leaned forward spreading me with his tongue, forcing his way between my labia to reach my clit. I reached out for the wall to brace myself, pushing forward to ride his face.

"Stop doing that!" James said, playfully pulling at my arm in the bathroom after our shower.

"Doing what?"

"Scrutinizing yourself in the mirror."

I had been standing in front of the mirror pulling at my stomach and love handles, sucking in my gut and pushing my breasts up. Imagining what it would be like if I were just five or ten pounds lighter or had the balls and money to go under the knife.

"You're a hot piece of ass. I don't know how Tom was able to convince you otherwise."

I huffed a soft laugh and rolled my eyes. He came up behind me, a towel draped provocatively on his hips, water still dripping off his body.

He put his hands on my waist. "*These* are not 'love handles,' you don't have any, look, I have nothing to hold onto, why do you think I grab your ass so often? And what on earth would you want to change about your tits? After your brain, they're your best feature." He joked with a grin, reaching around to squeeze my boob.

I rolled my eyes again, and he brought the other hand up to caress the other breast, twisting each nipple with a playful smile. I gasped and then quickly sighed, dissolving into his skilled hands and feeling that oh-so-divine stirring of need in my belly.

"Nice save on the 'best feature' thing, there, stud. But they're starting to sag. I used to be able to put a pencil under them, and the pencil would fall they were that perky. Now, look!" I grabbed an eye pencil and stuck it under the bigger breast. The pencil disappeared. He started to laugh.

"How do you know that they just haven't gotten bigger?" He chuckled, lifting my boob to retrieve the pencil before pinching the nipple again causing me to squeak.

"Oh, they have, ever since I went back on the pill when I left for Europe. But I failed the pencil test long before that. It's just something I have to accept. They've started to sag." I did a giant fake pout and reached for my moisturizer.

"Well, I happened to *love* your tits. You're not allowed to change them. And on that, I am unwilling to compromise." A salacious smile danced across the plains of his handsome face as he towel-dried his hair.

"Thanks." I suddenly grew serious. "But I'm a former fat girl who was bullied over my weight, for years. And these insecurities don't just disappear."

I dabbed a retinol cream under my eyes. "So, when an old crush or I guess any guy really, that I would have considered way, *way* out of my league, you included, shows interest or gives me attention it's a giant high. My ego was doing backflips today when Elliot told me he'd always had a thing for me."

He raised his eyebrows, surprised with my honesty.

I shook my head. "I'm sorry if that upsets you, but it means a lot to the middle school Emma, the insecure, ugly duckling who used to eat her lunch sitting in one of the bathroom stalls to avoid being made fun of or having to talk to anyone."

His face fell.

"You don't have to feel sorry for me," I said quickly, loathing the notion of his pity. I motioned for him to move out of the way so I could grab my pick-comb. "I'm over all that now. But I need you to understand where my head is. I'll never betray you, but honestly, I like the attention… most of the time."

I began combing out my curls, hanging my head to the side, so my body was bent almost ninety degrees. He watched me with fascination.

"I will try very hard not to get myself into similar situations in the future. But the former fat Emma does a really terrible, but kind of adorable happy dance inside when a good-looking man gives me a second look or hits on me. It's sick and sad, but it's the truth." I shrugged, flipping my head to the other side and combing it out.

"I… I had no idea it was that bad," he muttered. "I'm sorry." His voice was hoarse with remorse. I watched him in the mirror as he finished toweling off and then went on the hunt for his boxers. "You need to know that you are beautiful, drop-dead fucking gorgeous, and Tom and all those other jackasses that made fun of you are fools, and it's their loss. You are exquisite, inside and out." He came up behind me again, wrapping his big, strong hands around my body. "I find every inch of you sexy as hell, and I wouldn't change a thing. Please, stop putting yourself under a microscope and looking for imperfections that aren't there."

He was right in a way. I do have a pretty decent body, but we look at ourselves with such loathing and criticism sometimes, seeing countless imperfections until all of our good qualities get over-scrutinized and we think they're imperfect as well. And unfortunately I still saw the Emma from middle school, still heard the echoes of Tom's insults and it hurt. Like a deep cut that kept having the scab picked; I just couldn't heal, not properly anyway, and certainly not without an everlasting scar or two.

"I'll try." I shrugged. "But it's not going to be easy. It's become a habit."

"I just don't want you thinking negative thoughts about yourself," he said, fishing around for floss in his toiletries bag. "It's not healthy."

"I know." I turned around to face him, draping my arms around his neck. He nuzzled his nose against mine.

"Can I spend the night?"

"Yes, please."

"I wish you weren't so hard on yourself. It worries me to see how negatively you view your body." We were lying in my bed, James' head rested on my chest, and his fingers traced provocative figure-eights around my bellybutton and hipbone.

"It's hard not to be. But I used to be a lot worse. Tom really fucked me up."

"I hate him."

"Join the club," I huffed. "We meet on Thursdays."

"But it wasn't just Tom, you've said. He just perpetuated an already existing insecurity, right?"

My hip jerked away from him when he tickled a particular spot, but then a sweet caress had me melting back into him, my body craving more.

"Yeah. How do I put this? When I was in middle school, I wasn't popular, far from it, in fact. I had a few friends, but not really. Our school was incredibly cliquey. I was overweight, not obese, but puberty hit me in unfair waves. And then the acne came. And then the frizzy hair, that I can barely get a handle on now, just looked like a halo around my head because it was quite a bit shorter back then and it was before I discovered gel and mousse. And then add braces to the mix, and you've got yourself one insecure, ugly duckling."

He made a sympathetic noise in his throat. "It couldn't have been that bad. I'm sure you were adorable."

"You sound like my mother. No boys liked me. And we all know that the measure of beauty at that age is the number of boys who have crushes on you, call you or you or ask you to dance. That's how you tell if you're pretty and popular. I was scared shitless I would end up needing glasses like Peter as it would have made things even worse, unbearably worse."

I took a deep breath, watching his head rise and fall on my chest as I inhaled. "There was a day where my mum took me to the orthodontist, and I had hoped that he was going to give me a date that I could get my braces off. Only he added on another year instead. On the drive home I shut down. Wouldn't talk to anyone for three days. I locked myself in my room and started devising illogical plans to run away. I had visions of launching myself out my second story bedroom window headfirst to the driveway below to just end it all. I would never be pretty and believed I would die a virgin. Die unloved." A small tear trickled down my cheek, and I pulled my hand from James' hair to quickly wipe it away.

He lifted his head off my chest and pulled me up, wrapping his arms around me and pressing his body against mine, absorbing my pain. I let the tears fall, watching them run down his muscular back.

"That's all in the past now," he said, his voice a low and reassuring boon in my ear. "You're... you're not an ugly duckling. You are exquisite. Sexy, funny, smart. You're the whole damn package, Emma. I only wish

I could have been there when you were in so much pain. Taken it away then."

"I'm over it now." I sniffed, lifting my head from his shoulders to look him in the eyes. "Well, mostly. Therapy helped a lot. And Max and Alex. And you. I know I'm not fat, or ugly. But it's hard not to let the demons creep back sometimes."

He shook his head. "Kids are assholes. It breaks my heart." He looked so lost, the man with all the answers, Mr. Fix-it, at a loss at how to mend his damaged girlfriend.

"It's over now. I'm over it. Or at least I tell myself I am. And one day I truly will be. Don't worry about it. I... I don't want to talk about it anymore." I wiped my eyes and swallowed the hard lump in my throat. I was tired of being the center of this pity party. "Will you just hold me?" I wrapped my arms around him, and we slid back down to lie on the bed.

He pressed his lips to my temple and squeezed me tight. "Forever."

It was two fifteen on Wednesday when my phone buzzed in my pocket. My students were writing a test, so I had a moment and checked the name. It was James. I stepped out into the hallway to answer it.

"Hey. I can't talk long. I'm in the middle of class. What's up?"

"Hey, Baby. Just a quick question. What's Tom's last name?"

"Hunter. Why?"

"No reason. Just curious. I'll let you go. Have a good rest of your day."

"Uh... yeah... you too. Bye."

"Bye."

Well, that was strange.

19

The week went by in a flash and James, and I seemed to get right back into our sick but beautiful infatuation with one another. I wasn't overly worried about meeting Amy, from everything James had told me about his sister, she and I would get on like a house on fire. And I was excited to see another side of James, the older protective big brother. However, I wasn't looking forward to seeing Patricia again, and thankfully she had made herself scarce since the last time she had been over. I'd heard James on the phone with her now and again, but she hadn't visited when I'd been around, for which I was grateful. But I was sure that I would have to see her again this weekend as she would want to spend time with Amy, and Amy and Garret were staying at James' house.

"So, are you going to have a dinner or something when your sister is here and invite your parents? Or is your mother doing that?" I asked. We were lying in bed on Thursday night after a very acrobatic and energetic bout of lovemaking. James had been away for two nights in San Diego and had just got back. Extra horny and desperate for each other, he'd attacked me when I walked in the door after the gym, stripping me naked in the foyer and throwing me over his shoulder, taking the stairs two at a time up to his bedroom. Thank goodness I'd had a protein shake at the gym, as it didn't look like we'd be having dinner anytime soon.

He was lying face up with his hands tucked behind his head, and I was face down lying on top of him with my head on his chest. His cock still nestled safely inside of me. We were both short of breath and very sweaty from our naked reunion.

"Oh... yeah..." He made a perturbed face. "I guess I should. I hadn't really thought about it yet. What would be easier for you? Here or at my mother's?"

"Well, here, obviously. But if family dinners are usually at your parents' I don't want you to change things for me. It would just give your mother another reason to dislike me."

His fingers traced lines up my back. "Yeah, I've addressed that with her so she should be better."

"You have? When?"

"On the phone last week. I asked her not to judge you until she knows you better. I told her I'm crazy about you, and you make me happy, and that's all that should matter. She needs to deal with her issues and not take them out on innocent people. I even offered to go back to therapy with her if she's having some challenges. My dad offered too."

I lifted my head up and looked at him. "Whoa. And how did she take it?"

"She was not happy." He rolled his eyes. "She protested and said that she wasn't mean to you. But then she relented and agreed that she doesn't like you. She thinks you're too young for me and only after my money and the family name. Same song and dance she gave me before."

"And you told her I'm not, right?" I tucked my hands under my chin so I could look him in the eye.

"Yes, of course. But she doesn't believe me."

"So, now what?"

"Well, I told her that she needs to give you a chance, and should try to get to know you. Don't be surprised if she overcompensates this weekend and is very chatty. Patricia Shaw struggles at finding a medium. She's either really *off* or really *on*."

"Okay..." I clenched my internal muscles around him, and he moved his cock inside of me. We both laughed and then I climbed off him and walked to the bathroom.

"I love that ass," he purred.

I gave it a little shake before I turned the corner and closed the door. Hmmm, maybe I should initiate some anal activity this weekend with James. He was such a skilled lover that I could only imagine he was just as skilled when it came to ass-play. The thought of James with his finger in my ass as he worked me over with his tongue, started to turn me on. Could he go again tonight? We'd already gone twice since I'd gotten home, once in the shower and once in bed. But it was still early, maybe in an hour or so. I walked back into the bedroom, and he was right where I'd left him; spread eagle, buck-naked on the bed with the covers pushed down to the end. His arms were still behind his head, and his eyes were closed. A small smile danced on his lips.

I didn't even bother to pretend not to stare at the magnificent package between his legs as it grew harder by the second and lay thick and ready against his stomach. I guess we *could* go again. My mouth watered, and I tiptoed over to the side of the bed and bent down to kiss him. He must have sensed my presence though because with cat-like reflexes he pulled me down and flipped me over onto the bed, so I was beneath him.

"There's no sneaking up on me, princess," he growled, moving his hips, so they were grinding against me in an oh-so-wonderful way. I could feel his erection against my pelvic bone, so I started to grind my hips into him as well; moving my body into his so that eventually he could just slide on in.

"How do you feel about a little ass-play?"

Seriously? This guy's a mind reader.

"I can't get enough of that sweet ass. I need more of it. What do you think?"

"I was just thinking that myself." I grinned. "What did you have in mind?"

"I dunno," he hummed, intertwining his legs with mine.

We rocked left to gather momentum. He wrapped a hand around the back of my neck and rolled us across the bed so that I was once again on top of him. A big, calloused hand snaked behind me and fingers curiously began to dip and explore my wetness, trailing it back up along and over my anus. I let James set the pace, and within moments he had slipped inside me. I was on top, so I braced my arms on either side of his and angled myself forward, moving back and forth and loving the feeling of him. He continued to run his finger up and down my bottom, gently slipping a fingertip inside to lubricate me with my own slippery arousal. One finger slowly pushed into my ass and then began to move back and forth. The sensation was intense; I felt full. Full of James.

He was fucking my mouth with his tongue, my pussy with his cock and my ass with his finger. He was all consuming, claiming my body and making it writhe in pure ecstasy. I contracted my inner muscles, squeezing him, he moaned and slipped in another finger. I nearly lost my head.

"I want to fuck your ass."

"*Hmmm*... yes... please."

We were both out of breath, and I was already so close. The man was able to bring my body to levels of arousal that I'd never experienced before. I probably wouldn't even need a vibrator on my clit, and I'd still come from how turned on I was, and how good it all felt.

I moved forward and reached behind me to pull him out. Hastily he opened the nightstand and retrieved a bottle of lube. Squirting a liberal amount onto his fingers, he ran them up between my cheeks. His cock slipped out of me with a slippery *pop* sound, and he squirted more lube, this time onto my fingers. I stroked him, getting him good and silky. Once we were both slick, I lifted my hips while he grabbed his cock and angled it at my backside.

"Remember to push out as I'm pushing in, baby. It'll be easier and hurt less."

"Okay." I was panting, and so eager.

"And tell me if it hurts, I'll stop."

"O-okay."

He lifted his hips up, gently easing the head of his cock into my soft rosette. I pushed out with my muscles to help him enter me, taking long, deep, calming breaths, in hopes of loosening up my muscles. I'd need everything to relax if he was going to get up in there. There was a bite of pain, well more than a bite; I felt as if I was being stretched beyond my physical ability, he's just so damn big. I leaned forward and dug my teeth into his shoulder.

"Are you okay?"

"Yeah... I'm fine. Don't stop," I growled against his skin.

So he didn't. Pushing slowly, he stretched and filled me. And then suddenly everything started to feel unbelievably good, that is until he moved a hand between us and began to rub my clit with his fingers, then everything felt extraordinary. It didn't take long before the earlier stabs of pain were replaced by long ago forgotten pleasure, forbidden, naughty pleasure, that somehow felt so, so right.

I was getting close. Being so full, so consumed, so claimed was intoxicating. James was starting to get close as well, his pelvic thrusts, like my own, were becoming more erratic and random, the rhythmic pace we'd set was now just a memory.

He sped up and started hammering up with his hips, pulling down on mine, pushing his cock deeper inside my ass. We were both trying to make the other feel as much pleasure as we could while determined to reach our own climax. His fingers felt like pure magic as they continued to work my clit and his cock inside my ass was pushing on and reaching erogenous zones that had been ignored for ages.

I clenched my muscles again, and apparently, that was all that was needed. He grunted loudly and exhaled a groan, emptying himself inside me. His pulsing ejaculation crashed in waves against my sensitive walls making me lose all thought. Consumed by feeling and sensation, intense sensation, I let go, finding my release and allowing the climax to unfurl inside me. Unable to hold my weight any longer once the pleasure had subsided, I collapsed on top of him. My ear fell over his heart and I heard it beating loud and fast, much like my own.

20

Not wanting to "inflict" his mother on me any more than was necessary, James opted not to invite his parents over for dinner on the first night of Amy's visit; instead, he made reservations for us all to meet on Saturday at Primo Bucolo, a very ritzy Italian restaurant.

Friday evening around seven, found us in James' kitchen, pulling the crab out of the pot and grating parmesan on the Caesar salad. The doorbell chimed. Our guests had arrived and, grabbing the bull by the horns, nervously I offered to let them in. Best get the first meeting over quickly. I needn't have worried as both she and Garret greeted me with giant bear hugs, the kind of hugs usually reserved for close family and friends. Warmed by their embraces, I squeezed right back. After my rocky start with Patricia, it felt wonderful to be accepted by a member of the Shaw family. I hadn't seen any pictures of Amy so I had no idea what to expect but I liked her instantly.

They were a striking duo. She was adorable and edgy, with a blunt sense of humor and no-nonsense frankness. Her raven colored hair was cut in a sleek angled bob at her chin, and her honey brown eyes were warm and friendly. Garret was handsome as well—completely bald but, from the looks of things, it was by choice. Dark cacao brows framed bright leafy-green knowing eyes, hinting at a quirky sense of humor, which was up-played by a small but prominent dimple in his chin. He was a good foot and a half taller than Amy, but the two made quite the cute pair. She was petite, toned and fair and he was broad, built and had beautiful, flawless cappuccino colored skin.

"This Caesar salad dressing is fantastic," Amy said as she used the tongs to lift more onto her plate.

"Thanks." I grinned with a mouthful of crab. "It's all about the roasted *and* fresh garlic and way, *way* too much parmesan cheese."

We had all eaten ourselves sick to third-trimester food babies, as was evident by the ghostly pile of empty shells lying in the middle of the table. The crab had been decadent, especially when dipped in the melted garlic butter that James had made to go with it.

She turned to me and lifted a perfectly threaded eyebrow, taking a sip of her wine. "What are your plans for the morning? Do you run? Because I'm going to need to get in a workout after all this food."

The guys were talking animatedly about sports at the end of the table, so I appreciated Amy taking the time to engage me in conversation; it meant a lot, especially after how her mother had treated me.

"I go to a rebounder class on Saturday mornings at the gym. I do run, but not on Saturdays. Want to come with me?"

Her eyes alighted with interest. "Ooh, what's rebounder?"

"It's an awesome class. Everyone gets their own mini trampoline, and we do a series of drills. You should come."

"Wow, sounds like fun." She nodded at her brother when he offered her more wine. "But I'm afraid I'd fall off."

"Nah, it's harder to fall off than you think. And the instructor is great with beginners."

"Have you ever fallen off?"

"Well... yeah," I said with a snort. "But that was a long time ago, and I may have been either still drunk from the night before or heinously hungover. Either way, my inner ear was off kilter or something. Just come. You can always hop on a treadmill if you don't like it."

She nodded, and then we stood up and started to clear the table, but the men being the handsome and helpful modern-day knights that they are, took the dishes from our hands and shooed us out to the living room with another full bottle of wine.

The conversation with Amy was so easy; it was as if we'd been friends for ages. She was genuinely interested in my job and my travels through Europe and had some rather interesting stories of her own backpacking adventures. She'd spent a year in Holland on an exchange and had oodles of tales about Amsterdam, as I'm sure most people do. By the time the men joined us we were just pouring off the remainder of the wine into each of our glasses, fortunately, the boys brought more libations with them and topped us up.

James took a seat next to me and casually draped an arm around my shoulder, his hand slyly sneaking down to squeeze my boob. I gave him a sideways glance, but he just shrugged and grinned.

"So, how did you and Garret meet?" I asked.

Amy cleared her throat. "James brought me as his date to an event in Vancouver, and I met Garret there. It was the opening of a new cancer clinic, and Garret had been the lead architect while J.P.S Developing headed the project."

"It was love at first sight," Garret chimed in, looking lovingly at his soon-to-be wife.

Amy snickered. "Well, I won't go so far as to say *that*," she said, rolling her eyes. "You came off as a bit of a cocky bugger, remember? It was the first project you'd spearheaded the design on and were flying high. Chest puffed, ego blazing, strutting around like a horny and much too confident silverback gorilla."

"That's true, but you liked it," he chuckled. "You drove me home, gave me your number, and we went out the following day for breakfast." He waggled his eyebrows up and down with a cocky smile. "And then I took *you* home."

She shrugged. "I'm a sucker for a bum-chin, what can I say? I would never have given him a second glance if he had a normal chin."

We spent the rest of evening drinking, laughing and playing cribbage. I'd never played before but caught on quickly, and Garret and I even managed to beat the formidable Team Shaw. I couldn't remember a night where I'd felt so comfortable and at ease on a double date. Tom had always put me down and made me feel dumb when we were with our friends, often speaking over me and correcting me, drawing attention to my mistakes and any small error in an explanation or story but James just let me be me. He was complimentary, patient and funny, and I just couldn't stop myself, I was falling deeper and deeper under this man's spell each and every day.

Later that night as we climbed into bed I struggled to tame the giddy feeling that was bubbling up inside of me and a giggle—much too girlie for my liking—burst free as I turned down the sheets.

"What was that about?" James asked with his own laugh. "You okay? Female hysteria?"

I rolled my eyes. "No... I uh... I kind of bought something today... for *us*."

"Yeah? Something kinky?"

I rolled my bottom lip between my teeth. "Perhaps."

"Oh, do tell."

I opened the nightstand drawer and pulled free an impressive piece of bedroom equipment. A big purple vibrator with a vibrating head and a silicon bunny at the base for that extra bit of much-appreciated stimulation. James' eyes went wide with excitement.

"Miss Everly!"

I bit my lip again. "I dunno... last night was so much fun... I haven't been able to stop thinking about it all day. So, I ducked out on my lunch hour and walked a couple of blocks up to the sex toy store on Douglas Street. What do you think?"

"I think I want to fuck you in the ass with my cock and your pussy with that big purple beast. Does it have a name?"

I giggled again, this time much less girlie and more the sultry vixen —or so I hoped. "The *Thump-her* 3000."

"The *Thump-her* 3000, eh?"

Nodding, I slid onto the bed on my knees, turning on the vibrator and watching as the purple head started to rotate around and around.

"Oh, baby..." James purred.

And then before I knew it I was on my back, and James was straddling my chest. "Open up, sweetheart," he said, his boxers pulled down as he angled himself toward my mouth.

I gave him a challenging quirked eyebrow. "What no foreplay, not even a kiss first? Wow, way to take the seduction right out of the equation, Shaw."

I was mostly playing, but a part of me was a little peeved that he hadn't even kissed me before expecting me to go down on him. His face fell, and then in another blink, he was covering my body, and his lips were crushing mine, his tongue demanding access into my mouth as his hands roamed across my chest, up my neck, and into my hair. I smiled against his lips, yes, this was what I wanted. Always James' kisses. Always.

Inevitably, I grew hungry for more, for that cock that had been pressed against my lips and was now ramming itself against my hip as James ground his pelvis into me. I pushed him away, encouraging him to scoot back up.

I sucked him greedily, bent my neck forward, stroked with my hand and pulled at his hardening flesh with my lips, reveling in the gasps and sudden inhalations of his breath as I nipped at the soft head.

"That's right, baby, take it all. I love fucking your greedy little mouth."

I hummed in delight from the praise, loving how easily I managed to drive him insane. My cleft grew wetter by the second as I continued to suck and lick, the rest of my body humming with the need for him, craving and desperate for his touch elsewhere.

"All right, that's enough," he said just a few minutes later, pulling his cock from my mouth with a loud *pop*.

He slid down my body to where my legs were squeezing together, aching for pressure and friction. Pushing them apart, he bent his head low and began blowing cool air onto my swollen core. I bucked into his face immediately, whining and whimpering at the onslaught of pleasure that came from the sight of his dark hair bobbing between my legs; from the way his magnificent tongue lashed at my clit until it was screaming for release.

But he didn't stay down there long. He lifted up over my body again, covering me, kissing me, lapping at my tongue with his so that I could taste my own arousal, his chin and lips damp from my wetness. He slid two fingers into me, and I thrust my hips frantically into his hand, pushing his twiddling fingers into the depths of my body, gasping in pants as the pleasure swelled through me. I moaned incessantly and churned my hips as his long, skilled fingers stroked inside me with expert finesse.

"Oh, God, I'm close, already," I cried, as he rubbed his thumb over my clit in delectable circles.

"Come for me, baby," he coaxed, biting down gently on my nipple and sending me over the cliff.

He didn't allow me a moment of respite after my climax before the weight of his body pressed me into the bed, his hips swirling in circles as he dipped his shaft just centimeters between my pussy lips before pulling out and rubbing it against my throbbing clit. I ground and bucked my hips, frantic for attention, swiveling and churning my pelvis in a futile attempt to capture his cock and pull it into my body.

A soft rumbling chuckle emanated from his chest as he continued to torture me. I lunged at his mouth with my teeth, catching his bottom lip and tugging, but that only made him tease me more. Dipping and swirling, he evaded my cleft with every twist as I grappled and thrust up with painful need.

"Jaaamesssss..." I said, whimpering against his lips as they crushed mine.

"Do you not like this?" he goaded, rotating his hips and flicking his cock against my clit, making me spasm beneath him.

"Fuck me, damn it!"

"Well, all you had to do was ask." His voice gravelly and deep with equal parts passion and playfulness. He positioned himself right at my opening, gave me one hard look of lust and then with savage force thrust forward, sheathing himself to the hilt and hitting my cervix.

"Ouch!" I winced, but the jab of pain inside me was no match for how good the rest of me felt. My clit was hard and swollen and beckoning release while my diamond-hard nipples ached for his mouth.

"Oh! Sorry, babe." He eased back and started to fuck me gently and then harder and harder, his balls slapping my ass cheeks, the head of his perfect cock rubbing against my G-spot in rhythmic expertise and familiarity. I lifted my legs and wrapped them around his gyrating hips, digging my heels into his taut ass, pushing him deeper and deeper inside of me.

"I'm close again," I gulped, nipping his earlobe with my teeth. He hissed in excitement as I ran my tongue up along the perfect curve of his ear.

"Then I best get to work..." He grabbed the *Thump-her* 3000 from the other side of the bed and then encouraged me to flip over into the spoon position.

My inner thighs slid over one another as I positioned myself comfortably, willingly waiting for James' next move.

A soft buzzing sound drifted over my shoulder and into my ear as James' hand made its way tickling my hip and over my mound, dipping deep into my core, massaging circles around my never-satiated clit. There was no idle time with my skilled and devoted lover, he slid the pulsating purple vibrator into my pussy, and I squeezed my muscles around the thick silicon cock, pulling it greedily inside of me. But James only granted me mere moments of pleasure before he pulled the toy from me and put it to my lips.

"Suck it, baby, pretend it's me. Taste your delicious pussy." He was so commanding and dominating; I loved it. "Take it all, Emma. I know you can. I'm bigger than this." He continued to shove the rubber toy further down my throat while using his other hand to massage my clit.

I relaxed my throat and sucked greedily on the faux cock, feeling the bunny ears tickle my chin.

"Enough," he grunted. "This belong in your sweet little pussy now."

He pulled it from my mouth while using his clit stimulating hand to thrust the *Thump-Her* into my quivering core. All I wanted at that moment was to have James fuck me in the ass. I was so ready, so primed, so needy. With the vibrator working its magic inside me and on my clit, I was close and relaxed. James would have no problem claiming me in that forbidden way. I heard the squirt of the lube bottle and then felt the cool and slick liquid silk as he rubbed his fingers over my soft, sensitive hole, wetting my entrance and getting me ready.

"Easy, baby, you're greedy I know," he murmured as he moved the vibrator inside of me while pumping two fingers rhythmically in my ass.

"God, I'm so close. You need to do this. I... I need you," I said breathlessly, practically gasping for air at this point, frenetically awaiting another orgasm. All the sex we'd had so far had been incredible, but nothing was nearly as intense as this. He was all power, all beast and the way his eyes raked my body and his hands wielded their magic, I was under a spell and willing to do anything for more of him, for all of him.

James didn't need any more convincing; he pulled his fingers from me and positioned his cock at my wet and ready rosette, thrusting gently. But I was impatient, I moved backward onto him and pushed out with my muscles, welcoming his length and girth. There was no discomfort or bite of pain when he entered me this time; he'd stretched me out nicely last night, so tonight was easy. Just a bit of pressure as his cock fought the vibrator for space in my body. I was so turned on, so ready and so close to climax that everything felt incredible, like a never-ending parade of divine sensations taking over my body in waves and swarms, recklessly ripping through me.

The vibrations, the swirling head, the bunny ears, James' cock deep in my ass, his perfectly trimmed pubic hair rubbing roughly against my ass cheeks, it was all too much. I detonated instantly. Convulsing like I was being electrocuted I writhed on the bed, pushing and pulling at his cock with my hips and muscles. I screamed out his name before biting down hard on the pillow beneath my cheek as I kicked and curled my toes. James came seconds later, snarling an oath and then another, his crude and dirty words a canticle of male exultation as he spilled himself inside of me.

"Congratulations on your hat-trick tonight," I said as I walked back to the bed from the bathroom a few minutes later.

"What do you mean?" He cocked an adorable eyebrow as he laced his arms behind his head and grinned at me from the bed.

"Well, you managed to visit all three holes tonight. I'd call that a sex-capade hat-trick. I guess the next challenge would be to *come* in all three holes in one night, ending with the ass of course. I draw the line at ass-to-mouth play." I giggled as I slid my hand up his torso, lying down next to him and resting my arm on his chest, staring into those impossibly deep blue eyes.

"Challenge accepted, Miss Everly!" He nodded. "Though, not tonight." He reached around me and ran his fingers lightly down my back, cupping my butt. "You've drained me, woman. You are one insatiable little minx, you know that?"

"Ah," I sighed. "Mr. Shaw, what can I say? You bring out the beast in me."

21

"How was the gym?" James asked squeezing my sweaty bra-clad boob Saturday morning as Amy and I walked into the kitchen after the gym, with rosy cheeks and soaked clothes.

"It was good. Amy did well for a newbie," I said, chugging some water and batting his hand away playfully.

"Yeah, that class was intense," she agreed. "I'm going to have to see if there is a gym in Vancouver that offers rebounder classes."

Garret smacked Amy on the butt as she was filling up a glass of water. "*Ew*, my hand's wet, you're all sweaty."

"What the hell do you expect?" she laughed as she headed off to the garage apartment for a shower.

My eyes were closed, and my back was to the shower door as I savored the feeling of the heat massaging my tired muscles from every angle. It was a feat and a half to wash my hair given the length and thickness of it, but it was so full of sweat and had been a few days since I'd given it a good scrub.

I was rinsing out the conditioner when I felt two big, strong hands on my backside and a tongue snaking its way into my soft and wet cleft from behind. Despite the heat of the thrumming water, goosebumps danced across my skin, and my core and nipples tightened on instinct.

A hand came up my back and gently pushed me over, so my body made a ninety-degree angle giving the tongue easier access.

There was something so despicably wonderful about getting oral sex from behind. It felt, wrong and forbidden and I loved it. James slipped two fingers into my pussy and started fucking me hard, moving them in and out quickly and rhythmically.

And then, if the combination of sensations ravaging my body weren't enough, he slipped a finger from his other hand into my ass. I nearly fell over. Two nights in a row of ass play wasn't enough, I needed more of it. And James is all about giving me what I want. We shuffled to the tile bench, and I put my hands out for support, all the while he continued to swirl his tongue and suck hard.

"Fuck me... please," I pleaded, pushing into his face, urging him to sink his digits deeper.

He slid his tongue up my folds one last time, sending tremors or longing along my spine as he pulled his fingers out, but leaving the one in my ass, continuing with the exquisite and taboo torture. He kept me bent over with a gentle hand on my back and with one swift and confident thrust, sank in, balls deep.

"I love it when you beg," he growled, his fingers and cock moving in sync.

We'd quickly learned that we both loved having sex from behind; it was raw and carnal and oh so sexy. He controlled the pace, and I submitted willingly, allowing him to guide and coax my body to rippling orgasm, over and over again. I gripped my muscles around his cock liked a fist and moved back into him, feeling him hammer deeper and harder inside me.

A groan escaped him as he drove into me with force. He was on a mission, moving his free hand around to tease my nipples and pull on them, twisting and plucking until I cried out. The warm water was drumming our sensitive skin into melted butter, and the room was filling up with steam as my hair hung around my face and water dripped into my eyes. But I didn't care. It all just felt so damn good.

I looked down between my legs and saw his beautiful feet. His knees were slightly bent to get the right angle, and if I tilted my head just a little further I could see him sliding in and out of my pussy, the sight of him disappearing inside of me was all I needed. I could feel his balls hitting my ass, and the odd slapping feeling of it made clit throb and my body hum. I was nearly mindless as the orgasm in my belly brewed like a storm.

"Come for me." He snarled. "I know you're close. I'm close too."

His strained voice in my ear was enough; I came right then, and hard. It was almost too much to take in at once, the hot water pounding my back and sides, while James pounded my backside. Once again, this man blew my mind.

James was dressed and back downstairs with our guests before I was. I had hair to dry and makeup to apply; being a woman is time-consuming. We weren't going out to dinner until later, so I opted not to wear my evening outfit just yet and threw on a pair of skinny black jeans with a long sleeve shirt. The weather outside was superb, still cold, but the sun was out, and there was barely a breath of wind. I wasn't sure what the Shaw's had planned for the day, but I had a few errands to run.

As I walked to the top of the stairs, I could hear voices emanating from the living room.

"I've never seen you this happy. She's lovely," Amy commented.

"Ha, no? Was I such a grumpy fuck before?"

She snorted.

"Yeah, you were, actually," added Garret with a laugh. "Fucking miserable, in fact."

Amy gushed. "You guys are in that glorious honeymoon phase where it's all just sex and talking, aren't you? God, I love that phase."

"Hey!" Garret scoffed. "What the hell phase are we in now? We still have sex, and we talk." Affronted that his sexual prowess was being brought up and apparently challenged.

"Oh, be quiet." I could practically hear Amy rolling her eyes. "That's not what I meant. James and Emma are just in that exciting new relationship phase where they're learning about each other—obsessed with one another. You and I know everything about one another. Which is why you can make me come in under a minute. We're practiced. It's a good thing."

"Oh, Jesus." A cringe colored James' voice. "That's really not something I needed to know. Good job, Gare, but I didn't need to know that."

"Oh, whatever," his sister chirruped. "Get over it. All I'm saying is that I don't remember the last time I saw you this happy or chatty about a girl. You're all smiles. For God sakes you've called me at least six times since you met her, asking me for advice, and it's usually after you've screwed up. Jesus, dude, don't be such a jealous dick-head. Don't fuck this up with her. Besides, I don't think I have any more friends you can screw and ditch anyway."

James made a rude noise in his throat, and I heard Garret's low chuckle.

But Amy just continued to prattle on. "You just seem in a good place right now, and it's because of Emma. Content and calm. I think she's good for you. Either that or she's fucked the *miserable* right out of you."

Garret barked out a hearty laugh that echoed around the house. "That's probably it."

"Well, I... well... she's definitely something special. And lovely." He said the last word wistfully. I could only hear him, but I already knew his body language so well. James would be shyly half smiling and averting his eyes.

"Awe, my big brother is in love. *Finally!*"

"I... I never said... so... uh...so, let's talk about your upcoming wedding. When's the bachelor party, dude?"

I smiled at his blatant redirection. I wasn't hurt that he hadn't admitted he loved me. We weren't there yet, were we?

I walked into the kitchen to get a glass of water and also to make some noise, so my presence wasn't a surprise. They hadn't kept their voices down, and the open concept of the house turned the place into the cavern so you could hear everything that was happening on the main floor, but I didn't want them thinking I'd been eavesdropping.

By the time I entered the living room and sat next to James the conversation had drifted to Amy and Garret's wedding. Seeing me enter the room, Amy made space on the couch for me and grabbed my hand. Deftly, James' hand found my other, and we listened to Amy go on about the idiocy of the florist she'd met with earlier in the week and how the woman was trying to convince her to go with Plumeria in her arrangement.

"Anyway, less about us, what are your plans for the day?" she asked eventually when she'd run out of steam.

I took a sip of my water. "Well, I have to run a few errands. I need to go pick up some shoes that are getting fixed, hit the drug store for some makeup, and I wanted to go to the liquor store and get a bottle of wine or *five* for tonight before we take off for dinner."

"To take the edge off, before you have to deal with our *mother*?" Amy laughed.

I smiled sheepishly, but was unable to stifle the giggle that slipped between my lips. "What? Uh, no... okay, yeah, maybe a little."

They all laughed and nodded in agreement.

"Yeah." James winced. "We'll have to all have a glass or *three* and then cab down to the restaurant, if we're to get through an evening with Patricia Shaw."

"Don't worry too much about Pat," Garret said with a snort. "She didn't care for me either in the beginning, said I was only after the Shaw name and money."

"That's what she thinks I'm after as well!" I exclaimed, slumping deeper into the cushions and rolling my eyes. "To be honest, I was neither aware of the Shaw name nor the money until I met James, and even then I had no idea what kind of weight the name carried in town. For all I knew your family is to Shaw Cable."

"We are." Both Amy and James said in unison, with mirror image blank and serious expressions.

My eyes widened in shock. Were they? I looked back and forth between them, and then at Garret trying to get a read.

"Really?"

"Ha, no!" Amy nudged me playfully, the three of them erupting into laughter. I rolled my eyes again.

"Can I come with you on your errands?" Amy asked. "I'd like to pick your practical brain about more wedding ideas. Most of my friends are already married and idealistic. They think it should be a grand affair with doves and multiple dresses. I'm about ready to say 'fuck it' and dick off to Mexico. That's what Garret would prefer. Right, Gare?"

He nodded, screwing his face up in a look that said: "I'd rather get married in board shorts and a Tommy Bahama shirt."

James yawned and stood up, raising his arms into a big and muscle-popping stretch. "All right, well, you ladies go off and do your shopping, Gare, and I are going to go for a bike ride. Dinner reservations are for seven o'clock tonight, so should we say we'll meet back here around five thirty for drinks?"

I felt my mouth go dry just from watching him. Damn, he was perfect. He gave me a saucy wink and planted a kiss on my forehead before heading off with Garret.

"Sounds good," I squeaked after the guys had left the room. Amy just started laughing at me.

I chose my outfit for the evening with tremendous care. I didn't want to overdress and come across as trying too hard, but I wanted to make a good impression, to have my clothes reflect confidence *and* that I was taking this family dinner seriously. I decided on tight black pants that tapered at the ankle and a snug red sweater, but while Amy and I were out shopping, we came across an irresistible cobalt blue top for me to wear instead.

The new sleeveless shirt fit perfectly. Cut on the bias, it showed off my best asset or assets, my Double-D chest, without looking as though I wanted to flash my cleavage to the world. I paired the ensemble with the shoes I'd retrieved from the cobbler—my all-time favorite guilty pleasure, my five-inch, peep-toe leopard-print stilettos which I'd picked up for a steal. First time on, I'd rolled my ankle and busted the heel. I loved wearing heels, loved the way they changed the way I looked, but I wasn't the most graceful in them, that's for sure. To continue the jungle theme, I wore my matching leopard print bra and thong; a cheeky addition that only James and I would be privy to.

They were all standing in the kitchen clutching their wine glasses like life rafts when I walked in to join them. James came up to me and kissed me on the temple, taking great care not to muss up my makeup.

"You look beautiful," he whispered, "where have you been hiding these *fuck-me* heels?"

I smiled and winked at him, accepting my wine from Garret.

"Leave them on when we get home." He reached down and squeezed my butt, which, I must admit, looked fantastic in my black pants. I didn't do hundreds of squats and lunges each week for nothing.

22

I had only eaten at the Italian restaurant once before, with Alyssa for my birthday, but I remember my visit fondly. We'd sat in the bright, covered outdoor courtyard and the staff had been friendly and professional. The ambiance inside was different though. The rustic Italian-chic decor gave the space a more intimate, romantic feel and I would much rather have gone alone with James—to sit in a secluded corner and stare into each other's eyes like lovesick puppies than dine with the family, particularly Patricia—but she and Charles were already waiting at our reserved table when we arrived. Hopefully, James' dad would prove to be less of a challenge.

Outwardly Charles was exactly as expected; like an older, more distinguished version of James. Almost as tall as his son, with thick wavy salt and pepper hair, a broad chest and honey brown eyes that glowed warmly with humor and intelligence much like Amy's. He introduced himself bluntly, pushing James and Amy aside to get at me, insisting that I call him Charles or Chuck, not Mr. Shaw. Then when I offered my hand, he scooped me up in big hug similar to the one he'd given his daughter. And just like with Amy, I felt comfortable with him right away.

On the other hand, Patricia was polite and continued to be reserved.

She gave me a gentle impersonal hands-on-the-shoulders hug, a peck on the cheek, but the sham was palpable. So much for being overly chatty like James predicted. At least I had my allies next to me as James sat to my left and Amy on my right. My plan was to be polite and remain as quiet as possible through dinner so that Amy and Garret's wedding would dominate the conversation. Now, if I could just avoid Patricia's glassy stare.

No such luck.

"That's quite the top you have on," she said flatly. We'd only been at the table for roughly thirty minutes. I hoped at least to avoid talking to her until the dessert course.

I glanced up from my starter salad to see her looking at me; head cocked to one side with an amused expression on her face.

"*Umm*, thank you." What kind of comment was that? Was it a compliment? How should I respond to that? "Amy helped me choose it earlier, today."

"Did she? I thought her taste was more conservative than that."

Her gaze locked on mine, driving home her disparaging comment. Oh God, she was insulting me not flattering me.

"Mother!" James was quick to jump to my defense, as I was still too shocked to respond.

My mouth just hung open.

"There is nothing wrong with Emma's shirt, and I happen to think she looks beautiful." He put a supportive and protective arm around me rubbing my shoulder. I'm sure he could feel the knots building.

"Well, excuse me, dear, but don't you think her top is a little *inappropriate* for a family dinner? I mean she is practically *busting* out. No pun intended. And her shoes... well...." She shot a sideways glance across the table and down toward my feet.

I looked down at my chest, then down at my shoes, and then up. Everyone around the table fixated on the new topic of conversation and, embarrassingly, also had their eyes on my chest. Finding tops that would fit my body type properly is an ongoing change-room struggle. Tonight I believed I'd hit the right note for a meet-the-family dinner;

hardly any cleavage was exposed. Yes my new top had a V-neck, and yes I was big chested, but I didn't think it was so bad.

"I-I... I'm sorry," I stammered. "I'm sorry if my shirt and shoes offend you. I tried hard to look nice tonight. I'll... I'll just go ask the hostess for my coat."

I rose from the table and went off to find the hostess as if in a trance.

"Emma! No wait," James pleaded.

But I ignored him and headed off, though I didn't go to the hostess, I turned left for the washroom. I could hear the blended murmurs of our table reprimanding Patricia for her insults, but I didn't care, I needed to get away. I wanted to grab my coat and hail a cab, leaving the Shaw's to their martyr matriarch.

Thankfully the washroom was empty. I walked to the sink and looked in the mirror trying to figure out where I had gone wrong. I wiped away any last trace of my bold, cherry red lipstick and attempted to pull up the neckline of my top, but it was futile. It was no use. My tits were huge and apparently "inappropriately" on display for the remainder of the evening. I continued to stare at myself in the mirror, unshed tears welling up in my eyes. Amy came in moments later her face crimson and brows drawn down into a scowl.

"Holy fuck," she growled. "I am *so* sorry." She pulled me into a hug which was a little awkward given her petite stature and my extra five inches thanks to my heels. Her face was buried in my offensive cleavage. But she was probably used to hugs similar to this with Garret and James though with less cushiony boobage and more hard pectorals.

"It's okay," I lied, wiping my eyes with a piece of paper towel. "It's not unexpected. I knew she might say or do something. James hoped she'd behave, but I guess she could only be on her best behavior for so long. At least we got halfway through the salad course."

"We're all furious, just so you know."

"I think I should just go. Let you guys have a family dinner."

She shook her head. "Mum's a bitch. I love her, but she's a bitch. Your shirt is not too revealing. It's gorgeous. I wouldn't have suggested you buy it if I thought it was too slutty. Don't go. You're family too. You need to stay. Please don't let her win. And don't put your coat on."

I snorted a small laugh. "You sound like my therapist."

"We've all sat across from a therapist at some point." She smiled, resting her hands on my shoulders. "It's hard not to bring the lingo into your own advice. Come on."

I took a few more moments to compose myself; then I followed Amy back out to the table. The main course had arrived. Everyone had waited to start eating their entrees until Amy, and I sat down, everyone but Patricia that is, she was picking at her lamb with a pinched face. The remainder of the evening was uneasy, but détente had been achieved, and our meal went by without any further comments about my wardrobe.

When Patricia excused herself to use the washroom, James took the opportunity to tell me that he and Charles had a big long "chat" with her while Amy and I were away from the table. He explained that based on all their therapy practices, it was best to just move past things and discuss issues later on in private. James promised that he would go to bat for me against his mother again. He had no intention of letting this slide, but he'd do it when they were not in public and didn't have several bottles of wine down the hatch. I thanked him then put my head down and pretty much disengaged from the group for the remainder of the night, avoiding Patricia's gaze as hard as I possibly could.

I didn't bother ordering dessert, feared the foul taste of the evening would taint anything sweet. However, the rest of the table didn't hold back. James ordered an impressive array of the chef's finest for everyone to share.

"I know you don't want anything, but just try it. I ordered it for you." He held up a fork loaded with apples and streusel and an icy piece of dolce de leche heaven.

Rolling my eyes at him, I complied and opened my mouth. The moment the dessert hit my tongue my taste buds came alive—a circus of flavors danced around my palate, igniting notes of savory, sweet and salty. I closed my eyes to relish the bite and let the ice cream slowly melt and slide down my throat. God, it was good.

When I opened my eyes Patricia was staring at me from across the table, her expression inscrutable. I was on my second glass of wine for the night—well, fourth that night, second at dinner—and feeling a little more confident with myself thanks to the liquid courage. I looked her squarely in the eye, fixed her with the biggest smile I could muster and then subtly adjusted my shirt where it didn't need adjusting. Her eyes followed my hands only to return to my face and the look she gave me was enough to melt gold. Unwilling to be intimidated by her any longer, I smiled again, even bigger than before, and then asked James for another bite.

I'd had two more healthy-sized glasses of wine in lieu of dessert and was feeling pretty good. The fiasco with Patricia was temporarily pushed from my mind, and I was numb to her dagger glares, all I wanted to do was get home and get James naked.

I rested my head on his shoulder in the cab and dozed in and out, allowing the wine to wrap me in its warm cocoon of loveliness. However, the conversation in the car became heated—the Shaw children were livid with their mother, and with cause. Amy and Garret had plans to go to Charles and Patricia's in the morning for brunch, and Amy had every intention of taking advantage of their time together to lay into her mother.

"So help me God, James, sometimes Mum is a piece of work. Did you hear her telling me that we needed to invite the Goodwins *and* the Montgomerys to the wedding now because it is good form and good business? We have to reciprocate simply because they were invited, years ago, to their kids' weddings.

"It must be easy for her, considering she's not shelling out a fucking dime for this thing! And now Mother wants us to pre-book hotel rooms near the reception in the case last minute guests can't find a place to stay. We sent out the invitations in January for a July wedding. If you can't get your fucking shit together and book a hotel with that much notice, then don't come. Arghhhh."

It was neither the time nor place to laugh, but watching pixie-sized Amy get animated and curse like a sailor was pretty hilarious. I smiled like a drunk fool and grabbed her hand. "What happens when you tell your mother no?" I asked in a bit of a slur, a stupid smile still plastered to my face as my eyes struggled to stay open.

James and Garret both laughed, and Amy let out a series of expletives that had the cab driver inhaling.

"Oh, we tell her 'no' all the time," Amy said with disdain. "But the pig-headed woman doesn't let up until we give up. She's perfected the art of manipulation and guilt. Don't let the icy exterior fool you—she's been known to burst out in tears to get her way."

I half-opened one eye and looked at her. "And if you still don't budge?"

James answered this time. "We always end up budging. It's called keeping the peace, even though the only one who gets any true peace is her."

"Hmmm. Maybe you should just try not budging. Not matter what. See what happens." And then I put my head back on his shoulder and fell asleep.

I woke up to James carrying me up the stairs.

"Hey," he murmured, kissing my forehead. "You were a trooper tonight. Thanks for coming. I loved having you there, even though my mother ruined the evening." He laid me down on the bed gently and started taking off my shoes.

"Wait, I thought you wanted me to keep these on tonight." I pouted and then sat up on my elbows, yawning, delighting in the gentle massage he was administering to my arch and toes.

"You're tired. It's okay. We can wait until morning."

He grabbed the waistband of my pants and helped me shimmy out of them. I sat up and raised my hands over my head, allowing him to undress me like a child. I knew exactly when he'd seen my matching jungle print lingerie as he gasped softly followed on the heels by a low groan. He lightly ran a finger back and forth beneath the waistband of my thong.

"But I'm awake now," I said with a drunken purr. "Put those back on my feet and get naked."

"Were you going for jungle princess tonight?" he asked as he pulled his sweater over his head revealing his taut and bronze abs.

"More like jungle *warrior* princess. I figured I'd need to be a warrior to battle your mother."

I knelt on the bed and began to undo his belt and zipper, pushing his pants down over his firm ass, so they pooled at his big feet. Then raising my hands, I ran them along his body, dropping warm, wet kisses down his stomach.

"Yeah, Jesus, Em. I'm so sorry. Ames is going to talk to her tomorrow and then I will. Don't worry. She's not going to get away with how she treated you. We just have to deal with her properly. There's a process with Patricia Shaw. And for the record, I could have done with a bit *more* cleavage showing."

He traced the top of my bra cups, dipping a thumb and finger beneath the fabric to retrieve an already hard nipple. He pinched and pulled, sending a warm and wonderful quake through my body as he rolled the tender peak between his thumb and forefinger. I whimpered quietly, and nibbled on my bottom lip, a warm and needy feeling blooming in my belly.

"No more talk about your mother tonight," I said sleepily. "She's trying to come between us, so let's not let her."

I sat back down on the bed dangling my feet over the edge and pushed his boxers down so that he sprang free. He bent down and picked up my shoes putting them back on my feet while on bended knee. I felt like a sexy Cinderella, and he was my naked and hard Prince Charming.

"I'm okay with butt-stuff tonight," I said, playfully kicking my feet back and forth. "But be careful, I cut my crack shaving this morning."

"You what!" he choked, as he knelt on the floor in front of me and ran his warm hands up and down my abdomen, cradling my rib cage and softly kissing my neck.

"Well, I don't wax anymore, and we need to keep the backdoor trimmed, seeing as you're using it now, so I shaved. But I nicked myself with the razor, and it hurts a little, so just be gentle." I wrapped my arms around his neck and nipped at his chin and earlobe.

He growled, stood up and tackled me to the bed. "Emma Everly, you are quite the woman, and an adorable little drunk."

The rest of the night was a bit of a beautiful blur. All I remember is waking up briefly around 3 a.m. to pee and being sore in all the right places.

23

KNOCK, KNOCK, KNOCK... KNOCK, KNOCK, KNOCK

When consciousness claimed me Sunday morning, the world was far from pretty.

"What the fuck is that noise? Someone answer the fucking door," I moaned, rolling over in bed and covering my head with a pillow, trying to drown out the assault on my ears and brain.

"Babe, wake up." James was gently shaking me by the shoulder.

"Errmmmmmmm," I grumbled, sinking deeper into the covers and the darkness they offered. "Only if you promise to stop that infernal knocking."

"There's no knocking." He chuckled. "It's probably just the pounding in your head or maybe the ticking of the clock on your nightstand. You drank a fair bit last night. How do you feel?"

"Like I was run over by a freight truck full of elephants, and then it backed up and ran over me again."

He snorted another laugh. "Yeah, I figured. Here, sit up, I brought you some Advil and coconut water."

I wrestled free of the web of blankets and propped myself up on the pillows, but I couldn't bring myself to sit up completely; it hurt my head too much.

"Here."

He placed two little round pills in my hand and offered me a can of coconut water, which I chugged greedily. My mouth was dry and tasted like a sewer; had I forgotten to brush my teeth last night? I hated going to bed without having brushed my teeth. After years and years of braces, I had a keen sense of attachment to my perfect chompers. I took great care to floss and brush them multiple times a day, especially before bed.

"What happened last night?" I asked with a croak, swallowing the pills and letting the coconut water sit on my tongue and soften it. "Did I forget to brush my teeth? Am I still wearing makeup?"

He gave me a quizzical look. "How much do you remember?"

"I remember dinner, your mother being mean to me and then falling asleep in the cab. And then I'm pretty sure we had sex because I'm a little sore down there. It's a good sore, though." I smiled shyly, tucking my rat's nest hair behind my ears. My muscles thrummed and ached with remembered pleasure, even though I couldn't remember.

"Yeah, we did have sex. A lot of sex, you drained me, woman. You were pretty crazy." He raised his brows and opened his eyes wide "Crazy good, though. I'm not surprised that you're a little sore. I think we were both surprised with how flexible you are. However," he tilted his head to the side, and one eyebrow dropped, "you didn't get off."

"What?" I jerked my head up and looked at him, seeing black spots in my line of vision from the rapid movement. I had to close my eyes for a second until the nausea disappeared.

"Yeah, you weren't able to get off. We tried to get you there for a long, *loooong* time. Then you got upset and said you were too drunk that the alcohol had numbed your vagina." He smirked, apparently finding my inability to orgasm comical. "But that didn't stop you from rocking my world. You were quite amorous. Besides you not getting off, it was a rather fun night. I got to see an even wilder and uninhibited Emma. She's fun."

"Did I cry?"

He furrowed his brows. "Cry? No. Why would you cry?"

"Because I couldn't get off?"

"Oh... uh... no. You were upset, but it was more of a pissed off at your vagina upset, not a crying upset. At one point you got up and went over to the mirror to give your vag a pep talk. It was pretty hilarious."

"Oh, God." I cringed. "What did I say to it?"

"You said, 'vagina, you can do this, just give me one little orgasm, it doesn't have to be a big one, just a little one. Don't leave me hanging.' And then when I laughed you got mad at me and said I shouldn't make fun because what if your vagina was broken and you never got off again? Which made me laugh even harder."

I shook my head and closed my eyes, leaning back against the headboard. "Jesus, I'm a drunken fool. But I didn't cry?"

"No, you didn't cry. You smacked your vag a couple of times to try to wake it up, and I had to intervene when you started to get violent, but no, you didn't cry."

"Oh. Oh, good. I've never cried while drunk and I'm glad that I didn't do it in front of you. I hate crying drunks. A girl in high school bawled one night at a house party because she realized she'd never meet or marry Johnny Depp. I vowed then, and there never to cry while drunk." I heard him snort a laugh, and I opened my eyes to look at him. "And the pep-talk still didn't work?"

"No, you didn't cry. And no. The pep-talk didn't work. We just couldn't get you there. But you did do the Tarzan wail a couple of times and leaped at me across the bed." He started laughing when he saw the mortified look on my face.

"What?"

"Yeah, you took your jungle warrior princess character pretty seriously." He was still laughing, and I had a hard time remaining embarrassed. He was just so easy-going and accepting; it was hard not join in.

"Oh, God. I'm so sorry."

"Don't apologize. I loved it. You're an adorable little drunk. Affectionate, uninhibited and just a tad crazy." He kissed me swiftly on the lips and then jumped up from where he was sitting on my side of the bed. "Come on. It's ten o'clock, Ames and Garret are heading over to my parents soon. Have a shower and then come downstairs, drunky-face. And uh... Em..."

"Yeah?"

"Don't forget to brush your teeth." He smiled his gorgeous, makes-my-knees-quiver grin and then left the room.

I dragged my sorry hung-over ass out of bed to the bathroom and was horrified by what looked back at me in the mirror. My hair was a train wreck, full of knots, sticking out every which way, and the pillow creases on my face made it look like I'd had reconstructive surgery in a dark Mexican alley. Combined with bloodshot eyes and the raccoon mask from my mascara, the nightmare was complete. How was James able to even look at me?

When I finally turned off the shower, I felt like a new person. The headache was no longer repeatedly dropkicking my pre-frontal lobe; it was now more of a gentle tapping. James' Advil seemed to be working. I dressed in black yoga pants and a dark gray hoodie, throwing my wet hair into a quick French braid down my back, repeatedly pausing as I did so because the strain of having my arms up to do my hair was exhausting and causing me to see spots.

I needed to get a move on as I wanted to see Amy and Garret before they left. When I joined them in the kitchen, finally, they were all standing around cradling steaming cups of Joe. James handed me a mug of Earl Grey tea, and I picked at a bunch of grapes that were sitting on the counter while watching small, knowing smiles dance across their faces. They were sharing an inside joke, and I'm pretty sure I was the butt of it.

"All right, what?" I asked, cocking my hip to the side and into the counter while blowing on my tea.

"What, what?" James said giving me his best innocent face.

"What's got you all smirking and barely able to contain yourselves?"

And then I instantly regretted asking because Amy started beating her chest and let out a loud Tarzan wail. All eyes were on me instantly as I stood there, stock still, my eyes bugging out of my head. I could feel my cheeks getting warm, and it wasn't because I'd just taken a sip of my tea.

"Oh. My. God."

The three of them erupted with laughter and James came over and took my tea, set it on the counter, and enveloped me in a big hug. I buried my face in his chest, too humiliated to look at the other two.

"Oh, relax," Amy giggled. "It's funny. And I'm happy that my brother has a wild and fulfilling sex life."

I blushed and tried to hide my eyes again, attempting to make myself smaller or disappear altogether.

James' body shook with poorly contained laughter. "Hun, it's fine. No one cares. And I thought it was hot as hell. Isn't that all that matters?" He tilted my head up with his finger under my chin.

But I shook my head. "They were out in the garage apartment, James, and they still heard it. What does that say?"

"It says you were just trying to let all the jungle animals know that Tarzan and Jane were going to be making the beast with two backs," Garret quipped, causing the other two to start laughing again. "Though, to be fair, we slept in the house last night. The thermostat wasn't working in the apartment, and we were freezing, so we moved inside. But I'm pretty sure had we been out in the apartment we still would have heard you. *Jane*." He beat his chest as he walked over to stand beside his giggling fiancé.

"Okay, okay." I rolled my eyes and took another sip of my tea. "Let's all laugh at the crazy, horny, drunk chick. I can't remember doing it, so in my mind, it never happened."

"Oh, it happened, baby," James said sassily. "I was there. And it was *un-for-gettable*." He handed me a hard boiled egg, but the idea of an egg on my stomach made me want to retch, so I shook my head and grabbed another handful of grapes.

Amy flashed me a big grin. "Hey, like I said, I'm just happy you're making my brother happy. Fuck the miserable right out of him." She came over and gave me a small hug, whispering in my ear, "You're not the only one who got lucky last night. You just couldn't hear us over your own jungle fever."

I smiled, thankful that she was trying to make me feel better.

"All right, dear, should we head on over to your parents? Are you ready to tell off your mother?" Garret grabbed his jacket off the bar stool and took his empty coffee mug to the dishwasher.

"I'll never be ready to tell-off my mother," Amy sighed, giving her fiancé a stern look. "That's a horrible notion. But the fact of the matter is that she needs to be dealt with. Wish us luck, guys."

We wished them luck and then walked them out. As much as I enjoyed their company, the embarrassment of my audible sex-capade was a little too much, and I was looking forward to a bit of space. I had some paper grading to catch up on, as well as a few emails, and I wanted to check in with my parents and find out when they would be getting to town the following weekend.

"Hi, Mum."

"Hi, honey. How are you?"

"Hungover."

"Oh?"

"Yeah. James' sister and her fiancé are visiting, and we went out for dinner. And James' parents were there as well. His mother was mean to me, so I just decided to ignore her and drink until I was numb. Now I'm paying."

"How was she mean to you?"

My mum was my biggest ally; the epitome of a Mama Bear. She had taken it exceptionally hard when I told her about Tom. Before I'd even finished telling my parents the whole story, when I finally worked up the courage to fill them in, Anita Everly was in her car with the keys in the ignition and the engine revved, ready to go and "castrate the asshole" as she'd put it. It had taken every ounce of my persuasive power to get that impulsive, hot-tempered woman to turn the car off and go back into the house.

My dad, on the other hand, is a tad more stoic. When I told them about Tom, my dad had actually sobbed. He called himself a "failure as a father" and said that he should have seen the signs and protected me. He'd barely spoken to me for almost two days out of shame. It broke my heart to see him so emotionally thrashed and I spent countless hours with him in and out of therapy assuring him that he wasn't at fault that I'd hid it from everyone. And even now when the topic of Tom comes up, he still grows quiet, and a shadow of grief will wash over his face. I don't think he'll ever truly forgive himself and believe that he couldn't have saved me from the heartache.

"She hasn't liked me from the moment she met me," I went on, filling my mother in on the night. "She told me my shirt was tasteless and revealing and pretty much intimated that my shoes belonged on a hooker."

"She did what?" I could hear the anger building in my mother's voice. She probably already had her keys and purse in hand and was going to the hall closet to put on her shoes. She was getting ready to drive here to confront Patricia.

"Yeah. Anyway, Amy, James' sister, is over with their parents now and she's going to try to deal with her mother. And then James is going to talk to her as well. I'm not sure what to do, though. I've tried being nice, but she still treats me like shit. And then last night once she'd insulted me and I'd had some wine I just didn't care anymore—I egged her on by smiling smugly and adjusting my 'whore' shirt."

"Oh, honey, that's not egging her on, that's just asserting your confidence in your relationship with her son and your wardrobe. Was your shirt revealing?"

"No. There was hardly *any* cleavage, well pretty much none. You know how hard it is for me not to have cleavage showing. The girls are out no matter what. What should I do?"

"Well, is your relationship with this Patricia a make or break thing for you and James? Do you have to get along with his mother for the relationship to work?"

"I'm not sure, but I don't think so."

"Well, you need to find this out."

"Yeah, I guess. Should I maybe invite her out to lunch to clear the air? Explain that my intentions toward her son are honest and good? That I'm not after anyone's money."

"Wait and see what Amy and James say. But it might not be a bad idea. Worst case, she says 'no,' but you still get the satisfaction of being the bigger person and having tried. And James, if he's smart, will see that."

We continued to chat for a few more minutes, finalizing our plans for the coming weekend. And then the topic of lodging came up. I swallowed, took a deep breath and went for it.

"Don't book a hotel. If you guys are okay with it, James has offered you his garage apartment. It's an entirely independent two-bedroom suite, and it's private and free." I exhaled.

My mother and I had a great relationship, and Anita Everly is an open-minded woman, but it was still weird confessing to your mother that you are sleeping with a new man.

"Where will you stay?"

"Um..." I hesitated. "W-with James."

There was a brief pause on the other end. "I... um... I'll run it past your father, but that sounds good."

She didn't have to say it for me to know my mother was worried about me jumping so quickly into a new serious relationship.

"I'm excited to meet this new man in your life who has your heart all a flutter. I just hope he's good to you."

"He's so good to me, Mum," I assured her. "I'm really happy."

"That's what matters, honey." Her voice was thick with emotion. "I can't wait to see you."

"Me too, Mum."

"All right, sweetie. I've got to take the dog out for a walk before the rain starts again. I'll call you later in the week to confirm everything, okay?"

"Okay. Love you."

"Love you too. Bye-bye, baby."

"Bye."

By mid-afternoon, my head and stomach were feeling much better. There was no way in hell I would be getting to the gym or out for a run, though, and making it up the stairs without stopping to suppress the urge to vomit was a successful aerobic workout for the day. I retreated to bed for an hour, and although I was feeling all right, my muscles were achy, and I was tired. I curled up on top of the duvet cover and pulled the extra blanket, draped at the foot of the bed, over me and was asleep in minutes.

When I awoke, strong, warm arms were wrapped around me like a vine, and the deep and heavy breathing of James asleep beside me ruffled the hair on my neck. I stirred gently, too hot and uncomfortable in our current position, trying hard not to wake him.

No chance.

He parted his long lashes and looked at me sleepily. I became winded by a moment of overwhelming clarity, was struck dumb by the waves of emotions that coursed through me. Over the past several weeks I had felt myself falling, my feelings had shifted, but with Tom as my only comparison, I had never felt like this before so how would I know what it meant? I loved this man. I was head over heels in love with him. I knew it. It was scary and exciting and all kinds of wonderful. I would never be the one to say it first, though, but I knew then and there that I loved him more than I'd ever loved anyone. He smiled and squeezed me tighter for a moment before releasing me so I could find a more comfortable position.

"How are you feeling now?" he asked.

Still overwhelmed by my revelation, I struggled to compose myself and answer the simple question. My delayed response must have taken longer than expected because he cocked an eyebrow.

I swallowed. "I'm feeling a lot better. Thanks. This nap helped a lot. How are you?"

"Happy."

"Happy?"

"Yeah. Happy."

"Care to elaborate?"

He shrugged. "I'm just happy. Happy that you're here. That I found you. That you haven't gone running for the hills after the disaster at dinner yesterday. Happy when I think about my jungle warrior princess from last night. I'm just happy. Can't a guy be happy?"

I smiled. "Yes, of course, a *guy* can be happy, but I thought you felt uncomfortable expressing your feelings?"

"I'm trying something new. It was Amy's idea."

He leaned forward and nipped at my bottom lip with his teeth, his eyes darkening, brilliant cerulean turned from morning to midnight within seconds. I closed my eyes. He deepened the kiss and moved his body to cover mine. It wasn't long before we were both naked and James was inside me, making up for my lost orgasms from the night before.

"Amy loves you by the way. Dad and Garret, too." We were in the kitchen trying to figure something out for dinner and were perusing the freezer.

"Well, I'm rather fond of her myself. And I guess four out of five family members not hating me isn't terrible odds." I pulled out a steak for him and continued to dig around for something for me to eat. Amy had called earlier in the day to let us know she and Garret had been invited out for dinner with some friends, so they wouldn't be home until later. We were happy for the solitude.

"We'll deal with my mother, don't worry. I like this braid," James said, giving my long plait a healthy tug, so my head tilted back. We were working side-by-side in the kitchen chopping vegetables.

"Yeah?"

"Yeah." He planted a kiss on my lips and murmured, "I'd love to pull it and control you while I'm ploughing you from behind." His mouth stretched into a diabolical grin.

"Are you into that?" Things were suddenly growing very serious.

"Into what?" He straightened my neck and turned me to face him.

"Controlling me or... or women during sex. Are you into the kinkier side of sex? Like whips and flogs. Blindfolds and ball-gags?" I wasn't sure what kind of answer I was hoping for. I mean, I'd read all the steamy bestsellers and been *extremely* intrigued and turned on by them, but the idea of being handcuffed and whipped, with my emotional wounds from Tom still so fresh, I don't know. I wasn't sure I could handle it. I wasn't sure if I could be a submissive. He took the knife from me and put it on the cutting board; then he rested his hands on my shoulders, his face set into a patient half-smile.

"The fact that I want to pull your braid during sex does not mean that I want to tie you up, suspend you from the ceiling and cane you."

Suspend me? Canes?

He chuckled when my eyes nearly popped from their sockets. "I've dabbled a bit in that lifestyle and found that it's not for me. If we're going to use the correct terms, then yes, I am a top or a Dominant, but I would never ask you to be a bottom or my submissive. Even though sexually you are a natural submissive. But in everyday life, you're not. I would never ask you to be my submissive. Especially not after your experiences with Tom, but it's also not something I want."

"What do you mean you've *dabbled*?" I was nervous, and if I'm completely honest, a little turned on.

"A woman I was sleeping with for a little while was very into the BDSM lifestyle. She was a submissive and attracted to my assertive and controlling personality, she pursued me and then introduced me to the culture."

"Oh? What have you done?"

He lifted a shoulder and resumed his task of washing lettuce.

"Nothing too intense. I never trained as a Dom so I couldn't do too much. Some blindfolding, handcuffs, spanking, and I used a suede flogger on her a few times and a riding crop. Various other toys, that kind of thing. I went to a few parties and watched some demonstrations, but in the end, the lifestyle just didn't really appeal to me. I like to play, but the rest of it, the mental part of it just isn't my thing. That's not to say I still wouldn't love to blindfold and or handcuff you if you were willing. Spank your sweet ass until it's a beautiful rosy pink."

I bit my lip and looked at him, still not ready to resume the task of chopping vegetables, I felt like this topic required my full attention.

"So, it's not something that you'd miss or feel was missing in your life if I wasn't interested?"

He shook his head. "No, not at all. You're so sexually adventurous in your own way that I'm pretty sure we'll never get bored. And I'd like to remind you, that you were the one who bought the *Thump-her 3000*, *and* who got up on all fours last night and told me to spank you."

I blushed and averted my eyes. Another thing from Saturday night that I did not remember.

"Oh, yes baby, it happened." He smacked my butt and then headed out to the patio to check on the barbecue.

While I was in the washroom, James had dimmed the lights and lit a few candles, setting two lovely place settings at the kitchen bar.

We were just cutting into our meals when he abruptly put his utensils down and raised his wine glass. "To one month. And to the woman who, in that one month has managed to turn my whole world upside down."

I swallowed my broccoli and gave him a big grin, hoping that I didn't have anything green trapped in my teeth. "The feeling is quite mutual. You've made me so happy."

We clinked glasses, and he leaned across the bar to kiss me, grabbing my hand in the process. Only it wasn't his hand that he placed in mine it was a small, black velvet box. I cocked my head.

"What's this?"

"Just a small thank you, for letting me buy you that drink one month ago and changing my life, for the better. Open it."

Had it been a month already? I'd completely lost track, it felt like we'd known each other for so much longer, but at the same time, the month had just flown by.

"I... I didn't get you anything."

"You weren't supposed to." He shook his head. "What I want, I have. Open it." The look on his face was sweet but serious; I couldn't get a read on him. The box wasn't wrapped, so I just opened it.

"Oh, my... God." My eyes flew back and forth between his face and the box. It was the most beautiful pair of diamond earrings I had ever seen. They were round cut and although I'm no jeweler, at least three karats each. Just stunning. "I can't... this... these are too much."

"Of course you can." He made a dismissive face. "I saw them, knew they were meant for you and so I bought them. Plain and simple."

"But... I... I... They're gorgeous."

"*You're* gorgeous. They're two shiny rocks." He reached for my hand and pulled me into his lap. "I don't think you quite realize what it is you've done to me. You've turned my whole life upside down. Ask anyone. I haven't been this happy in years. You make me want to be a hands-on, always around, super-boyfriend. I hate the idea of having to leave you for any amount of time. I've deflected so many major projects all over the country to my associates because I just don't want to be away from you. I've never felt like this about anyone before." He gave a small half smile. "See, you even have me sharing my feelings."

I cradled his head in my hands and started sprinkling kisses all over his face. "Thank you. Thank you. Thank you. Thank you. Thank you." I'm fairly certain that he knew my thank yous were for more than just the earrings.

"Thank *you*. So, is it too early to ask you to move in with me?"

I stopped kissing his neck and murmuring all the filthy things I wanted to do him and looked him square in the eyes, mouth agape.

"Umm…" What could I say? I knew that I loved this man, but it had only been a month. And more importantly I loved living on my own, and I loved my independence. Granted James and I spent nearly five nights a week together, but I just wasn't ready to live with someone again. "Please, don't take this wrong way, but, yeah, I think it may be a bit too early."

I leaned back trying to take in his whole face to get an inkling of what he was thinking.

He was quiet for a moment. It was probably no more than three or four seconds, but with everything hanging in the balance, it felt much longer.

Was he mad I'd said, no? Did I just ruin our perfect evening?

"Okay." He finally shrugged, planting a swift kiss on my lips and reaching for the velvet box. "You're probably right. It was a lucky shot. I just wish I could wake up next to you every day."

My hair was still in a braid so with a broad smile on his face he grabbed it a pulled, angling my head to one side. And ever so gently he slid each of the white gold posts into my pierced ears. I closed my eyes; the tiny touches of his knuckles on my neck and cheek were driving me wild. The intimacy of James putting earrings in my ears brought me to a new kind, a new level of arousal.

"You look lovely."

I smiled shyly, fingering the large studs that now dressed my lobes.

I wasn't sure where to take the conversation from here. I'd just accepted an expensive gift from this amazing man, while simultaneously turning down his proposal for us to live together. Needless to say, the moment was a bit awkward.

"Um, so, just so you know, to continue our conversation from earlier, I wouldn't... be, uh... I wouldn't be opposed to blindfolds or handcuffs or both. I think it would be hot. I'm not too sure how much further I could go, but I'm definitely up for some experimentation."

There! I figured, if you can't add to the conversation, change it, and change it to sex. That should work.

His eyes perked up. "Really?"

"Yeah, well, I trust you. And I think it might be kind of fun. All the women in the books I've read seem to enjoy it." I winked at him as I made my way back to my stool.

"All right then." He picked up his knife and fork. "So, would you like me to take the reins and introduce new and kinky things as I see fit or would you like to discuss things first?"

I speared a broccoli floret with my fork and held it up to my mouth. "The tamer things you can probably surprise me with, but anything kinkier than a blindfold or handcuffs should probably be discussed."

"Okay, done!" He nodded, taking another sexy bite of his steak with a Cheshire Cat-like grin

24

The more I got to know Amy, the more I felt I was getting to know James as well. I was getting a glimpse, albeit a very faint and blurry one through Amy's eyes, into his past and the type of person he'd been before we'd met. Lucky for me, Amy and Garret had decided to stay an extra day, so I was getting an even longer glimpse. James had managed to snag tickets for us all to the St. Patrick's Day party at the Irish Pub downtown, so when I finished work at five thirty, I walked to his office to meet them.

For years I had walked past James' office and stared up at the looming building with its all-masking reflective windows. I had never dreamed that I would be dating a man who worked on the top floor. A man who could look out the windows of his commerce castle and watch the rest of society scurry around on the pavement below, like ants after crumbs, trying to survive and forage before the rains came. A man who preferred to look out those windows toward the horizon and watch as the sun sank slowly behind the West Shore than talk numbers or play the ass-kiss game.

I walked into his office unannounced. The receptionist had gone home for the night, so I gently tapped then poked my head around the partially opened door. He was on the phone, but he waved me in and held up two fingers. I wandered around the room, taking it all it. He mouthed the word "sorry" and made a sad face, apologizing for his lengthy call.

His office was the definition of him; powerful, bold, smart, confident and sexy. The color scheme was similar to the décor palate at his house, dark woods, and earth tones, homey and warm without seeming weak. In fact, it was just the opposite. You could smell the authority and power as it percolated throughout the room, and it was making me hot. I continued my survey, ran my fingers along the dark mahogany trim of the mantle, taking in his endless awards and diplomas that hung on the wall, discreetly. However, as impressive as this man's credentials were, I grew bored quickly. I'd had an awesome day at work, was happy to be spending more time with Amy and Garret so my spirits were high and my mood playful.

He was still on the phone, and from what I gathered it didn't sound like it was going very well, or that it would be ending anytime soon. I decided to take his mind off the frustrating person on the other end of the line and onto something more positive. He'd texted me earlier in the day to say that Amy and Garret had stopped off at the dollar store to buy something Irish, whatever that meant? Taking advantage of our time alone, I sashayed over to where he was sitting behind his desk in the large plush leather chair and climbed onto his lap, straddling him.

His eyes grew wide along with his smile as I slowly and seductively started to unbutton my gray blouse, revealing my very appropriate for the occasion, mint green with black lace balconette bra. Leaning in, I planted soft kisses up his neck, trailing my tongue along the curve of his ear and back down while running my hand up his chest and pulling mischievously on his sage green tie. His head came forward, and he laid his face between my breasts inhaling deeply, mumbling "yes" and "mhmm" into the receiver.

He rested the phone down and hit the button for the speaker; a male voice took over the room, booming out figures and deadlines. James continued to answer appropriately and timely, but his attention was severely waning. Two hands came up and caressed my breasts, pulling my cups down so he could pinch and pull at my nipples. I let out a yelp, causing the man on the phone to pause for a moment. But James didn't seem fazed; he continued to tease me, bringing his lips down around one and suckling it gently at first but then with more pressure and power, sending waves of pleasure through my body.

I ground my hips into him, feeling his erection growing against my pelvis. I was wearing a black mini skirt with black tights and short black ankle boots; not exactly the easiest outfit for a quickie, but I was game if he was. His hands came up, and he slipped them beneath my blouse cradling my rib cage and back in his hands. His breathing was becoming ragged as my grinding grew more intense while his responses to the man on the phone were delayed and short. I loved the effect I had on him.

"Listen... uh ... Bruce, I'm sorry, but I've got something *pressing* that I have to get at RIGHT now. So, I'm going to have to call you back tomorrow. This can wait. Thanks."

And without waiting for *Bruce* to reply, James ended the call, and I was pushed onto my back on his desk with a stapler digging into my spine.

A quick rummage through his desk drawer and James had managed to locate a black shoelace, he deftly tied my hands together and told me to keep them above my head, and then he went to work removing my clothes.

We didn't get too far into our impromptu office quickie before we heard a rather fake but an obvious cough by the doorway. Thankfully, we were both still fairly well covered, minus my open blouse and nipples and James' trousers around his ankles, and of course, my bound hands. He glanced up from where he had been furiously trying to pull off my tights, and I tilted my head over the edge of the desk, so I was looking upside down at Amy and Garret standing just inside the doorway, both wearing shit-eating grins.

"We can come back later if you guys want to finish," Garret offered as he and Amy laughed. James grabbed some scissors and freed my hands so we could scramble to redress ourselves and cover up my chest and James' conspicuous hard-on.

"Jesus, bro, lock the door if you plan on getting down to business, or at the very least close it all the way," Amy reprimanded as she made herself comfortable on the black leather couch opposite the fireplace and began pulling unidentifiable green paraphernalia from a plastic dollar store bag. "Emma, when you've finished tucking your nipples back in your bra, come see what I bought for us to wear."

I could feel the warmth from my cheeks working its way up into my hairline I'm sure my complexion rivaled a candy apple. The woman's blunt and playful chastising was going to take some getting used to. I hastily adjusted myself, hiding my chest and buttoning my blouse on my way to sit next to her.

"Perfect timing as always, Ames, just as I'm about to have a good time, you show up and ruin the fun." James, on the other hand, didn't seem flustered in the least by his sister. He zipped up his pants and walked over to where we were sitting on the couch going through her St. Patrick's Day garb.

We walked to the pub from the office in a convoy of green plastic crap. James' enthusiasm with regards to his green fedora was minimal, but he wore it with a smile to please his sister. I got the feeling that he did a lot of things that he didn't want to do to make her happy. I found it sweet, and I know my brothers have done the same.

Amy coerced me into wearing a green feather boa that was molting profusely. It had lost so many feathers already that it looked as though a parrot had been assaulted in the street—by the end of the night; I'd be lucky if I had enough left to cover a hummingbird adequately. But Garret, bless him, bore the brunt of Amy's Irish assault. She had convinced him to wear a green felt top hat and feather boa that was sparser than mine. Also, he wore a pair of white boxers printed with tiny leprechauns and pots of gold over top of his pants. And on the butt, it said, "Kiss me I'm Irish." Amy wore multiple green beaded necklaces as well as a green and gold bowler hat that had a giant shamrock stuck to the front.

Fortunately, we were neither turned away at the door for our garish attire nor were the most ridiculously dressed people at the pub. Irish pride was paramount, and the shamrock emblazoned clothing was plentiful. All patrons showed their love for the potato loving country to various degrees, and whether Irish or not, the green beer was being drunk with vigor.

We were shown to our upstairs table and, to my delight, Alyssa and Steve were already seated with a mug of holiday brew before them. My wonderful boyfriend had actually scored *six* tickets to the party and invited Alyssa and Steve as a surprise. Introductions were made, and soon we were all deep into our green nachos and green beer, enjoying the Celtic music and watching the antics of the university kids downstairs as they challenged each other and their livers to shots of Irish whiskey.

Amy was regaling Alyssa and Steve with my Jane of the Jungle nighttime antics and then this afternoon's coitus interruption when Alyssa's face suddenly went pale, and she mumbled "Oh fuck" under her breath. All conversation stopped. Apparently, she had caught sight of something unexpected out the window. She snapped her head to look at me, then over at Steve, then James, and then back at me. Pure panic etched on her face.

"What is it?" I asked. What could she possibly have seen to garner such a dreaded response?

She avoided my eyes and took a healthy sip of her beer. "It's nothing, I-I thought I saw something, but it was nothing."

"You're lying." I pulled on her shoulder until she faced me. "What was it?" For a lawyer, the woman was a terrible liar, good thing she primarily did mediation and not litigation.

She shook her head. "Em, don't."

"Don't what?" Now, I was getting kind of pissed. I was on my third glass of beer and feeling it, so my irritability was floating on the surface.

She let out a huge sigh. "It was Tom, *and* Jennifer and they were pushing a stroller."

I don't know why, but I jumped up from the table and took off downstairs and outside, green feathers flying. My mind was blank while my body was running on impulse and adrenaline. I looked up and down the street hugging my arms as I'd forgotten my coat in my hurry. I ran half a block down the road and then spun around, forgetting why I'd burst from the pub in the first place.

A trio of intoxicated, green-clad guys walked past me stopping to say, "May your luck be like the capital of Ireland, always Dublin" but didn't wait for my response and kept on going, reiterating their proverb to the next pedestrian they came across. I sat down on a bench and put my head in my hands.

A hand rested on my shoulder, and a silhouette fell across me blocking out the final light of the day. Without even looking up I knew it was James.

"Care to tell me why you ran out of the pub after your ex like that?" His voice was calm and quiet, but I knew him well enough by now to know that he was having difficulty holding back his frustration.

"I... I don't know. I just needed to see him."

He moved around to stand in front of me. He didn't sit next to me or crouch to be at my level, and this sent the hair on the back of my neck straight up. He was using an intimidation technique on me whether he was aware of it or not. I looked up. His face was devoid of emotion, and his blue eyes were shadowed to black by the streetlight.

A muscle ticked along his jaw. "Why did you need to see him? I thought you never wanted to see him again."

"I don't. It's just... I don't know!" I threw my hands up in the air and then covered my face again, unwilling to look him in the eye, the man was able to see right through me.

"You told me that one of your biggest fears was running into Tom and Jennifer with their baby and not knowing what to do."

I watched as his fists bunched and then relaxed, bunched and then relaxed. He was trying so hard to keep his temper in check.

"And yet when you find out they're nearby you run to them. Why?"

"I don't know." My head just continued to shake. "I don't *fucking* know."

"Are you still in love with him?" His voice was like jagged steel piercing my heart.

"What?" I looked up from the ground into his face. Maybe the shadows were playing tricks on my eyes, but he looked mean, fierce almost; nothing like the man with whom I had fallen in love. His chiseled features were hidden, his smile a distant memory. The man in front of me was frightening to look at; his anger was building, was being reined in but just barely. "God no! How could even ask that? Knowing what you know, and what he did to me?"

"Then why run after him?"

"Fuck!" I threw my hands in the air. "I don't know. Maybe... for closure? I haven't seen Tom since he kicked me out of our apartment. I don't even know what Jennifer looks like. Is she pretty? Does she look like me? I don't know. For validation that he wasn't lying just to get rid of me that there actually *is* a Jennifer and a baby. Fuck, James, I don't know."

"Does any of that matter?" His voice was cold; it reminded me more of the voice he used when he was doing business. It was cutthroat and to the point.

"Obviously it does if I ran out of a pub after them, doesn't it?" I sighed, his lack of compassion was quickly starting to piss me off.

"Are you over him?"

"Are you serious?" I stood up and looked him in the eye, angry with the anger that was coming out in his voice. How could he be mad at me?

"Emma, clearly you haven't been entirely honest with me and you have some unfinished feelings for Tom that you need to sort out."

"Clearly!" I snapped. "Clearly? Fuck you, James. I thought you understood how Tom's behavior damaged me, psychologically. That you understood what some of my triggers are, but *clearly*, you don't!" I turned away and began walking down the road toward the pub to get my purse and coat so that I could leave.

He grabbed my arm and pulled me to face him. "Stop fucking running." He growled. "Of course I understand. It was all I could do not to kick the living shit out of him when he walked into my office, the pompous little cocksucker. What I don't understand is why you needed to see him."

I stopped and stared at him. "What are you talking about? Walked into your office? When did you see Tom?" I was panting, he had a firm grip on my arm, and his fingers dug into my bicep; his chest was heaving against mine, and his jaw flexed. He was riding the edge of fury.

"Your *boyfriend* came into my office to introduce himself as the newest member of my bookkeeping and accounting team. Tried to get me to sign some shit." His use of the word *boyfriend* stung something fierce, which I'm sure was his intention. "It would appear that Edwin Hall appointed him to the team because Arthur would never have made such a mistake. I had the asshole removed and subsequently fired from the firm."

"What? Why? Why did you do that?" I couldn't think of anything else to say.

"Why?" He bared his teeth in a snarl. "You have to ask me, why? Do you honestly think I could allow a man like that to work for me, handle my money, my company's finances after knowing who he is, what he is capable of? Knowing what kind of person he is. What he did to *you*?"

"James ... I—"

"You're angry with me? I thought you'd be pleased." His fingers kneaded my bicep, his grip unrelenting.

"I don't know. It's just... I... it's just a lot to take in. You're hurting me." I tried to shake him off my arm, but he adjusted his grip and wrapped his arms around me, pulling me to his chest.

"I told you I wanted to take care of you. If you can honestly say that you're not still in love with Tom, that you're over him, then I'll believe you, and we'll be done with this." His face softened. "And I didn't get him fired. I asked that he be removed from my accounting team, made some vague shit up when I gave my reasons as to why, and I guess the firm found him to be too much of a liability, so they fired him. Apparently, he's been pissing off a lot of people, and they've been looking for a reason to terminate him. Building a case. But, how do you think it would have worked if I had kept him as my accountant? It wouldn't have. Not in any way, knowing what I know about him now. And it wouldn't have been fair to you." His speech had become gentle, his words kinder.

He tilted my head up with a finger, so our eyes met. The shadows no longer wreaking havoc on his beautiful face. His eyes were no longer fearsome empty holes, but rather they permeated my soul with their endless blue depth.

"I... I'm s-sorry I ran off like that," I said, the words tumbling out of my mouth in a stutter. "I wasn't thinking. I went blank, was on autopilot. I don't even remember getting up from the table and leaving the pub. I guess I just wanted to see for myself. I'm sorry. And thank you for—"

He cut me off. "Are you still in love with him?"

Enraged, I pushed out of his arms. "How dare you! You actually feel the need to ask me that? After all you know? Who fucked you up? Why are you such a jealous ass?"

"You haven't answered me." The frost was back in his voice.

"NO!" I yelled, walking away and then rounding back on him. "Of course I'm not *in love* with him. I don't think I ever was. I didn't even know what love was until I met you! I don't love him. I love you!"

I clapped both my hands to my mouth, my eyes wide in horror, surprised and infuriated with myself that I'd let such a thing slip. But before I could even think or move he was on me, his hands in my hair and his lips crushing mine. I was not normally one for public displays of affection, let alone public displays of anger, but there wasn't much else I could do.

He had me in a vice grip. His lips left mine and traveled to my cheek and temple to my ear and down my neck. My mind was at war, the beauty of his kisses and my admission of love dueling within me. He was murmuring incoherent words; words I couldn't make out over the arguing voices in my head. I tried to turn the voices off so I could hear him.

"Oh, Emma, I love you. I'm sorry my love. So, so sorry. I love you too. Forgive me."

I looked up into his eyes they were sparkling again and filled with passion.

"I am *so* in love with you, Emma. And I'm sorry for my reaction. I should have been more understanding. Jealousy has always been a problem, and I let it get the better of me. Please don't give up on me. Say you forgive me. I'm an idiot." He was blathering on like a fool, and a chuckle wormed its way up my throat.

I choked back a sob, only able to squeak out, "Okay."

Tears stung my eyes, but I quickly wiped them away as he pulled me closer and wrapped his arms even tighter around me. James was coatless too, and even though our kiss had been feverish, our body heat was no match for the clear night and the whipping wind. He grabbed my hand, and we ran back to the warm embrace of the pub.

All eyes were on us as we sat back down at the table. It seemed as if we had been gone for hours, but it was probably no more than five or ten minutes, my green beer glass was still frosted and the nachos warm. I felt like I owed Amy and Garret a bit of an explanation. They had been so welcoming and friendly to me that the last thing I wanted was for Amy to think her brother was dating a nut job who ran after her exes. I gave them enough of my backstory with Tom for them to understand my impulsive flight and then, after a few probing questions, the vibe at the table resumed back to normal.

When we got home, we all shared a quick nightcap and then retired to bed, promising to rise early enough to see Garret and Amy off before they left.

I emerged fresh-faced, and sexy pajama-clad from the bathroom into a bedroom filled with flickering white candles. The fireplace danced with bright orange flames, and the linens on the bed were turned down. Only James was nowhere to be found.

I wasn't sure what he intended, but I decided to lie on the bed, trying hard not to try too hard, avoiding any cliché come hither poses.

Moments later he came through the door dressed only in his black boxer briefs and carrying a stainless steel bowl.

He looked good enough to eat. Was I drooling? I wiped my chin as discretely as I could, then licked my lips, eager to get my mouth on him. His grin was wicked and wolfish as he climbed onto the bed, setting the bowl on the nightstand. I was beneath him in seconds, his body pressing mine into the mattress, his hands cradling my head and his lips tasting my own with soft but passionate licks.

Lifting his head, he looked me in the eyes and smiled.

"I love you, Emma Violet Everly."

I grinned. "And I love you, James Parker Shaw."

Our eyes stayed locked, letting the moment sink in. His smile grew wider, and he lowered his head to the crook of my neck, snaking his arms beneath my body, holding me, hugging me, loving me. We rocked once, twice, three times and then rolled so that I was straddling him.

I studied his face. "Are we okay?"

I was pretty confident in the answer, but I wanted to clear the air and make sure before we decided to take the evening any further.

His smile stretched across his face. "Yeah, we're okay. We're better than okay. You love me."

"Indeed I do." I nodded. "And you love me."

"I do." He nodded. "And now I'm going to make love *to* you."

"Are you now?"

"Yep. But you're wearing far too many clothes, Miss Everly. This just won't do."

He lifted the hem of my top and pulled it over my head. Sitting up he propped himself against the headboard and leaned back, extending his arm over to the side table and the bowl, grabbing what was inside.

"Close your eyes, baby."

I did as I was told.

Suddenly there was a warm *and* cold sensation on my nipples. I opened my eyes to find James' nipping and sucking my swollen bud; his mouth was cold—he had an ice cube! My nipples instantly pearled as he delivered the two opposing sensations. The mix of extreme temperatures was divine. Pulling the ice cube from his mouth he rubbed it on and around my breast, causing my skin to gooseflesh while taking my crimson nub back into his mouth to warm me up again; I moaned from the pleasure. Then he began delivering the same delicious attention to the other.

His fingers beneath my shorts were doing all kinds of wondrous things as well; I was already so slick that his digits slid around and between my folds with ease, plunging two fingers inside me and then pulling out, and drawing luscious circles around my clit with his big thumb. I didn't notice when he lifted his hand from my breast to get another ice cube, but when the ice touched my clit, my eyes flew open. Thousands of tiny nerve endings shocked and awakened by the cold. His smile was salacious as I squealed and tried to roll off him, only his puma-like reflexes prevailed, and I was once again pinned beneath him.

"Do you not like the ice, my love?" he asked playfully.

I exaggerated a shiver. "It's just a little cold. A little *too* cold in some places."

Two could play this game. I grabbed the ice cubes from him and put them in my mouth. Using all my strength, I pushed him off me, but he didn't put up much of a fight; he could keep me pinned and spread at his will so easily. He kneeled on the bed in front of me, and I pulled his shorts down, releasing his red-blooded masterpiece from its fabric confines. He was rock hard. I wiped off the glistening bead of pre-cum with my finger and licked it, enjoying his quick inhale, and then the low groan that traveled down into his belly.

My mouth was cold, almost painfully so, I spat the larger ice cube into the bowl, placing it on the bed beside me and then taking James into my mouth. He sucked in air as the coldness touched him and my tongue swirled around his length bringing the ice with me, up and down and around, paying close attention to the crown where he's most sensitive. The ice quickly melted, but I continued to suck, warming him up with my mouth and enjoying the moans of pleasure that thundered through him.

"Oh baby..." he growled as he pulled me up, so I was kneeling in front of him. "That mouth." He captured my mouth with his, forcing his tongue between my lips, tasting me with gentle but possessive thrusts.

He guided me to my back, our lips never coming apart, as his fingers slipped beneath my shorts and pulled them off, his hands guiding and molding my body, urging me to lift my hips and bend my legs, helping me to hook my arms behind my knees. I was needy and greedy; the emotional storm we had both faced that evening was rumbling in the distance, and I needed the physical connection to confirm we were okay.

But James had other ideas. Just when I hoped he was going to impale me, he dipped his head to the apex of my thighs and started running his tongue up and down my pink, slippery folds. I was burning up, hot, but somehow his tongue and lips were cool like a balm, infinitely provocative yet soothing.

"Please," I panted. "I-I need... fuck me... now."

He lifted his head smiling, his lips shiny and wet, the gleam of me on his strong chin. I reached out, and he covered me. I thought at first that he was going to thrust forcefully, full throttle, but to my surprise, he eased himself in with languid luxury; teasing my entrance with the head of his cock and gently pulling in and out before slowly embedding himself inside. Our foreplay may have started out playful with the ice cubes, but it was quickly turning into heated passion.

As we lay in bed a tangle of limbs and sheets in the afterglow of our lovemaking; satiated and near comatose, our chests still rising erratically, the sweat glistening on our naked bodies, I started to cry. I'm not sure why—I hate crying, but cry I did. In fact, I sobbed as I laid in bed with the man I loved, watching the candles cast dancing shadows on the ceiling above while tears streamed down my cheeks.

"Hey, hey, baby, what's wrong?" James asked, propping himself up on an elbow, wiping my tears away with his thumb.

I gasped a few times, struggling to catch my breath. "I-I... I don't know. I guess... it's just that tonight was such... a... an emotional roller coaster. And I'm finally coming down."

He made a small pout. "What do you mean?"

I took a deep breath and rolled over to onto my side to face him.

"Well... we started out almost screwing on your desk, except we were caught pants down by your sister, which was mortifying. And then I stupidly ran after my ex, which caused us to fight and created a commotion in the street, and I hate 'scenes.' And somehow I ended up telling you I loved you, which I promised myself I wouldn't do first, and then you told me you loved me too, which was great, but it's still not how I hoped it would happen.

"And then we made out in the street, and I abhor PDA's almost as much as *scenes*, and then we came home, and you fucked me senseless until I cried. And you won't tell me why you're so jealous. I don't know anything about your past. I feel like I hardly know anything about *you*, besides your family. So, yeah, today was a roller coaster. You beguile me, James. I've never been in love before, not really, and it terrifies me."

He moved, closing the gap between us until our bodies were once again intertwined. "Tonight was an emotional night, you're right. I'm sorry for getting so upset and for our fight in the street, I overreacted and let my jealousy take over... again." He grimaced. "But I will never apologize for kissing you, no matter where we are. Not ever. And there's nothing to be afraid of. I've never felt this way either. We'll just have to figure out this *love* thing together. What does *abhor* and *beguile* mean? You use really unusual words! *Abhor... beguile...*" he muttered against my temple.

I giggled softly, sniffing and wiping away more wretched tears. Why was he avoiding my questions? Why wouldn't he tell me about his past relationships? Who hurt him? What has made him into such a jealous person? But now was not the time to pry. I was too exhausted to push... maybe he'd tell me when he was ready... I could only hope.

He kissed my forehead and then rested his chin on the top of my head, letting my tears trickle onto his chest.

"And, no, it wasn't all roses and violins when I told you I loved you, but it doesn't make it any less real because there weren't any. And who cares that you said it first? I thought the way you told me was raw and romantic, spontaneous and in the heat of the moment, what more could I ask for? Why does it have to be planned out? Why does it matter how we said it or where we said it? Or who said it first? What matters, is that we said it and we mean it. I love you, Emma. I want to spend the rest of my life with you."

I looked up from under his chin into his eyes, the depth of sincerity stole my breath. Tilting my head up to his perfect lips, I kissed him heatedly and hungrily—

"I love you too."

And this concludes Sex, Heat and Hunger: Part 1
Stay tuned for Sex, Heat and Hunger: Part 2
The Dark and Damaged Hearts Series: Book 4

IF YOU ENJOYED THIS BOOK

If you've enjoyed this book, please consider leaving a review. It really does make a difference.

Thank you again.
Xoxo
Whitley Cox

SNEAK A PEEK - SEX, HEAT AND HUNGER: PART 2

Sneak a peek
Sex, Heat and Hunger: Part 2, Book 4 of The Dark and Damaged Hearts.

SEX, HEAT AND HUNGER: PART 2 - CHAPTER 1

I was in love. Hopelessly, mind-bogglingly, head-over-heels in love. I was blissfully happy despite the fact that I was forced to say goodbye to the man I loved Tuesday morning, wishing him a safe flight to Seattle and a productive work week.

I missed James terribly, especially at night when I was forced to sleep alone, staring at the empty space in the bed next to me that was usually reserved for his big, gorgeous body. At the same time, as much as I missed him, it was nice getting back into the routine of things—hitting the gym, vegging out in my pajamas in front of the television before bed. Mundane and monotonous, maybe, but they were things I looked forward to after a long and busy day at work.

Having finally said those three magical little words to each other was the glue we'd needed to solidify and finalize our commitment to one another. I no longer felt as though I was suddenly going to have the rug ripped out from beneath me, that he'd call it quits or just stop calling. We were in this, both of us, for the long haul. For the happily ever after, for forever.

Wednesday night after the gym Alyssa and I grabbed dinner, where we re-hashed my stupid St. Patrick's Day run-out. She agreed that I had yet to find closure when it came to Tom, that the memory of him still haunted me regardless of how much Max, Alex, and James had changed my opinion of men and my own self-worth and exorcised the demon from my life. She also gave me shit for how I handled things, calling me ridiculous and childish, and agreeing that James had every right to get upset. As seems to be the case these days, I conceded and told her she was right.

Friday was here before I knew it. I was excited to see my parents but more excited to have James home. My addiction to him was becoming a bit of a problem, but I just couldn't stop, nor did I want to. He couldn't have gone on business at a better time, though, for the day he left I got my period, and the day he returned it ended.

I drove home after work, packed a bag for the weekend and then made my way out to his house. The lights were on when I arrived, which was surprising as James had texted me when he got back into town to let me know he didn't expect to leave the office until six thirty or so. When I opened the door, and the most mouth-watering aroma embraced my senses, I was nearly knocked off my feet. Oregano, basil, and roasted garlic—someone was cooking Italian!

I walked into the kitchen to find my man, wooden spoon in hand, wearing a dark green apron on over two pieces of his tailor-made suit, white dress shirt, black vest, and the sky blue tie I'd bought him last week. His sleeves were rolled up, and a dish towel flopped casually over his shoulder; marinara sauce simmered enticingly on the stove, and garlic toast was ready to broil. He even had a salad sitting in a big bamboo bowl and something delicious baking in the oven. Chicken parmesan maybe? He knew it was one of my favorites. His back was to me as he stirred the sauce, the Sinatra on the stereo had muted my entrance. I walked up behind him and slid my arms around his waist kissing that sexy spot between his shoulder blades and inhaling his intoxicating James smell; woodsy, spicy and all man.

Turning around and taking me in his arms, he kissed me soundly.

"Hi," I managed to say after I caught my breath, his cobalt eyes twinkling with love. I ran my hands up and into his hair, pulling ever so slightly on the dark silky strands.

He growled low and manly. "God, I missed you." His lips against my neck, peppered kisses up one side and down the other.

"I missed you too." I put the grocery bag up on the counter and went over to peek inside the oven; it was chicken parmesan—yum. "I thought we were just going to take my parents out for dinner tonight, and then maybe eat in tomorrow night. You said you had to work late."

He lifted one sexy shoulder. "Yeah, I know, but I worked so much over the last three days that I'm just drained, and I want to make a good impression on your folks. And I'm *dying* to fuck you. Serious blue-balls here." He pinned me against the counter with his hard body. "It's been a long hard week. *Very* hard, if you get my drift. And you smell so damn good." He thrust his hips into mine, deftly rotating them, my eyes closed from the delicious friction against my clit. Even with layers of clothes between us, the man drove me wild. "Do we have time for a quickie before they get here?" He quirked an eyebrow then tilted his head down to nip at my neck.

"Probably not." I pouted. "They'll be here any minute. Are you nervous?" I reluctantly pushed out of his grasp and started putting the groceries away in the fridge.

"No. Well, maybe a little. I haven't really done the whole *meet the parents* thing before, and I really want them to like me. I'm kind of in love with their daughter, you know? *Besotted* in fact." I glanced at him and raised my eyebrows. "Oh yeah, I bought a Word of the Day Calendar, I need to keep up with your *verbose loquacity*, and today's word was *besotted*."

He poured a glass of zinfandel and handed it to me as I giggled at his use of the new word, his playful grin making my knees weak and my core tighten in need.

"I know." I wrapped my arms around his neck and stood on my toes, so I was eye level with his mouth. "They'll love you, don't worry. And I'm *besotted* with you too."

Suddenly there was a knock at the door. I looked at the clock, and it said six thirty—show time!

"Mum! Dad!" I opened the door to find my parents standing on the front steps in quiet awe of the house.

"Hi, sweetie!" My mum dropped her bags and pulled me into her arms, one of my favorite places to be. I love how my mum smelled; scents from my childhood, clean linen, Pantene shampoo and chalk from the pre-school. I'd inherited my coloring from my mother, we both have peaches and cream skin, hazel eyes and honey blonde hair. But unlike my mermaid tendrils, my mum chooses to keep hers in an adorable pixie cut that shows off her long neck and high cheekbones. Without a doubt, Anita Everly is a very attractive fifty-three-year-old woman.

I heard an impatient throat cleared behind my mother. "Hey, what about me?"

"Sorry, Dad," I laughed, letting my mum go. "Hi." I wrapped my arms around my father, giggling like a child as he lifted me off the ground and spun me in a circle. My dad was the fire chief and had been on the rowing team in university, he was anything but a slouch, and didn't show his fifty-six years at all. This was a man who still ran thirty miles a week and could bench press a smart car; he was built like a "brick shit-house" as his friends liked to say. And although all three of the Everly children shared their mother's hazel eyes, my brothers got their coloring from my dad.

All the men in our family shared that naturally tanned skin with dark blond wavy hair, though my dad kept his cut quite short and it was starting to thin. As a child, I had whined about not getting my dad's eyes. In my opinion, they were his best feature, bright green with flecks of copper and yellow, alert and wise with humor and passion bubbling beneath the surface. The running joke in our family was that if you looked up "Daddy's Girl" in the dictionary, there would be a picture of me clinging to my father's legs and standing on his feet as we danced at my Uncle Dan's wedding. Phil Everly rarely said no to his little girl.

I wasn't sure if James had followed me to the door or if he was waiting in the kitchen for us, but I had my answer when my dad dropped me abruptly, and I stumbled to get my footing.

"Oh shit, sorry. James, this is my dad, Phil, and my mum, Anita. Mum, Dad this is…," I said with a sigh as I looked at the man I loved, "this is James." They all shook hands, and I could tell that my parents were eyeing him up warily. James, on the other hand, tottered back and forth on his feet and licked his lips nervously; it was a whole new look for him.

"Come in... come in," I urged. "We're going to put you in the garage apartment, but we can take your stuff up there later. James made dinner, and it's almost ready."

I grabbed my mum's bag, and James reached for my dad's. However, my dad reached for his bag at the same time, and they had a little awkward hand-over-hand moment. Poor James' face went crimson.

"You have a lovely home," my mother said as we lead them through the foyer into the open floor plan of the house.

"Thank you, Mrs. Everly."

"Oh, please call us Phil and Anita."

"James designed the house himself, Mum, and did most of the work as well, bringing in his most trusted contractors only when he had to. I'll give you the full tour later."

"Can I get either of you anything to drink? Wine? Beer? Water? The bar's fully stocked so just name your poison," James asked, as he made his way back into the kitchen and started decanting a second bottle of wine.

"I'll have a glass of wine please," my mother said.

"Wine for me as well," my dad said but didn't bother to turn around. He was too busy wandering around the living room examining the rockwork around the hearth and the wood beams of the ceiling. My dad had designed and built my parent's house as well, although not as complex or grandiose as this, I could tell he was sizing James by his craftsmanship and style.

James seemed to relax once the meal was on the table and the wine had calmed his nerves. And his chicken parmesan had us all sporting some pretty righteous food babies.

"So, Mum, are you still interested in coming to my rebounder class in the morning?"

"Yes, honey, I'd love to try your trampoline class. I'm just afraid I'd fall off."

I scoffed. "Nah. Nobody falls off. James' sister came with me last weekend, and it was her first time, and she didn't fall off. You'll be okay. You do yoga; you've got core strength and balance. Dad, what are your plans for tomorrow?"

"Well, sweetie..." He took another sip of his wine while rubbing his stomach. "I would like to get to a running store or two, I need some new shorts, but it doesn't have to be tomorrow, it could be Sunday on our way home. We're just here to see you."

"Well, I think James wants to do some work on his boat this weekend. Wasn't that right, James? You wanted to try to get the boat out of winter storage and put it back in the marina?"

James nodded while taking a sip of his wine. "Oh, uh, yeah, but that can wait if your parents wanted to do something specific."

"What kind of a boat do you have?" my dad asked.

I knew my father, the avid fisherman and boating enthusiast, would have his interest peaked the moment I mentioned James' boat. I hoped that this would earn some brownie points for James and dissolve any last bit of awkwardness between him and my dad. I was right. My question spurred a thirty-minute discussion about fishing spots, lure preferences and boats of all sizes. As we were clearing the plates, I could tell by my dad's questions that he was eager to see James' boat and check it out.

"Tell me, James, do you golf?" We were all sitting in the living room enjoying more wine and discussing our upcoming Caribbean holiday when my dad abruptly changed the subject to one of his key "are you worthy of my time and worthy of my daughter?" questions. Fortunately, however, it was a subject I had prepped James for. My father hates golf. Despises it. He calls it the "lazy man's past time" and spits when anyone calls it a *sport*. Plus, as the fire chief, he loathes the amount of water it takes to hydrate the courses, especially during the hot summer season when the rest of the city is on water restriction, and there are severe fire-bans because the tinder is so dry.

James was ready. He shook his head. "No, sir, I don't. Not unless I have to, that is." And he was telling the truth, James didn't golf, in fact, he hated it as well and shared many of the same reasons as my father.

"Ah, I getcha." My dad nodded, indicating he understood the pain of having to do something you hated for the sake of the greater good. "Like a golf tournament for charity or a schmoozing, elbow rubbing, ass-kissing event."

"Yeah, exactly. But I don't consider it a sport. After golf I still have to go for a run, get a real sweat going, you know what I mean?" And that was that. James was my father's new favorite person.

"Your father and I really like James, dear. We think he's very kind and he seems to be crazy about you," my mother said as we stopped into a drugstore on the way home from the gym the next morning.

"Yeah? That's good. I'm glad you guys like him. He was so nervous."

She ran her hand affectionately down the back of my head like only mothers can do. "And he's one heck of a cook, and handsome. Boy, is he ever gorgeous. And he's won your father over entirely, boats, fishing, running and a mutual hatred for golf. It's like your dad has found a new BFF."

I snorted, picking up a perfume sample and sniffing the nozzle, wrinkling my nose at the over-powering scent of musk. "Yeah, I figured Dad would love him."

"Do you?"

"Do I what?"

"Love him?"

I gave her the side-eye, a small smile playing on my lips. "Yeah... I do. I'm crazy about him, Mum."

"Awe honey, that's wonderful." She beamed, resting her hand on my shoulder and giving it a motherly squeeze. "And he feels the same way? Why am I asking? Of course, he does, I see the way he looks at you." I smiled, picturing James' handsome face and the way he lights up when I walk into a room.

"Do you think our age difference is going to be a problem?"

"How old is he?" We were now perusing the cosmetics section, mindlessly putting samples on the back of our hands while having one of our many heart-to-hearts.

"He just turned thirty-eight. His birthday is in January. Do you think he's past the time of wanting to get married and have kids?"

"He's thirty-eight?" She raised her perfectly tweezed eyebrows. "Wow, he looks *really* good for thirty-eight. I don't know, honey. What has he said? Does he want kids?"

"Since meeting me, he said all his priorities have changed but I've never asked him to elaborate, so I don't know what he means."

She smiled, her classically symmetrical face rosy from our workout and her eyes twinkled as we talked about love, my mother has always been a hopeless romantic. "Then that's exactly what he means. A man like James puts his career first and his love life on the back burner, waiting for the right woman to come along. And *you,* my love, are that right woman. I don't think you have anything to worry about."

"What's your key to a happy and long-lasting marriage, Mum? You and Dad have been together for almost thirty-five years."

"Keep the fights clean and the sex dirty, honey." And she wandered off to look at the Elizabeth Arden makeup leaving me stunned.

"Mother!" I chased after her.

She rolled her eyes and exhaled with a chuckle. "Oh, chill out."

We were giggling so much we were drawing attention. My sides hurt and I had to go on the hunt for a tissue to wipe the tears from my eyes. A hopeless romantic she might be, but my mother was also a straight shooter, she tells it like she sees it and doesn't beat around the bush. And as much as I didn't want to hear about her and my father's sex life, I'd rather know that they still had plenty of romance in their relationship, then find out that they were in a loveless marriage and only stayed together out of habit.

I felt my phone vibrate and checked my text messages. It was James.

J: **Your dad and I are going out in the boat. What are our dinner plans?**

"Well, it looks like Dad and James are still hitting it off. They're taking the boat for its first run of the year."

She gushed. "Oh, your dad must be in his glory right now. Anything having to do with boats and he's like a child at Christmas."

"James just asked what we want to do for dinner. What do you think?"

She shrugged, holding up her hand to show me a foundation shade. "I'm good with whatever."

I shook my head and made a face; it was much too dark for her complexion.

"Well, how about Thai? I can make reservations for later in the evening, so we're not rushed. Are we going to go downtown after our showers?"

My mother nodded. "Yeah, sure, that sounds good."

E: **Thai for dinner. Will make a reservation for 7:00. Have fun. Xoxo**

J: **Sounds good. Love you.**

A small tingle ran through me at the sight of "Love you" in his text. I hoped the feeling never got old.

ALSO BY WHITLEY COX

Love, Passion and Power: Part 1
The Dark and Damaged Hearts Series Book 1

Love, Passion and Power: Part 2
The Dark and Damaged Hearts Series Book 2

Sex, Heat and Hunger: Part 1
The Dark and Damaged Hearts Book 3

Sex, Heat and Hunger: Part 2
The Dark and Damaged Hearts Book 4

Hot and Filthy
The Dark and Damaged Hearts Book 4.5

True, Deep and Forever: Part 1
The Dark and Damaged Hearts Series: Book 5

Snowed In and Set Up
Featured in the *Season of Seduction* Boxed Set

Upcoming in 2018

True, Deep and Forever: Part 2
The Dark and Damaged Hearts Series: Book 6

Lust Abroad

Quick & Dirty

Book 1 of the Quick Series

Quick & Easy

Book 2 of the Quick Series

Hot Dad

Hard Hart

Book 1 of The Hart-y Boys

Hard, Fast and Madly: Part 1

The Dark and Damaged Hearts Series: Book 7

ACKNOWLEDGMENTS

There are so many people to thank who have helped me on this daunting journey to becoming a published writer. First and foremost, my editor Stephanie, whose honesty and patience has been invaluable. You're a beta-reader, editor and surrogate mother all rolled into one. Thank you, Stephanie, I couldn't have done this without you.

Tara at Fantasia Frog Designs, your covers are fantastic, and you are a peach. Keep 'em coming, lady!

The ladies in Vancouver Island Romance Authors, your support and insight have been incredibly helpful, and I'm so honored to be apart of a group of such talented writers.

And lastly, the husband. Thank you for being so encouraging, supportive and understanding. For suggesting I go and sit and write in Starbucks for countless hours on a Saturday while you play tea party and have daddy-daughter dates with the Small Human. You are my inspiration for happily ever after, my everything and I love you.

JOIN MY STREET TEAM

WHITLEY COX'S CURIOUSLY KINKY REVIEWERS
Hear about giveaways, games, ARC opportunities, new releases, teasers, author news, character and plot development and more!

[Facebook Street Team](#)
[Join NOW!](#)

DON'T FORGET TO SUBSCRIBE TO MY NEWSLETTER

Be the first to hear about pre-orders, new releases, giveaways, 99cent deals, and freebies!

Click here to Subscribe
http://eepurl.com/ckh5yT

YOU CAN ALSO FIND ME HERE

Website: WhitleyCox.com
Twitter: @WhitleyCoxBooks
Instagram: @CoxWhitley
Facebook Page: https://www.facebook.com/CoxWhitley/
Blog: https://whitleycox.blogspot.ca/
Multi-Author Blog:
https://romancewritersbehavingbadly.blogspot.com
Exclusive Facebook Reader Group:
https://www.facebook.com/groups/234716323653592/
Booksprout: https://booksprout.co/author/994/whitley-cox
Bookbub: https://www.bookbub.com/authors/whitley-cox

ABOUT THE AUTHOR

A Canadian West Coast baby born and raised, Whitley is married to her high school sweetheart, and together they have a spirited toddler and a fluffy dog. She spends her days making food that gets thrown on the floor, vacuuming Cheerios out from under the couch and making sure that the dog food doesn't end up in the air conditioner. But when nap time comes, and it's not quite wine o'clock, Whitley sits down, avoids the pile of laundry on the couch, and writes.

A lover of all things decadent; wine, cheese, chocolate and spicy erotic romance, Whitley brings the humorous side of sex, the ridiculous side of relationships and the suspense of everyday life into her stories. With mommy wars, body issues, threesomes, bondage and role playing, these books have everything we need to satisfy the curious kink in all of us.

Made in United States
Orlando, FL
22 September 2025